Colt had figured out the imposture as soon as he'd gotten into the cab with Dana. In the confined space, the differences between the sisters were obvious.

Rail-thin Nickie starved herself, while Dana, though far from *zaftig*, had a few extra inches here and there. Not enough for most people to notice, but Colt, couldn't help but notice that Dana's breasts filled out her dress in a way that made his mouth water and his cock stand straight up.

He'd decided to go along with the joke, wondering where and when Dana would 'fess up. In bed, maybe?

That quickie with Dana in the elevator told him that his brother had set his sights on the wrong girl. On the other hand, Max might be angry with Colt for wrecking his relationship. Better shut up, he advised himself. And, though she was incredibly hot, he couldn't see Dana again.

Besides, though he'd liked her responsiveness, she wasn't his type. But who was?

Forbidden, charming Dana, whose attempt to imitate her sister's sophisticated veneer would have been pathetic if she weren't so damn transparent, obvious, and ... cute. She'd avoided his eyes, stuttered occasionally, and refused to engage in any of the sexual banter that had made her sister such an exciting date a year ago. Warming her up had been a challenge as well as a pleasure.

She was adorable, and Colt felt a little guilty about getting her toasted and taking advantage of the situation.

But not very.

The Wilder Brother

Suz deMello

Liquid Silver Books
Indianapolis, Indiana

Copyright © 2006 Suz deMello

Published By:
Liquid Silver Books
10509 Sedgegrass Dr.
Indianapolis, IN 46235

Liquid Silver Books publishes books online and in trade paperback. Visit our site at
http://www.liquidsilverbooks.com

Manufactured in the United States of America

ISBN: ISBN Ten: 1-59578-448-9
ISBN Thirteen: 978-1-59578-448-3

Cover: April Martinez

The Wilder Brother

Chapter One

November Boston, Massachusetts

"I'm bored."

Dana Newcombe's jaw tightened. Whenever her twin, Nicole, announced she was bored, bad things happened.

She had to think of a diversion—fast. "How about, um, Monopoly, or … Scrabble?" Dana looked around the living room of her cozy apartment, wondering where she'd stashed the board games.

Pressing her oft-photographed lips together, Nickie picked up a silver-backed hand mirror and scrutinized her image. The victim of a chemical peel gone awry, her sister's face reminded Dana of a molting snake, with brownish, discolored patches alternating with areas of fresh pink flesh. Nick wore tinted glasses as a disguise, and had come to stay with Dana to prevent anyone in Manhattan from seeing her looking any less than perfect.

Both Dana and her sister sprawled on identical plush couches upholstered in deep, velvety green. The smoked glass coffee and side tables reflected the crackling flames of the fire glowing in the white brick hearth. Unable to use make-up herself with her skin so bad, Nicole had been experimenting on Dana, so open containers of cosmetics—blusher, nail polish, and lipsticks—littered the coffee table between them.

"You could read your latest magazine." Dana reached for a copy of *Vogue*. The cover of the November issue featured her sister's famous face, eerily like her own, but with the features made up with Chanel's latest line of cosmetics. Dana figured that it had been shot before that fateful visit to the incompetent aesthetician who'd come close to ruining the career of supermodel Nicole Newcombe.

Rolling her eyes, Nicole groaned. "Spare me."

"Max and I are going to the Ingmar Bergman revival at the Arts Theatre downtown. Tonight they're showing *Cries and Whispers.* Why don't you come along with us?"

Still staring into the mirror, Nicole picked at a dead patch of skin. "After which the two of you will go to the Boring Cafe, drink hot cocoa, and discuss logarithms."

"It's the Boolean Cafe, and it's more likely we'll talk about the film." Dana adjusted her glasses.

"Whoa, exciting. As exciting as a funeral dirge." Nick scowled at her reflection.

"Look, I'm probably going to marry Max. The two of you ought to do some bonding."

Nicole dropped the mirror. It clattered onto the coffee table. "You can't settle for Max! He's too dull for you. Not like…"

"Colton?" Dana knew that Nickie and Colton, Max's brother, had been hot-and-heavy last summer. That had ended when Colt traveled to Europe. "Look, I don't want to poke a sore spot…"

"Colt didn't hurt me." Nicole tossed her mane of long, platinum blond hair.

"Whatever. Look, Ms. Supermodel, I'm not exciting like you. I'm just a dull little scientist. Max and I are perfectly suited."

"Mr. Meticulous has his head buried so far into his stocks and bonds that he can't even tell you and me apart."

"Oh, nonsense. Of course he can. He loves me."

"Can not."

"Can too." How on earth did her sister manage to reduce her to a bickering little brat?

"Bet you I'm right, and if I win, you can't marry him." Nicole wagged her index finger, decorated with a French-tipped nail, back and forth.

Dana stared at her twin, eyes widening. The stakes had definitely risen.

"Unless you're afraid." The taunting note that had always irritated Dana had entered her sister's voice.

She told herself not to let Nicole get to her. Unfortunately, Nick knew exactly how to crawl under Dana's skin. "Afraid of what?" Dana asked.

"Afraid I'm right."

"Max knows me. He loves me! There's no way he'd be fooled."

"No doubt you both think so. And if you're right, you have nothing to worry about." Nickie's voice was smooth as a con artist homing in on a rich old lady. "Does he know I'm in town?"

"Umm, yeah, I told him you'd be here this weekend."

"Is he coming to pick you up?"

"We were going to meet at the theatre."

"Okay. I'll wear your coat and tell him I—you—whatever—I have a headache, or something, and didn't come down from New York."

"You're mixing up your pronouns."

Nicole waved a hand. "You know what I mean."

"No way!"

"Why not? It's just a little harmless fun. You scared?" That taunting note had entered Nick's voice again.

"I'm not scared." Pissed-off, she infused her voice with equal contempt. "I'm not going to let you push me into something I don't want to do."

"Bullshit. You're gonna wimp out on me, aren't you?"

Dana bit her lip. When she put it that way… "I'm not a wimp!"

"Okay, okay." Nickie sounded mollified. "So let's visit your closet."

~ * ~

After pawing through Dana's clothes and rejecting most items, Nicole picked black wool pants, a loose, thick black sweater, and a sensible parka. She touched up her face to partially conceal her mottled skin, then donned a red beret and red knitted gloves. Pirouetting in front of the full-length mirror, she asked, "How do I look?"

Her mouth dry, Dana swallowed. "Like me."

"Perfect!" Nicole pranced out the door in Dana's borrowed black waffle-soled boots, leaving Dana's heart sinking to her ankles and her head throbbing.

What would happen if Nickie won the bet? Dana's comfortable life with its cozy relationship would be blasted to smithereens.

She poured a glass of Cabernet and raised it to her lips with a shaky hand. In her heart, she knew Nicole was right. Dana cared for Max, maybe even loved him, but he didn't light her fire. He never had. Actually, she'd pretty much given up on finding a man who would really, truly do it for her. A stroke book and a vibrator were so much more reliable.

On the other hand, Dana looked forward to the life she and Max could share. Security, home, comfort, affection … children, maybe, when the time came.

Nicole didn't understand. Men didn't fall at Dana's feet the way they swooned for her glamorous celebrity sister. Males weren't attracted to cerebral women. She was lucky to have Max. A stockbroker, Max valued her intelligence and looked beyond her academic façade. Or so she hoped. What if Nick was right?

Dana bitterly regretted the bet. It scared her. Had she wagered her future on impulse?

She took off her glasses to massage her temples, then found a bottle of aspirin in the bathroom cabinet and washed a couple down with the rest of the wine. She was crazy. Why was she letting this happen? She had to stop this disastrous bet. She grabbed Nicole's long, elegant leather coat and flung it on, preparing to leave.

The door bell chimed, and Dana wondered why neither Nicole nor Max used their keys. Both her sister and her almost-fiancé had them. And who else could it be?

She opened her door. A dark-haired male in denim leaned on the jamb. She recognized him immediately.

Her heart stuttered.

Her stomach dropped.

Her palms sweated.

She overheated like an ancient Studebaker laboring up a mountain.

She wasn't a coward, but she was tempted to slam the door before hiding in her darkest closet. The man at her door scared the starch out of her usually upright backbone. Why, she couldn't define, and that bothered her all the more.

But for no reason she could pinpoint, Colton Wilder, Max's younger brother, spooked her right down to the tips of her toes.

"Hey, Nick." Colt straightened to his full six-foot-two. "Can I come in?"

Without waiting for permission, he sauntered past her, brushing the coat's fur trim with his arm. The touch tingled through her as though he'd caressed her breasts, which lay directly beneath the fur.

He didn't say excuse me, either.

Maybe that was why he pissed her off, Dana thought. He was the rudest man she'd ever met. Like a predatory hawk, Colt liked to swoop in, take what or who he wanted, then fly away again.

He was so different from Max that Dana couldn't fathom how they'd emerged from the same womb. Perhaps Colt's rough streak was the result of being Son Number Two instead of the firstborn, she mused as she watched him strip off his sheepskin-lined denim jacket and take a seat on her plush sofa.

"Wha-what are you doing here?" she asked. She tried not to stare at his chest, clad in a snug turtleneck, which outlined incredible pecs. The cobalt fabric accentuated his brilliant blue eyes.

"I flew into LaGuardia earlier today and called you in Manhattan. After I listened to your phone message, I decided to come rescue you from my brother and your sister. Last time we went out you told me they bored you to tears."

Dana's mouth dropped open. Nick, that traitor, had called her *boring?* She'd get her.

Colton spread long arms along the back of the couch and eyed her. "Come on over here, Nickie, and say hello properly." He patted his lap.

Torn between deception and truthfulness, Dana hesitated. For all his faults, Colt was a prime piece of manflesh. He wasn't a mere boy toy. He was FAO Schwartz, Toys-R-Us, and Santa's workshop at Christmas rolled into one mouthwatering package.

He'd swooped in last summer and they'd double dated, with Dana and Max showing Boston to Nick and Colt, who'd indulged in a torrid affair lasting all of three weeks. Then he'd flown away in wham-bam-thank-you-ma'am style.

Nicole never discussed Colt, but that really wasn't odd. She tended to be casual about her affairs, and Dana hadn't pried, assuming that Nicole had set another notch into her lipstick case and moved on.

But Dana wouldn't lie. "I'm not Nick."

Colt laughed. "I love your sense of humor." He stood. "Okay, if you're not in the mood, we can go over to the Four Seasons and eat."

"I'm not dressed for the Four Seasons. Why do you want to go there?"

"They burn a good steak. Why don't you change your clothes?" Colt eyed her jeans and fisherman's sweater. "I'm sure you brought more than that from New York."

Nick had, of course. "What about you?"

"I won't matter. I'm sure they'll be delighted to seat the famous Nicole Newcombe whenever and wherever she pleases. Remember last time?"

Dana did. The four of them had gone to the racetrack; with Colt's contacts in the horse-racing business, they were able to see the horses up close and personal. Afterwards, even though they reeked of the stables, Nicole had swept into the Four Seasons as though she owned the place and demanded an early supper of champagne and hors d'oeuvres. The maitre d' had seated them without a flick of an eyelash or a twitch of his nose.

Dana decided that getting confused with her sister might not be so bad. She figured she could do a credible Nickie imitation for one evening, especially if the deal came with Colt's company. Why not? After all, Nick was enjoying a night out with Max. Why should Dana stay at home alone and let her sister have all the fun?

She went to the bathroom to freshen up a bit and stared into the mirror. The long, fur-trimmed coat looked jaunty, rakish and dashing, but her plain-Jane demeanor reminded her that she was Dana the scientist, not Nicole the cover model. No one in their right mind would label her jaunty, rakish, or dashing.

How did Nickie do it? Dana wondered for the umpteenth time. Although she wore Nick's crimson lipstick and matching nail polish, she definitely felt like a pig in a poke. They shared the same DNA down to the ends of their platinum hair, had the same hazel eyes and six-foot height. Yet Nickie had a stellar career as a model while Dana dated staid, dull-as-dirt Max. An astronomer, she studied the stars at the Massachusetts Institute of Technology in nearby Cambridge. Glamour girl Nickie danced with them in Manhattan's trendiest clubs Even at age twenty-five, Dana felt eclipsed by her famous sister.

Dana immediately berated herself for her disloyalty to Max and her jealousy of Nick. It wasn't Nicole's fault that Dana had always felt insecure. Max wasn't dull.

There was nothing wrong with being known as Mr. Meticulous. He was steady, not staid. Reliable.

Like her father.

Dana shunted her mind from that icky thought. She stripped off her clothes, then raided Nick's suitcase for a long, spangled slink of a dress. Of cream and gold jersey, the gown was cut so low that Dana had to take off her bra rather than expose her under things.

Examining her reflection, she saw the dreaded VPL—visible panty line—ridging the clingy knit.

She bit her lower lip. No undies in this freezing weather? Nick would skip them, she reminded herself. She stripped off her bikini panties, put on pantyhose, then rearranged the gown.

Hoping for the best, she left her glasses where she'd tossed them on the counter. Big risk. In terms of their appearance, the glasses were the major difference between herself and Nickie. When Nick wore glasses, they were an affectation or a disguise. For Dana, the vision in her left eye was permanently impaired, and she needed them to see. She had contacts, but they couldn't completely correct the damage done by an errant soccer ball at the age of four.

She tended to avoid analyzing the blow to her psyche caused by that soccer ball and the resulting injury. But she knew that she was less tough, less secure, and less outgoing than Nickie.

Squinting into the mirror, she popped in her contacts before she smeared a little of Nicole's coverstick over the tell-tale red marks on each side of her nose where glasses usually rested. She then draped

Nicole's long leather coat over her arm and returned to the living room.

Colt leaped to his feet. "That's more like the Nickie I know and love." He ran his tongue over his teeth.

"Love? A strange word coming from your mouth."

He came closer. "Now, darlin'. We said no regrets, remember?" He ran a hand across her bottom, sheathed in snug, cream-colored jersey.

Her flesh rippled. With shaky fingers, Dana wrapped Nicole's spangled muffler around her neck and picked up her keys, ready to leave her home with Colt.

Forbidden, frightening, scary, *exciting* Colt.

"No regrets," she said.

Chapter Two

Tugging off Dana's parka, Nicole shoved the red
gloves into the pocket and settled herself into a
plush seat at the front of the Arts Theatre's first
balcony. So far, so good, she thought. She'd finished the
toughest test: keeping up an innocuous conversation
with Max while standing in line to get tickets for the
movie. It had been easy.

When Max had kissed her on the cheek she'd
accepted the caress, and simply said she was fine when
he'd asked. She'd explained that her sister had stayed in
New York, and Max had said that they ought to send
Nickie flowers if she was feeling poorly.

Nick was touched. That was sweet of him.
Obviously the dullard didn't know that she considered
him in the same class as P. B. and J. sandwiches. Nice,
but not in her league.

Then they'd stood in line and people-watched,
exchanging their observations in whispers, punctuated

by occasional giggles from her and guffaws from him. Max was witty and clever, and Nicole had finally begun to appreciate why Dana wanted to marry him. He was more entertaining than she'd thought.

Eyeing her, he'd asked if she'd tried a make-up that had hurt her lovely skin. Picking up his lead, she'd given him a rueful smile and said, "Nickie insisted that I try a new cosmetic. You're right. It didn't agree with me."

She'd enjoyed a little secret chuckle when he'd tut-tutted and said, "That Nickie! Always up to something!"

After he'd seated her, he'd gone to fetch refreshments, leaving her alone with an opportunity to relax and reflect.

She realized she felt different, here in Boston with Max, rather than she did in Manhattan with the men she usually dated. She'd become so well known in New York that she couldn't stand in a line in public without someone recognizing her. Whispers behind upraised hands usually started, followed by requests for an autograph or a photo.

The males she was with—generally other models—didn't seem to mind the constant interruptions. Relished them, even. Nicole had been set up more than once by publicity-hungry dates who'd told paparazzi where they'd be going. She'd never objected to that kind of manipulation, figuring that it was par for the course. Besides, any publicity benefited her career, too.

Now she saw that her social life had been missing a few things. Intelligent conversation, for one thing. And, instead of feeling exploited, Max made her feel protected.

Sheltered.

Safe.

Nicole gave herself a mental shake. Safe is not Nicole Newcombe, she reminded herself. Safe is tame. Boring. Remember? You like risk and excitement.

Max reappeared. He sat next to her, handing her a bucket of popcorn without butter, as she'd requested. She rested it in her lap.

"Off butter tonight, darling?" He laid an affectionate arm over her shoulders.

It was on the tip of Nicole's tongue to explain that she never ate butter because it made her break out, but she remembered to shut up. It had been so long since she and Dana had gone to the movies that Nicole didn't remember how her sister liked her popcorn.

The thought made her mood darken a tad. Maybe she should spend more time with Dana. Nicole couldn't recall her twin's favorite salad dressing or how she wanted her steaks cooked.

That was bad.

"Um, yeah, I read that butter's unhealthy."

"Everyone knows that." Max laughed. "Did you get your head out of the stars long enough to hear about good and bad cholesterol?"

Nicole imitated Dana's shy smile. "I kind of remember something about that."

Max roared. "I do adore you, Dana." Hauling her close, he gave her a deep, wet, open-mouthed kiss.

Nick stiffened, but Max didn't seem to notice. Then, to her embarrassment and shame, sensual heat flashed through her, cutting off her thought processes. The feeling was so powerful that she had to slide her arms around Max's neck and return his kiss.

Her skin heated, and an erotic sizzle zapped through her. She rubbed her palms over the close-cut hair at the base of Max's skull, inhaling his scent. She thought she recognized the cologne as Aramis, but beneath it he was all male.

He slid his tongue into her mouth, and her body reacted as though he'd entered her with something longer and harder. Why, Max, I didn't know you had it in you, she thought while moaning with delight.

Guilt seized her, and she jerked away. She was sure that this bet with her sister didn't include dancing the tongue tango with Max in the balcony of the Arts Theatre. Shit. What if Dana found out?

Nick would be dead, embalmed, and buried. Her sister might maintain a cool academic demeanor, but Nicole knew that beneath the calm surface there lurked a broad streak of self-righteousness that, when crossed, easily turned into anger. Dana could be a total bitch, as tough to deal with as … as…

Well, as tough to deal with as she, Nick realized with a grin.

"What's that Mona Lisa smile about?" Max fondled a strand of her hair.

"Uhm, nothing. Isn't it time for the movie yet?"

"Yes. I wonder what's taking them so long?" He twisted his head, evidently trying to see inside the square hole of the far-away projectionist's booth.

A harassed-looking man in a tuxedo strode across the stage in front of the Arts Theatre's red velvet curtain. "Ladies and gentlemen, I regret to inform you that this evening's showing of *Cries and Whispers* will be postponed. The print we received from the distributor is severely damaged. We at the Arts Theatre are dedicated to bringing you the finest in filmmaking, and we can't bring ourselves to torture you with a flawed interpretation of Bergman's masterpiece. You may pick up tickets good for another film here at the Arts on your way out."

"Bummer," Nicole said, hoping she hid her relief. After a long week, which ended with the trip to Boston, she didn't think she could last through the monotonous Bergman movie without falling asleep. Max would surely see through the deception if she didn't snore … because Dana did.

"That's all right." Max smiled at her. "I just enjoy being with you. How about going to my place and finishing what we just started?" He nuzzled her neck.

His caress made her quiver, damn it. "Er, um, I'm kind of hungry. How about going to the Four Seasons for a bite to eat?"

~ * ~

Nicole waited in the atrium of the restaurant, pulling off Dana's gloves and hat. She tried to avoid tapping her toe with impatience as the maitre d', a slimy creep with an awful *faux* French accent, told Max that no tables were available.

"That's nonsense." Max opened his wallet and took out a twenty. "I'm sure you can find something."

The maitre d' ignored the tip. Instead, his contemptuous gaze wandered over the parka Nicole wore. His lip curled, and he said, "I am sorree, but…"

"Oh, there's Nicole and Colt," Max said, looking over the maitre d's tuxedoed shoulder. He turned to Nicole. "This is great. Colt's back! And Nickie must have made it after all."

What? Nicole walked past Max and the phony French maitre d' to look. Yes, Max was right. Occupying the biggest, best table in the house—where Nick she herself would normally reign—was Dana, with her boobs practically hanging out of one of Nick's own dresses. The brat, Nicole thought. She's way fatter than me, and she's stretching the knit. I'll never be able to wear it again.

Worse, there was Colt, holding a champagne glass tipped onto Dana's lower lip, and she was sipping, her eyes fixed on him as though she was a Juliet who'd found her Romeo.

Nicole gasped. "That—that two-timing…" She cut herself short.

Max touched her shoulder from behind. "What, darling?"

She gulped and said, "It's great to see the two of them having a good time."

His arm wrapped around her shoulders. "If they can find half of what we've got, they'll be lucky. But I'd be surprised. Colt and Nickie are free spirits. Neither wants to be tied down. Their lives are too divergent, I'm afraid, for them to ever be a real couple."

Says who? Nick wanted to scream. Instead, she controlled herself and said, "I don't know about Colt *(that slime-sucking scumbucket!)* but Nickie might surprise you one day."

"How so?" Max steered her toward Dana and Colt, who were now giggling as Colt spilled champagne down Dana's neck and cleavage. Despite her red-faced embarrassment, he started to lick it off her throat. His tongue slid lower and lower...

Nicole gritted her back teeth, then consciously focused to pick up the thread of their conversation. "Nick can't model forever," she said. "One day, she'll have to settle down. And I'm sure she'd want to go out on top, not as a has-been."

"Well, she's barking up the wrong tree if she thinks she can snag my brother. Colt's nowhere near settling down. He's been away from the farm for months." Nicole knew Max referred to the Wilder family's horse farm in Kentucky. Max continued, "He'll want to get back home, not stick around the East coast."

In a couple more steps, they reached Dana and Colt's table. Colt's arm was around Dana's shoulders, his fingers tickling her neck. Both were laughing.

Dana's giggles turned to a horrified gasp when she spotted Nicole with Max. She flushed, radiating guilt that only Nicole saw. Colt and Max were oblivious.

And Nicole knew exactly how to punch Dana's buttons.

Dana's gaze trailed over Max's arm securely anchoring Nicole to his side. Nick turned her head and smiled brilliantly at Max.

Visibly, thoroughly smitten, he beamed at her. Nicole looked back at Dana and smirked.

Colt said, "Now, look who's here!" He stood, and the males engaged in masculine hugs and macho slaps on the back.

"Hi," Dana squeaked as they separated. Her eyes skittered to Max's face, then to Nick's, and back again. Her mouth firmed. She seemed about to speak when a waiter interrupted.

"May I set two more places?"

"Sure, that'd be fine," Colt answered, his tone mellow and easy. He glanced at Dana. "We can snuggle later, huh, darlin'?"

Nicole consciously unlocked her tense jaw as she allowed Max to help her take the parka off. "Thanks, sweetie," she said to him.

He winked at her, then took off his jacket and handed it to the waiter.

Dana sat ruler-straight, glaring at Nicole. The nerve, Nickie thought. She's going out on her boyfriend with my former lover, in my dress, pretending to be me. She's got no right to be pissed off.

Colt's arm still rested casually over Dana's shoulder. "How ya doin', dude?" he asked Max.

"Great." Max took Nick's hand. "You're so cold, sweetheart."

She smiled at him. "You can heat me up later."

"We ordered some appetizers." Dana's voice sounded stiff. "The chicken satay in chili-peanut sauce should help."

"Or we can order some soup for you, *Dana*," Colt said, staring at her.

Had she imagined his emphasis on the name? Nickie scrutinized him, noting the twinkle in his blue eyes. Colt was far from stupid. Did he know? She bit her lower lip, wondering if she should say anything.

Colt leaned back in his seat, lifting Dana's hand and bringing it to his lips. Closing her eyes, she hummed with obvious pleasure.

Nickie's body jerked, and she bashed her knee on the underside of the table.

"Are you all right?" Max jumped up.

"I—I don't know." Nick stood. She rubbed her knee. "I'm sorry to break up the party, but I think I should try to walk this off."

"Let's go to my place for the night," Max said. "It's not far."

She glanced at Dana, who was flaunting Nicole's dress, Nicole's makeup and, at that moment, the man Nicole wanted. "Yes, let's do that," she said to Max.

~ * ~

Stricken, Dana watched her almost-fiancé leave with her sister.

Max hadn't known who she was. When would he figure it out? When he bedded Nicole?

Whatever happened, it was clear that Nickie was right, Max was clueless, and Dana couldn't marry him.

Supper passed in a blur of champagne, appetizers and conversation. Nicole and Max's betrayal loosened the chain that had prevented Dana from enjoying Colt's company. Now she could admit to herself that she was attracted to Colt, handsome, funny, interesting Colt. He paid a flattering level of attention to her, touching her frequently. He played footsie under the table and kissed peanut sauce off her fingers. She accepted the caresses, wondering what Nicole and Max were doing. Two bottles of champagne later, Dana didn't care.

Colt left only to pay the bill at the desk rather than at the table. He took several minutes. She wondered why, and took the opportunity to freshen her lipstick.

After his return, he took Dana's elbow and steered her toward the elevator. She didn't know why, but decided she didn't care when she stepped inside. "Oh, wow." A modern, glass-walled structure, the elevator car afforded a view out of the hotel. The night sky was punctuated by the city's glittering lights. "Ooh, pretty." She stared with fascination.

As the double doors closed, he punched a button. The city's lights winked and glowed, turning into shining streaks of color as the car rose.

Colt leaned her against the elevator wall, pressing his hips against hers. He dug one hand into her hair, fisting it, holding her face steady as he kissed her. Slow and sensual, his mouth leisurely explored hers. She parted her lips, impliedly saying yes to whatever he

chose to take. He slipped his tongue inside for a deep,
sexy soul kiss, and heat flashed through her body.

He must have rented a room when he paid the bill,
she realized hazily. Did she want this?

The memory of Max leaving the restaurant with his
arm around Nick taunted Dana. But did that really
matter? Max didn't know.

Anyway, did their acts excuse hers?

She tried to squirm away from Colt, but his weight
pinned her. With his tongue stalking hers, stroking hers,
she couldn't protest.

She didn't want this. Did she?

She turned her head away, detaching her mouth, and
panted for air. He kissed along her jawline and down
the side of her throat, parting his body from hers only to
glide his free palm against her breast, plucking the
nipple until she moaned. He rocked his hips against
hers again, using one thigh to urge her legs apart, then
wedging himself against her.

His hard-on nudged the sweetest spot. Pleasure
flared, intense and sharp. She bit his lower lip without
thinking, then pulled away with a gasp. If he kept doing
that, she'd come, and she didn't want that. She did not
want an orgasm with Colt.

Or did she?

His hand left her breast to fumble at the strap of her
dress. He tugged it down, exposing her. His fingers
took her breast again, cupping her as he recaptured her
mouth. He plunged deeper with his tongue and rubbed
his erection back and forth across her mound. Every
stroke of his hard cock against her clit took her higher

and higher, forcing jagged shards of pleasure through her body.

The fifth time he did that Dana came, tearing her mouth away from his to draw ragged breaths. He feathered his lips along her throat toward her ear. A tender afterglow enveloped her in ecstasy.

But he wasn't done. He lifted her skirt and palmed her inner thigh, reaching toward her pussy. His busy fingers found a tiny rip in the crotch of her pantyhose. He tore the hole wider and pushed a finger into her moist folds, caressing her clitoris, then probing her slit.

With a long, low moan, Dana continued coming. Colt lifted her leg high and set her heeled foot onto the elevator rail while unbuttoning his fly with hasty fingers.

A condom packet crackled, and then he was inside her, easing into her welcoming, wet pussy. His thick cock opening her brought her to her senses.

"C-colt?"

"Yeah, baby?" Rotating his hips into hers, he slid a hand between them and stroked her bud.

Another blaze of pleasure shot through her, and she sucked in a breath. Colt didn't stop, and she couldn't.

But she had to.

"We c-can't do this."

He laughed. "We are doing this."

"It's wrong for me."

"Shh. Do me, baby, real good. Come for me."

With one of his hands rolling her nipple and the other playing with her clit, she did. She was on fire, way out of control, her entire being centered on his hard cock stretching her sheath, his eager hands exploring every inch of her body he could reach, his tongue filling her mouth.

Dana dropped her head back against the glass elevator wall, turning her head so her cheek touched its coolness. Her panting breaths gradually calmed as the aftershocks mellowed into a gentle, soft bliss.

Colt nibbled on her earlobe and asked, "You're not going to marry my brother, are you, Dana?"

Every muscle in Dana's body spasmed, and she sobered in an instant. She shoved Colt away from her. "You—you—you…" She clawed for the elevator's control panel, stabbing randomly at buttons before grabbing a round red knob marked STOP. She yanked on it, and the elevator halted with a jerk. An alarm sounded.

Howling with laughter, Colt clutched his sides as Dana frantically punched at the button she hoped would open the elevator doors. The doors finally slid apart. They'd stopped between floors, with only a two-foot space at the level of her head. She could see light and carpeting in the gap, and that was enough for her. She grabbed onto the rim of the sixth floor, trying to haul herself out of the elevator.

Colt's laughter increased to guffaws interspersed with snorts. "Dana, Dana. Stop, honey. You'll hurt yourself."

She dug her elbows into the carpet. Her hips and legs were still inside the elevator, and she could feel one of Nicole's high heels slipping off her foot. She curled her toes, trying to keep the shoe on. She didn't care about explaining the loss of a shoe to Nick, that traitor. But Dana needed the shoe to get home.

Colt grabbed her hips. "Seriously, darlin', what if the elevator starts up again?" He wasn't laughing anymore.

"Let me go, you scumbag!"

"I'm a scumbag? You're steppin' out on your boyfriend and *I'm* the scumbag?"

"You—you knew!"

"Yeah, I knew. I knew you and your sister were making fun of my brother."

"We're not making fun. This—this is serious.'"

"Then what are you doing?"

"None of your business." She tried to squirm out of his grasp.

"Didn't expect me to stop by, did you?"

"I tried to tell you…" The alarm bell clanged again, and she could hear running feet. Someone shouted from the floor below, "Don't worry, we'll get you out!"

She decided that dying would be better than continuing to endure this humiliation. "To hell with it," she snapped. Kicking Colt away, she flipped the shoes off her feet. She climbed out of the elevator and ran along the carpeted hotel hallway toward a door marked EXIT.

Leaning against the elevator wall, Colt continued to laugh so hard that tears leaked from his eyes. He slapped his palm against the red STOP knob, shoving it in. The elevator doors closed, and the car again started to rise. When it stopped, he tapped the lobby button, intending to catch Dana and see her home when he arrived in the lobby.

He'd figured out the imposture as soon as he'd gotten into the cab with Dana. In the confined space, the differences between the sisters were obvious. Instead of sniffing the flowery fragrance of Nicole's favorite *Joy*, the warm aroma of doughnuts had perfumed the air. Colt had figured that Dana wore a vanilla-scented body lotion. Very pleasant, but definitely not Nick.

And her body was different. Rail-thin Nickie starved herself, while Dana, though far from *zaftig*, had a few extra inches here and there. Not enough for most people to notice, but Colt, having banged one sister and shamelessly ogled the other, couldn't help seeing that Dana's breasts filled out her dress in a way that made his mouth water and his cock stand straight up. Her sensual enjoyment of the food was something that model Nicole could never share.

Just for kicks, he'd decided to go along with the joke, wondering where and when Dana would 'fess up. In bed, maybe?

Colt had never before been attracted to Dana, but he'd never seen this wild, daring, fun side of the sedate scientist sister.

And what was going on between Nicole and Max?

He'd enjoyed the hell out of the unplanned meeting in the restaurant. The twins' jealousy and competitiveness had kept him highly entertained, at least until Nicole had left. The belief that he could have either sister in the sack pleased him immensely.

Even though he hadn't come when he was inside her, he'd dug getting it on with Dana. But now, regret stabbed. There were two billion women in the world, but Colt had only one brother. He shouldn't have dished his brother's dirt, and hoped that Max would never find out.

While buttoning his fly, Colt frowned. He'd thought Dana would be a fitting mate for Max, his serious and sedate brother. But, given the game she'd played tonight, Colt wasn't so sure.

That quickie in the elevator told him that his brother had set his sights on the wrong girl. On the other hand, Max might be angry with Colt for wrecking his relationship. Better shut up, he advised himself. And, though she was incredibly hot, he couldn't see Dana again.

Besides, though he'd liked her responsiveness, she wasn't his type.

But who was? He had to admit that he'd never really met a woman who matched his fantasies of the ideal mate. He had always compared women to horses and found them wanting. Oh, he liked girls well enough. All kinds, shapes, and colors, in every way possible, and in every conceivable combination.

But horses were another matter. Thoroughbreds only. The only woman he'd ever met who came close to matching his love for horses had been Dana's sister Nicole. His ex-lover's flowing platinum hair and elegant body rivaled the most graceful Arabian. Like an untamable steed, she'd driven him crazy, especially when she'd flirted with other men.

That was why he'd left. They'd fought as he packed, especially when he'd told her that flirtation was as intrinsic to her personality as whinnying was to a mare. She'd never change, and he'd be miserable if he stayed with her.

And now, Dana. Forbidden, charming Dana, whose attempt to imitate her sister's sophisticated veneer would have been pathetic if she weren't so damn transparent, obvious, and … cute. She'd avoided his eyes, stuttered occasionally, and refused to engage in any of the sexual banter that had made her sister such an exciting date a year ago. Warming her up had been a challenge as well as a pleasure.

She was adorable, and Colt felt a little guilty about getting her toasted and taking advantage of the situation.

But not very.

He suspected that Nicole was behind whatever had happened. Well, he'd do his best to make it right, even if that only consisted in getting Dana home okay. The elevator doors opened, and he strode through the lobby. No Dana. Checking the coatroom, he learned that she'd already picked up her coat. He figured she'd high-tailed it out into the night and had taken a cab home.

Chapter Three

Max didn't understand his Dana's mood. Though a sweet girl, she rarely showed strong emotion. But tonight, she seemed imbued with an unusual liveliness. More than normally flirtatious, she didn't miss a chance to touch him, casually stroking his fingers when they shared popcorn at the theatre, bumping her hip against his as they walked to his apartment, meeting his glance at every opportunity. Her wide, hazel eyes held a hot promise he'd never seen in them before.

He wasn't normally uptight around her. Quite the opposite. He loved the sense of comfort and caring he felt with Dana. But tonight was different. A nervous excitement possessed him, tautening his muscles, igniting his need.

He unlocked his door and ushered her in. After taking her outerwear and putting it into a closet, he settled her on the couch in front of the fireplace. With quick movements, he turned the key to light the gas poker in the hearth.

"Instant atmosphere," she said. "Nice."

Odd, he thought. Dana preferred a wood fire, or so she'd once said. But he didn't care. Weren't women famously inconsistent? "Wine?" he asked.

"Sure. What do you have open?"

"I have a nice Cabernet, and some California Chardonnay in the fridge."

"I'll take the Cab."

After he'd poured wine for both of them, he tucked himself next to her, laying an arm across her shoulders. She turned her head and gave him her brilliant, heartwarming smile.

He lifted his glass, admiring the ruby red color of the wine backlit by the fire. "To the night."

She winked. "To a hot and heavy night."

"Um-hmm," he said, grinning. She was ready and very willing, and he could hardly wait to get her naked and underneath him. He captured her glance while sipping wine.

His heart raced. Should he pop the question? She seemed to be in a receptive mood. But maybe after sex would be better. Soft and compliant in post-orgasmic bliss, she would say yes to whatever he asked.

She put down her glass and reached for him. Lips met lips in a wine-flavored kiss, and he dove into her delectable depths. Tasty, but not enough, not with his cock raging to get inside her. He pulled at her enveloping sweater and, lifting it to touch bare skin, reached for her breasts.

Nicole panicked. Her breasts were about a cup size smaller than her sister's, which was why she'd picked a heavy, concealing sweater for the deception. Most people wouldn't notice, but one touch on her tits would tell Max something was very, very wrong.

He cupped her and squeezed. "What the hell?" He squeezed again, his hands searching.

"Shit!" She bolted, jumping over Max, spilling red wine over his previously immaculate camel-hair pants.

"Honey, what's going on?" Ignoring the damage to his trousers, Max reached for her, voice anxious and brow furrowed with concern.

"I'm sorry, I … I can't do this."

"What? Dana, talk to me. Please, talk to me!"

"I'm not Dana."

"What?" Then his brow darkened. "Nick, you bitch! What the hell is going on?"

She backed away, frightened by the anger on his face. "It was … it was a bet."

"A … a what? A bet?" His mouth dropped open. "Between you and Dana?"

She nodded. "We bet that you couldn't tell the two of us apart. She was sure you could. I was sure you couldn't."

He reached for the collar of his shirt, loosening it.

"I was right. You couldn't, could you? Not even when you kissed her, um, me." She refused to let herself feel guilty. She wasn't the man who couldn't tell his girlfriend from her twin sister!

"And I thought I was going to marry her." His voice was quiet. "I guess that's not such a good idea, is it?

Not if I feel more for you in one evening than I've felt for her in the last eighteen months."

Overwhelmed with shame, Nicole closed her eyes. "Max, I'm sorry."

"Don't be, but right now, I think you'd better leave. I have a lot of thinking to do."

She blinked back tears, knowing she'd deeply hurt a good man. "Are you mad?"

"No, I'm not. I'm sad, not mad." He went to the closet to retrieve her coat, hat and gloves. "I'll see you later, okay?"

~ * ~

Dana returned to her apartment to find it empty. Footsore, freezing, and miserable—she'd had only her keys, and no money for a cab—she ripped off Nicole's clothes and turned on the shower full blast. She stepped into the stall before the water had heated, believing she deserved an ice-cold drenching.

She'd behaved like a total slut. How could she face Max? And what was she going to do about Nicole?

She could break up with Max in a letter. Pushing remorse away, she decided that his failure to tell apart the sisters was enough to make guilt unnecessary, especially since he was probably busy shagging Nicole.

The water had heated, so Dana rubbed soap into a washcloth and attacked her filthy, beat-up feet.

As for her queen bitch sister, Dana would be quite happy to cut off all contact. She'd tried long enough to have a normal, loving relationship with her twin.

Nicole's competitive streak had always gotten in the way, and Dana was finally convinced that she shouldn't waste any more time on Nick, who always spoiled anything Dana had.

No doubt she'd be aided by Nick herself. Mercurial Nickie was capable of disappearing from Dana's life for months at a time. Maybe this would turn out to be one of those lucky instances. In any event, Dana would do her part to minimize or even eliminate contact with Nicole. No problem.

Scrubbing off the makeup, she heaved a sigh of relief. Disaster had been averted. All was right—sort of—in her world. She'd find another boyfriend somewhere, one who truly understood her and knew who she was. And she'd keep him away from Nicole.

Nicole entered the bathroom, and Dana's slightly elevated mood washed down the drain with the soap bubbles.

"So you're here," Dana said truculently. "I thought you'd be in the sack with Max by now."

Nicole ripped back the translucent shower curtain. Cold air poured into the stall, chilling Dana's skin. "What kind of remark is that?" Nick asked. "He figured out who I was."

"When?" Dana closed the curtain with an angry swipe of her hand.

"When we were kissing on his sofa."

A spasm of rage gripped Dana. Making out on Max's sofa was usually a prelude to lovemaking.

"He was feeling me up and knew immediately I wasn't you." Nickie cast a jealous glance at Dana's breasts. "You're about a cup size bigger than me."

At least Dana had something better than Nicole. Two things, actually. "But why did he take so long to tell us apart?"

"Because he's not the man for you. Admit it." Nicole stuck her face in the slit between the end of the curtain and the shower stall. "I'm right and you're wrong. You can't marry him."

A pang jabbed Dana's heart. Or was her ego taking the shot? "You're right. I'm wrong. I have no boyfriend and I'm a 'ho'." She reached for the shower head and aimed the stream of water at her sister's smug face.

Yelping, Nicole backed off, then took a towel and dried herself. "Did you sleep with Colt?" she asked.

"Obviously not, since I'm here, not there." She put the shower head back into its holder.

"You didn't get any at all?"

"Well, not really." Dana evaded. What she'd done wasn't any of Nick's business. From now on, nothing she did, and no one she saw, was any of Nick's business.

Again jerking open the curtain, Nick eyed Dana. "You better not have done anything, and don't get attached. I have it on very good authority that Colt isn't going to settle down."

"Don't worry about it. The only silver lining about this crappy evening is that I never have to see either Colt or Max Wilder again. Umm, did you see Colt at Max's apartment?"

"No. If he went there, I'd already gone." Nicole looked closely at Dana, who resisted throwing a washcloth at Nickie's face. "You're okay, aren't you?" she asked.

"Yeah, fine." Dana turned off the water and stepped out of the shower, elbowing Nicole out of her way. Grabbing a towel from the rail, Dana began to dry her skin.

"Weelll … if you're okay…"

"What?" Dana snapped.

"What if … what if I went out with Max?"

Something in Dana's belly twisted. She shoved it aside, considering, then blew out her breath. "I guess it's okay. I can't marry him." So what difference could it make? She felt sure that Nicole and Max wouldn't last long. They were too different.

Chapter Four

Dana got off the plane from Boston at two p.m. Pacific time. The unbelievable heat of Los Angeles in June hit her like a fist to the face. Dragging a wheeled carry-on suitcase behind her, she staggered along the airport concourse searching for her parents as she choked on the smoggy air.

She stopped to pull her pale pink sweater over her head, exposing a matching polo shirt, and twisted the sweater around her waist, tying it in the front of her khaki pants. She undid the top button on her shirt while wondering what she was doing in a city she detested, attending the wedding of a sister she disliked.

How on earth was she going to make it through the next few days?

She'd just have to brazen it out. After the debacle in November, she'd broken up with Max and limited her contacts with Nicole, just as she'd planned. But her sister and Max had filled any gaps in their lives with each other.

Now they were getting married. Dana had tried to back out of the event, but her mother was an expert manipulator who'd knocked down every excuse Dana manufactured. She'd finally caved in rather than suffer more of her mother's cross-country nagging.

So Dana would have to endure the parties, pomp and circumstance surrounding a big, fat, not-Greek but very pretentious wedding. She wasn't a party girl, hated pomp, and lately had avoided every circumstance that took her away from her studies and her work.

Was she jealous of Nicole? The question would surely arise, and Dana had to figure out how to deal with it. The answer would be the truth: she'd broken up with Max, who'd turned to Dana's sister for comfort. A meaner person than Dana would imply that he'd settled for second best, but she was above such pettiness. She'd keep a smile on her face for the next few days until she left on Monday, no matter what happened.

A less easy question was posed by the possible appearance of Colt Wilder. After the Four Seasons screw-up, he'd phoned and left a message saying he'd hoped she'd made it home safely, but hadn't given a number for a return call. She hadn't contacted him through Max—too crass, she decided.

Maybe Colt wouldn't show up.

She had prayed for the whole thing to go away, but noooooo, Nick had to mess everything up by dating— and then becoming engaged to—Max Wilder.

And how could Dana face his parents? They had to know something about what had happened. She'd been invited to the Wilder horse farm in Kentucky for both Thanksgiving and Christmas. She'd let Max's mother know she couldn't attend, but surely Colt or Max would have seen their parents over the holidays and told them what had happened. The entire Wilder family probably had shared some good laughs over Dana and Nicole's antics.

Dana's guts writhed. What must the older Wilders think of the Newcombe twins? She was surprised that they were supporting Max in his decision to wed Nicole. If she'd been in their position, she wouldn't.

And what did her parents know?

When she spotted her father's smiling face in the crowd, she realized that maybe they didn't know anything. Out on the west coast, her parents weren't heavily involved in their twin daughters' lives. Dana had merely told them that she'd broken up with her boyfriend, and neither parent had asked for details.

Reaching her dad, she hugged him around the neck, then slipped her arm around his waist. Tom also wore khakis and a polo shirt with the top button undone at the neck, though his shirt was green, bringing out color in his hazel eyes. He ran his hand through his pale hair and glanced at her. "How was the flight?"

"Horrible, but you're worth it," she said, walking with her father toward the baggage claim area.

"Worth what, punkin?"

"Worth that late flight with the bad food and the screaming baby. Worth the unbelievable heat and bad air in this disgusting city. It's great to see you, Dad."

"So the plane trip was not unbroken joy?"

"Hardly. You know I hate air travel."

He chuckled. "Not enough time to come by rail?"

"No, but I'll go home by train," she said. "I had to stay in Boston until yesterday because of final exams. But now I have a few weeks before I have to be back, if I want to wander."

"I didn't realize you still had finals, as a post-grad student. I never did."

"I don't take them," she said. "I graded a few for my thesis professor. You know how that goes. I'm his unpaid flunky if I want to get my doctorate anytime before I'm thirty."

Tom snorted. "You should skip getting more degrees and work for us, or even for Netscape or Microsoft. You have enough talent as a programmer…"

"Please, let's not go there again, okay?" They'd been over and over this issue a gazillion times. She'd gotten tired of explaining to her parents that she had a great opportunity at M.I.T., liked her job on the Juno project and enjoyed living in Boston.

They reached the luggage carousel and stopped near the tunnel where the baggage would pop out of the chute.

"You're going to stay in Boston? I think your mother is going to want you to live here eventually."

Shuddering, Dana reached forward and grabbed a green tapestry suitcase. "Nothing would induce me to

live in this Godforsaken wasteland." Certainly not
Mother, she thought.

Tom snared her matching garment bag. Together,
they made their way to an exit.

"It's not so bad. We've been very happy here."
Behind tortoise-shell glasses, his mild eyes regarded her
with their usual serenity.

She frowned and pushed her glasses further up on
her nose. They exited the building and walked until
they could see the Newcombes' big blue Volvo sedan
approach. When it chugged to a stop, she saw her mom
was at the wheel and her older sister, Sabrina, was in
the front seat. Dana's niece Rose, a three-year-old,
napped in a child safety seat in the back.

Gabrielle, a brunette Frenchwoman, hopped out of
the car, and briefly hugged her daughter. She looked at
Dana's shoulder-length bob with disapproval. "You cut
your hair off," she observed, in her lightly accented
English. "Well, I guess we can get you an extension eef
your sister wants you to wear a French tweest."

Dana gritted her teeth. She'd cut her hair soon after
the Max/Colt disaster, deciding once and for all she
would never, ever again be mistaken for her sister.
"Nice to see you too, Mother," she said. "How are you
doing?"

"I'm fine. She wants all zhe bridesmaids to look
alike."

Fat chance, thought Dana. She walked around the
car to kiss Sabrina. "I'm a bridesmaid? How did I get to
be so lucky?"

Sabrina winked at her. "You're maid of honor. You didn't know?"

"No." So much for keeping a low profile.

Gabrielle opened the Volvo's trunk. After Tom loaded Dana's luggage, they piled into the car. Seated behind Sabrina, Tom smiled at her across the captured Rose.

"I haven't talked to Nick for weeks," Dana said. A slight misstatement, since she hadn't talked to Nick since November. She'd felt even less inclined to communicate with Nicole after the wedding invitation had arrived six weeks before, preferring to spend her time concentrating on her work and trying to figure out how to avoid the wedding—impossible with steamroller mama in control.

"Well, you're zhe maid of honor, of course, and Sabrina is zhe matron of honor," Gabrielle said. "Your dress is being shipped. Did you bring the black *peau de soie* heels I told you to buy?" She accelerated onto the freeway before turning eastward.

"Yes, Mother."

"And try on zhe dress right away when it arrives. Several of zhe ozher bridesmaids have felt zhey are too big."

"Yes, Mother," Dana said. "Sabrina, are you and Steve staying with us?"

"No, we're going back and forth to the Valley," said Sabrina. "It's a lot of driving, but it's better for Rose and her routine if we stay at home in Northridge. And, we just found out I'm pregnant again," she added. "Two months."

"Congratulations, sweetie," said Dana affectionately. Unlike her fractured relationships with her mother and her twin, she'd always been close to easy-going Sabrina, who turned around in her seat to smile at Dana. Her older sister looked great; Sabrina's long brown hair was shiny and thick, and her hazel eyes twinkled. "Pregnancy becomes you," Dana said.

Sabrina grinned smugly. "I feel good, too. I think I was born for motherhood."

"Miss working?"

"Oh, heck, no. No insult intended, Dad." Sabrina's degree was in programming and she had worked for their father.

"None taken," Tom said. "I hope all my daughters are happy with their lives, whatever they do."

"What, um, do you think of Max?" Dana asked.

"He's a fine young man," Tom said. "Seems very stable, which will be good for Nicole. She needs to settle down."

Good heavens. Did her parents know that Nicole had broken up Dana's relationship with Max, then snagged him for herself? Apparently not. "When will I see him?"

"Soon. The groom ees staying in zhe guesthouse," Gabrielle said.

Damn. "The groom is staying with us? Isn't that a little unusual?"

"There's nothing improper with eet," Gabrielle said stiffly. "His brozher will be coming in shortly and will also be staying zhere. Zhe parents are already here, and their group is at zhe Marriott."

Great, Dana thought. This weekend, the Wilder brothers would be as ubiquitous as the California sunshine. She'd hoped to avoid them as much as possible, seeing them only at the ceremony. Damn, damn, damn. Could she manufacture an excuse to stay at a hotel, or with a friend?

"It sounds like it'll be really crowded at home," she said. "Maybe I should stay with Leta Weller, or at the hotel."

"What?" Gabrielle's voice rose. "Stay in a hotel?"

Rose, startled awake, let out a wail. "Aw, Rosie," said her grandfather, "where's your lolly?" Tom hunted around the tan leather seat to find a sticky bit of purple candy on a stick. He jammed it into the child's unresisting mouth. Rose was immediately content.

"Dad, that's about the worst thing you could teach her," Sabrina said. "Now she'll expect a sweet whenever she cries. Plus, it'll rot her teeth."

"Honey, I'm her grandfather. I'm expected to spoil her." Tom looked fondly at the child, who opened her budlike mouth and stuck out her purple tongue at her grandpa. Grape saliva dribbled down the child's chin.

Dana dug for a tissue in her pocket and wiped her niece's face. Rose screamed. Gabrielle, startled, slammed on the brakes, and everyone in the car was sharply jerked forward and back.

"What happened? What happened?" Sabrina cried.

"I only tried to clean her face…"

Rose's wails drowned out the rest of Dana's explanation.

"You touched her face? She hates to have her face touched. She doesn't let anyone touch her face. Don't touch her face, Dana," Gabrielle snapped.

Dana sighed. "Yes, Mother." In this family, no good deed goes unpunished, she thought gloomily.

"And there's no need for you to stay in a hotel," Gabrielle said. "Your father and I have been looking forward to spending some quality time with you."

Dana looked at Tom, vainly trying to comfort the screaming Rosie.

It was going to be a long, long week.

Chapter Five

Colton's plane had been hellaciously late leaving the ground. Normally a family member would have picked him up from the Los Angeles airport, but he had phoned his parents from the airport in Louisville and told them not to try to meet his unpredictable flight. Instead, Max had arranged for a "limo"—actually a van—to meet Colt and take him from L.A.X. to the Newcombes' home in Glendale.

Toting his garment bag and a battered backpack, Colt paid off the overpriced cabbie and approached the Newcombes' front door. Ho-oly cows and cranes. Pillars, porticoes and all, the place was a freakin' mansion. He bet the upper level balconies of the big white house would have a great view of Los Angeles's urban sprawl, but he'd take the green hills and open country of his Kentucky home any day.

Cars and limos choked the wide, circular driveway in front of the house. Through an open window, he heard laughter, the clatter of china, and the distinctive clink of cut crystal. A champagne cork popped.

With a start, he remembered that his mother had mentioned a cocktail party the Newcombes planned for the families to meet each other before the wedding. Well, he'd better get a move on. He didn't care if he offended the bride and groom, but upsetting his parents with bad manners wasn't on his agenda.

Unfortunately, his true plans would probably bring about a certain amount of tumult. Disrupting the wedding would surely result in chaos. So be it. He had to try. He just couldn't bear to see his brother marry Nicole Newcombe, a manipulative bitch who'd deliberately broken up Max's relationship with her sister so she could get him for herself.

Colt also questioned Max's motives. Although Nicole and Dana were twins, they weren't interchangeable parts. What the hell was Max thinking?

He was determined to put a halt to this ridiculous wedding before it led to a mess of a marriage. And he was sure that any marriage that included Nicole Newcombe would be a match not made in heaven, but spawned in one of the fouler pits of hell.

The door swung open. "May I help you, sir?" The doorman, attired in a white dinner jacket, gazed with blatant disapproval at Colt's beard, jeans, wrinkled T-shirt, and battered cowboy hat.

Colt looked ratty from a long day of travel and he knew it. Still, what wasn't appropriate for the stuffy Newcombe mansion was perfect for the Wilder horse farm, and if this white-coated clown didn't like it, well, too bad. He had the mother of all headaches, really didn't want to be here anyway, and now the doorman gave him the evil eye.

What would be next? A cheery evening of watching Max make goo-goo eyes at Nicole? Nicole gushing all over Max? This party—no, the entire weekend—would probably be like living in a Hallmark card, one corny, saccharine moment after another. Colt hoped he wouldn't have diabetes come Monday.

He took off his hat and slapped it against his leg. A puff of dust rose from his grubby jeans into the air. The servant's moue of distaste at the sight made Colt grin. He probably smelled like a horse, too. "I'm Colt Wilder, the groom's brother. I'm staying here."

"Ah, yes, Master Colton. You are staying in the guest house." The elderly butler tipped down his nose a fraction and opened the door to admit Colt. "Could you come this way, please?"

He stepped into a large, dimly lit entry, floored with marble tile. The hall was decorated with cherry wood antiques, a grandfather clock, and crystal bowls filled with cut roses. Their lush, heady scent pervaded the room. A wide staircase flowed down into the hall from the second floor. From above, a flash of color and movement caught his eye.

Maybe it was Dana. He really wanted to bump into her. Bump and grind, actually. Naked. That would be cool, or rather, hot. He didn't really have a letch for her, but this week would be a lot more fun if they could share a night or two.

"Right this way, sir." The butler took Colt's garment bag.

"In a minute." Putting himself in Dana's place, Colt guessed that this wedding was just as distasteful to her as it was to him, and he'd be delighted to give her wounded ego a little sexual healing. Weren't they both staying in this mansion for the week? He'd have lots of opportunities to finish what he'd started with her.

As the descending footsteps thumped closer, he could see that neither pair of well-shod feet belonged to Dana. Instead, Max and Nicole came into view. Damn. Pasting a phony smile on his face, Colt braced himself.

"Colt, my bro'! Good to see you." Max's dulcet bass filled the room.

Colt hugged his brother, slapped him on the back, and then stepped back to check him out. Attired in a tailored navy blazer and slacks, Max still wore his short, black hair parted on one side. He epitomized the successful young stockbroker on his way to the top. As for Colt, the only stock he'd ever break would be fillies and colts to saddle.

He didn't want to be openly rude, so he turned to greet Nicole as she arrived at the bottom of the stairs. "Hey, Nickie, you look wonderful." But he was lying. Though attractive, Nicole didn't cause the instant physical reaction he'd had when he'd hung out with her knock-out sister … which made no sense at all, since the Newcombe twins swam in the same gene pool.

"Thank you." Nick's fair hair flowed down her back. A slinky black dress encased her tall figure. Wisps of some filmy fabric floated from the sleeves and neckline of the floor-length gown. She reminded him of a blond Morticia Addams.

"Remarkable dress," Colt said.

"I designed it. This is the first Nicole Newcombe original." Nick pirouetted.

"Uh, cool." *I guess she could sell it at Halloween.* Amazing that Nick suffered by comparison to her babe-licious sister. They're identical twins, Colt reminded himself. Two peas from the same pod. Cast from the same mold.

"I'm hoping to break into couture when I get pregnant." Nick smiled at Max.

"But that won't be for awhile," Max said. "You ready to go to the party?" he asked Colt.

"Oh, Lord, no. Everyone will be in suits or dresses. I need to shower and change."

Nicole looked dubious. "Well, okay, but hurry. You're pretty late. I'll tell everyone you're here, and you'll join us in a few minutes. Max, would you take him to the guest house and get him settled?" She bustled toward the back of the house.

Max, with a lovesick gleam in his blue eyes, watched his fiancée until she'd left the room. Colt bit back a sarcastic remark or two. Or five.

"Come this way. It's not elegant, but it's the most direct route." Max led Colt down a hallway into a large kitchen, dominated by stainless steel appliances and jammed with hordes of caterers. Waiters rushed in and out, bearing bottles of champagne and trays of tasty-looking canapés. Cooks removed hot, savory hors d'oeuvres from the three ovens, deftly sliding them onto silver salvers.

"Nick's certainly going for maximum effect," Colt said.

"You know she always was a party animal. She gets that from Gabrielle."

"Who?" Colt asked.

"Mother Newcombe. You'll meet her soon. She's quite a character."

As a caterer opened the door of one of the two refrigerators and Colt caught sight of a generous mound of peeled shrimp. His mouth watered and his stomach rumbled. He grabbed his brother's arm. "Let's move along. I'm starved."

Max grinned. "Good thinking. It's a great party. The Newcombes are first class, all the way."

He led Colt out a back door and over to a guest house nestled in a stand of trees at the back of the property. In the distance, tiny candles floating on the water lit the surface of an Olympic-sized pool. Several guests standing near it appeared to be drinking champagne. Their distant laughter drifted over the rich lawns.

Opening the sliding door of the guest house, Max guided Colt to one of the bedrooms. "Ah, Mannering." The Newcombes' servant had already started to hang Colt's clothes in the closet.

Colt asked the butler, "How crushed is my suit?"

The aged servant examined the garments. "Not too bad, sir. I'll hang it in the bathroom while you shower. The steam should take care of the matter." Mannering left with the offending suit in hand. A moment later Colt heard water running.

"What is *he*?" Colt hissed to Max.

"Mannering is an old family retainer. Like I said, the Newcombes are first class all the way. Gabrielle is especially picky, almost feudal, really." Max rolled his eyes. "You know, the family butler, the family cook, the housemaid, et cetera, et cetera. Now get into the shower. I'll see you at the party."

Startled, Colt stared after his brother. Max had taken to this high-falutin' environment like a horse to fresh alfalfa.

$\sim * \sim$

Wearing a new white linen suit, with his long hair neatly tied at his nape, Colt wandered toward the swimming pool. More people crowded the deck now than he'd seen a half hour before.

He snared a flute of champagne from a tray carried by a passing waiter. Maybe a sip or two would soothe his headache. He looked around for familiar faces. Finding none, he entered the house through the French doors that opened onto the pool area.

He stepped into a large, brightly lit room full of elegantly dressed partiers. Near the door, a tuxedo-clad musician sat at a baby grand piano, playing jazz standards. Seated on a couch at the other end of the room, Colt's parents seemed engrossed in conversation with another couple. Nick's parents?

Then he saw *her*.

Gold sandals with criss-crossing straps imprisoned delicate arches. Shapely, bare legs shimmered with a light suntan. She wore a sleeveless lime green dress that ended several inches above her knees, its simple lines emphasizing her lush figure. She seemed a few inches slimmer around her hips, but her breasts were as enticing as ever. He longed to bury his face between them.

He hadn't had a chance to come inside Dana back at the Four Seasons, as he'd planned. He'd wanted to shag her all night long, not for only five minutes. Now he realized he'd felt deprived for seven months.

His cock began to harden. He prayed that Dana would be the silver lining in the dark cloud of this week.

The soft light shone on her platinum blonde hair, now trimmed to shoulder length. He strolled over, intending to greet her, and tripped over a fold in the thick Oriental carpet. His champagne flute flew out of his hand and hit her square in the tits, emptying over her. She squealed, and every head in the room turned to watch the show.

Colt found himself on his hands and knees, looking up Dana Newcombe's wet mini-dress.

Whoa, baby. Green lace panties and a very lush bush. He jerked his head back and struggled to his feet while she tried to clean herself off.

Shit. "I'm really sorry, Dana." He grabbed a nearby cocktail napkin and dabbed at her front. His hands made a beeline for her breasts. He couldn't help it.

They were the choicest set he'd seen in a long time. In seven months, to be exact.

Bits of the paper cocktail napkin formed tiny damp balls on her dress, and she swatted away his hand. "Haven't you done enough? I'm going to change." Whirling, she strode out of the room.

Colt sighed as his mother slipped an arm around him.

"What happened, son?"

"I've really blown it with Nick's sister," he muttered.

"Don't be silly. Anyone can stumble. You've done nothing wrong." Judi Wilder hugged him around the waist. "By the way, it's good to see you, dear. Would you like to meet the Newcombes now?"

She walked him over to the love seat where Dana and Nick's parents sat.

"Mr. Newcombe, Mrs. Newcombe, I'm happy to meet you." He shook their hands, one after the other. "I'm Colton Wilder. Congratulations. I'm sure Nick and Max will be very happy." He hoped he didn't sound too fake.

"Call me Tom, and this is my wife, Gabrielle." Thomas Newcombe's hazel eyes assessed Colt from behind a thick pair of tortoise-shell glasses. "Please, sit down."

Colt sat in a nearby chair. "Hi, Dad."

Alan Wilder nodded. "Good to see you, son. How was your trip out?"

"Slow. Maybe if I'd driven with you and Mom I would have gotten here faster." Colt reclined in his chair and tried to relax. He met Nick's glance. She stood behind her parents' love seat with her arm around Max, who smiled and gave Colt a "thumbs up" sign.

Tom leaned forward. "I hear you graduated from Northwestern. What was your field of study?"

"Business management." Colt sat up straighter.

"That's an intelligent choice." Gabrielle Newcombe had a light, charming French accent. "You then traveled, eh? Where did you go?"

Colt grinned. "I went anywhere they have beautiful horses, ma'am, and a few other places besides. All over the U. S. of A., Europe, parts of Africa and Asia. It was great, the trip of a lifetime."

"Did you happen to go to Boston?" Mrs. Newcombe asked.

"Yes, I've been through there a time or two."

"Have you met our other daughter, Dana? She's at the Institute of Technology there in Cambridge."

"M.I.T.?" Colt asked, faking innocence. Evidently neither set of parents knew anything about the multiple relationships between the Newcombe twins and the Wilder brothers. "She must be very bright."

Tom smiled proudly. "A scientist like her old Dad."

"You must be very gratified by your children," Colt's father said. "They're beautiful, talented young ladies."

"What, exactly, does Dana do?" Colt asked. If he could find some common ground with the prickly woman, he might be able to forge a connection that would lead to her bed.

"She's in a doctoral program and works part-time with a group called the Juno project," Tom said. "She analyzes the data sent back to Earth from the Juno space probe, which is orbiting Jupiter. Dana has a special interest in the moons of Jupiter."

Colt blinked. No help there, he thought.

Tom went on. "She's considered one of the nation's top authorities on the satellite Europa."

Colt blinked again. "Very esoteric."

"Oh, but it has tremendous future promise." Tom's eyes glittered, weirdly magnified behind his Coke-bottle glasses. "Europa is one of the few places in this system that has colonization potential."

"Colonization potential?"

Gabrielle cut in. "I'm sure Colton doesn't want to hear about Dana's silly planet. Would you like some shrimp?" She flagged a waiter.

"Actually, yes," Colt said, even though he would have liked to hear more about Dana's work, which sounded interesting, if obscure. "I haven't eaten since lunch, and plane food is never any good."

Gabrielle loaded a plate with several shrimp, as well as two caviar canapés. "You like caviar, eh?" Smiling, she handed the appetizers to Colt.

A little girl jumped into his lap, giving him a big, sloppy, kiddie hug. The sticky midget upset his plate of food, and shrimp tumbled everywhere, all over his immaculate white trousers, into his shoes, onto the floor.

"Unka Max?"

Colt looked down at the child. A pink, rosebud face stared up at him, then emitted an accusatory wail. "You're not Unka Max!"

"No, Rosie, this is Uncle Colt," Gabrielle cooed, lifting the little girl out of Colt's lap.

"I want Unka Max!" screamed the brat.

Colt's head already throbbed, and the child's screech cut through his brain like the whine of a Black and Decker lathe.

"Over here, over here." Max came over to scoop Rose away from Gabrielle, who glared at him.

Rose howled.

"Colt, this is Rose," Max said. "She's Sabrina's little girl."

"Have you met our oldest daughter, Sabrina?" Gabrielle asked.

"I'm right here, Mom." A brunette pulled Rose out of Max's arms, laid the child over her shoulder, and patted her small back. Rose's cries softened to a whimper.

Standing, Colt smiled at Sabrina. "I'm Colton Wilder, and I'd shake your hand but I see you're occupied."

She smiled back. "I'm Sabrina, and I see from your clothes you've met my daughter, Rose. Someone should have warned you *not* to wear white around her. She's in a very messy stage."

"That's all right. She was only trying to hug me— well, actually, Max. Besides, I'm sure the pants can be cleaned. Luckily, there wasn't any cocktail sauce on the plate."

Sabrina laughed. "Colton, this is my husband, Steve Drake."

Steve, dressed casually, had a trim dark moustache. Colt shook his hand.

Dana pranced into the room, wearing white denim shorts and a CalTech T-shirt. She looked Colt up and down. "Well, I see you've received your karmic comeuppance."

Colt zeroed in on Dana's gorgeous thighs. "Huh?"

"Don't be mean, Dana," her mother reproved.

"Yes, Mother."

Nick said, "Colt, go change. I'll send Mannering to the guest house, and he'll do something with that suit."

~ * ~

After he changed into jeans, Colt reentered the Newcombe house via the kitchen, where the caterers were cleaning up. He wished he'd grabbed some food on his way out. The house had quieted. Judging from the chatter from the front of the house, the party had wound down, and the remaining guests had gathered in the foyer.

He listened for the tinkling piano, hoping that there'd be some munchies left in the last remaining party room. He followed the song to its source, and discovered the musician playing "Unforgettable" in the back room near the pool area. Otherwise, Colt was alone. He picked up a cut crystal tumbler from the sideboard and filled it from a decanter. He sprawled comfortably on the love seat to enjoy the fine old Scotch.

Soft, strong hands kneaded his shoulders from behind him. "Penny for your thoughts?" a female voice murmured in his ear.

Colt turned his head to identify the girl rubbing his muscles. Based on the A-cup breasts, as well as the hairstyle and clothing, it had to be Nicole. Max was nowhere in sight.

Chapter Six

A grandfather clock chimed midnight. The musician stopped playing, closed the piano, and left the room. Colt heard the soft click of a computer keyboard. The slight, shifting light of a monitor emanated from an adjoining den, creating odd patterns and shadows.

"Where's Max?" he asked.

"He went to see some guests to their cars. We're alone, darling."

"What's up with this 'darling' stuff? Aren't you about to marry my brother?"

"Just teasing you a little bit, dear. You don't mind, do you?" Nicole walked around the love seat to sit next to him, trailing her fingertips along the back.

"As a matter of fact, I do mind. I think I mind the entire thing."

"What thing?" Her knee was close—too close—to his.

"This thing. You marrying Max." Standing, Colt walked away. She seemed too seductive for a woman in love with another man, and he wouldn't let his brother marry a two-timing Jezebel.

"Max said he thought you were upset. I guess he was right. Well, I must say, I'm flattered."

"Flattered? Why?"

"Obviously you're lovesick. I'm sorry to have led you on, Colt." Nicole's voice held no remorse.

His pride was stung. "Hey, *I* left *you*, remember?"

"So what's bugging you?"

Colt breathed deeply. The computer no longer clicked, and the room was so quiet he could hear the rasp of his breath. "What you did to Dana, to begin with. And on top of that, I haven't heard you tell me that you love my brother, either."

"My feelings are none of your business. Max offers me what I need, and I'll be a good wife to him."

"That's not the same thing, and we both know it. Dammit, Nick, what if you're making a big mistake? You'll be ruining three lives. Is that right?" He sat down on the love seat next to her, taking her hand.

Dana burst into the room from the adjoining den. "I don't believe my ears. Who are you to decide they're making a mistake?"

Colt dropped Nick's hand. Of all people to catch him, it had to be Dana Newcombe. *Now she'll think I'm a total scumbag.* Since all was apparently lost, he decided to go on the offensive. "And who are you to be interrupting a private conversation? This is none of your affair."

" 'Affair' seems to be the operative word. But if you want to have a private *tête-à-tête*, don't chat in a public room in someone else's house," Dana snapped. "Do you realize how upsetting this conversation could be to our parents, or to yours? Or to Max? Clearly, there's something still going on between the two of you. I suggest you straighten it out before Saturday night." She stomped out of the room.

"Dana!" Shit. If she thought he was hung up on Nicole, he wouldn't have a chance with her. "I wonder how long she was listening. Think she'll tell anyone?" he asked Nicole.

"No, Sabrina was always the snitch," Nick said. "Look, Colt, I appreciate how you feel, really I do." She stood and walked to the bar. "But Max and I are both adults, and believe me, we've discussed you and Dana more than once. We're sure we're doing the right thing for both of us. We're sorry you two are hurt, but…"

"I didn't say we were hurt. I don't know how Dana feels. I haven't talked with her."

"Whatever." Nicole shrugged. "There's nothing either of us can do about how you feel."

"An amazingly sympathetic reaction. I'm starting to feel sorry for Max."

"Face it, Colt, you're not truly hurt. Like you said, you left me. The fact is that you won't commit to anyone or anything but that damn farm. I wasn't even as important as another filly to you."

Enough was enough. If she wanted a quarrel, she was gonna get one. He let all his pent-up resentment explode. "I dumped you because you're a flirt and a cheat. My brother deserves better."

"Don't you dare interfere in my relationship with Max! You want to know why I'm marrying him? Because he values me. You never did. I don't have four legs and whinny." She stalked out of the room. The filmy black streamers of her gown trailed behind her.

Nick still refused to say that she loved his brother, so shouldn't he discourage Max from a marriage that would be a disaster? Colt rubbed his forehead again, realizing that any attempt to warn Max might come off like sour grapes.

~ * ~

Dana went to the front of the house to help her parents assist their guests into cars and taxis. Seeing the partiers safely on their way was no small effort, but kept her mind off the disturbing scene she'd witnessed between Nick and Colt … at least for a few moments.

She pried Rose away from Gabrielle's prized Lladro collection, and handed her sticky-fingered niece to Sabrina and Steve, who were heading home for the night. Dana then checked her room to make sure her cross-dressing French cousin hadn't ransacked her lingerie drawer. Again.

Her clothing secured, she wandered through the dark, quiet house to the back yard. Rambling past Mannering's kitchen garden, she admired the neat, raised beds of herbs and vegetables. Trellised beans and peas marked the boundaries of the butler's agricultural domain. She passed her mother's roses, breathing in the flowers' perfume. The pale saucer-shapes seemed eerie at midnight.

She strolled to the swimming pool and sat cross-legged on the diving board, gazing at the wavering silver reflection of the half-moon in the still water. The tiny, floating candles lighting the pool earlier in the evening had flickered out and drifted over to one side of the pool, near the filter. She hoped none of them would be sucked into the mechanism.

She sat for a long time as she contemplated the evening's events and, of course, Colt. Why, oh why, couldn't he have stayed away?

The memory of what she'd done in the elevator with him still scorched as though his hot cock had branded her from the inside out. Though she'd dated in the last seven months, no man she'd slept with came close to turning her on as much as Colt had. With a newly-grown dark beard, bedroom-blue eyes and seductive smile, he looked like a romance novel hero, even if he acted like a horndog. Unfortunately, she'd always been attracted to the Wild West thing, even though she'd never been to a ranch and horses scared her.

Last time they'd seen each other, he'd been a total cad, using sex with her to make a point about her relationship with Max, which really wasn't Colt's business. And tonight, he'd turned goofball. Not only had he tripped and dumped champagne all over her new linen dress, but he'd taken the opportunity to peek at her panties. Sick, sick, sick. Where did he think he was, a hoedown?

Maybe she was being unfair, since Colt hadn't planned to stumble or to peek. But he apparently intended to persuade her sister to call off the wedding. He'd even been holding Nick's hand. Did he want to seduce her? How could he be such a low-life? Dana wondered whether Max knew of disloyal Colton's plans.

Nick, at least, seemed to behave. But what was really going on inside her heart? *I haven't heard you tell me that you love my brother*, Colt had challenged, and Nick had replied, *Max offers me what I need, and I'll be a good wife to him.* Dana shook her head. That sure didn't sound like true love.

She wanted to talk with Sabrina, who always understood her worries. Too bad she'd gone home with her husband for the night.

Sabrina and Steve were an example of the way a romance should be … the way Dana wanted her life to be. And, even though her mom could act screwy and neurotic, her parents had been happy together for nearly thirty years. That accomplishment seemed impossible to Dana.

She sighed, and a voice came out of the darkness. "That's a heavy sigh. Sounds like you've got something on your mind." Emerging from the night, Max sat next to her on the diving board.

Damn. She'd managed to avoid being alone with Max for days, but it seemed that her good luck had run out. Well, she could keep the conversation light and avoid any touchy topics. She uncrossed her long legs and stretched them out in front of her.

"So what's going on?" He turned and fixed her with a keen glance. "We were close once, Dana. Why can't we be friends?"

She hesitated, searching her feelings. She liked him, but wasn't in love with him and never had been. Sure, her ego had been a little bruised, but she'd gotten over it.

"I guess we can," she said slowly. "It would certainly make family gatherings easier."

"It's a weird situation, but we're all adults here."

"True." *And if I'm fortunate, you haven't found out that I boinked your brother in a glass-walled elevator in front of downtown Boston.*

"So what's on your mind? You know you can tell me anything."

Oh, no I can't. "Nothing in particular, I suppose. Just trying to keep my head in all the excitement."

"So, are you getting along with Colt?" Max's eyes glinted mischievously. "Last time I saw the two of you together at the Four Seasons, you seemed … close."

She gave an embarrassed chuckle, wondering how much Max knew. "I didn't really get much of a chance to talk with him tonight, considering that both of us spent most of this evening changing clothes."

He laughed. "I was afraid you and Colt got off on the wrong foot tonight."

She blessed the darkness, which hid the blush heating her cheeks. How could she explain the situation to Max, the innocent bystander and potential victim?

She'd feel like a heel if Nick, prodded by Colt, ran off and left poor Max at the altar, while she, Dana, knew about the situation but did nothing. Alternatively, what would happen if she told Max about the conversation she'd overheard? What if she caused the breakup by telling him what she knew?

Yikes. This was way too much responsibility. She decided to play for time until she could talk with Sabrina and figure out what, if anything, to do.

"I'm sure we'll work it out." She faked a yawn. "I'm pretty tired… Excuse me. Well, I suppose it's time for me to say good night." She retreated into the house, wondering if every evening with the Wilder brothers would be as unsettling.

~ * ~

Overtired, Colton slept late, awakening to find Max gone. After putting on his favorite denim cut-offs, Colt poked through the small refrigerator of the guest house. It contained only a carton of milk and an apple that had seen better days. He decided to raid the main kitchen for breakfast.

Opening the door of the guest house, he noticed a brunette woman in a large straw hat roaming through a fragrant rose garden nearby.

" 'Allo, Colt!" Gabrielle called. "You slept late, eh?"

"Good morning, Mrs. Newcombe. How are you today?"

"I am well," she said, wielding her clippers, "but tense. It was like this for me before Sabrina's wedding, also."

"At least you don't have to worry about tonight. That's my parents' responsibility." He stepped out of the guest house into the California sunshine. Already intense at eleven o'clock, its heat hammered his bare shoulders.

"Yes, but I recommended the restaurant where they are hosting the rehearsal dinner. If all is not right, I shall feel to blame."

"Oh, don't worry. If you picked the place, I'm sure it will be terrific." He figured it wouldn't dare to be otherwise. He'd seen the steel beneath Gabrielle's charm when she'd reprimanded Dana. "Is that where my parents are right now?"

"Yes, they are there, with Max and Nicole. Also they visit the church to make sure all is ready for the rehearsal. They will come back to take you to pick up your tuxedo. Have you eaten breakfast yet?"

"Actually, no."

"Go to the kitchen," Gabrielle said. "There should be coffee and croissant. It's late, lunch will be soon."

Colt fetched himself a mug full of hot, fragrant French roast coffee and a flaky croissant. After spreading the roll with butter, he took the meal out to the poolside patio. He made a mental note to swim or run later, otherwise his visit to Los Angeles would leave him big as a pony and pudgy as Miss Piggy.

He put his mug and his plate on a small glass table beneath an umbrella, sprawled into a handy deck chair

and started eating breakfast. As he munched, Dana
Newcombe stepped out of the house. His hormones
jumped to record levels.

Ostentatiously ignoring him, she dropped her towel
and headed for the diving board. Her red bikini showed
off her exquisite figure. He adjusted his cut-offs, which
had become uncomfortably tight around his growing
hard-on.

She ran four steps along the diving board, bounced,
and executed a sloppy swan dive into the pool, then
surfaced. Her platinum hair, slick and dark from the
water, gleamed against her skull. She swam over to the
end of the pool, then did laps in a steady Australian
crawl for several minutes. The water flowed past her
shapely body in a smooth stream. Fast and fit, she
obviously worked out.

After a few minutes, she climbed out of the pool,
and went again to the diving board. This time she
bounced high, coming down into the pool with her long
frame tucked into a ball, arms wrapped around her legs.
The cannonball, a favorite of every kid Colt ever knew,
splashed torrents of water over the pool, the deck, and
him. Howling in surprise and dismay, he leaped out of
his chair to give her a piece of his mind, but she was
underwater and couldn't possibly hear his angry shout.

When Dana surfaced, she saw her mother frown at
her from the edge of the pool.

"Dana, you splashed our guest. Please apologize."
Gabrielle turned and walked into the house.

"Yes, Mother." Dana looked up at Colt. Water
clung to his shaggy dark hair and beard, glistening off

his chiseled torso. He rubbed his chest, moist with water from the pool. Droplets lit by the bright sun clung like tiny crystal stars to the black, curly hair on his sculptured pecs.

The smirk crossing his face made her want to slap him silly, and she realized she'd been staring.

"Well?" he asked.

"Well, what?"

"Where's my apology?" Colt sat down at the side of the pool and dangled his bare feet into the water.

"Oh, that?"

"Yeah. You owe me, darlin'."

Dana gasped at his nerve. "I don't owe you squat, dude!"

"I heard a very definite order for an apology, and I'm not leaving until I get mine."

"You'll get yours, all right!" She grabbed both of his arms and, bracing herself against the side of the pool, tugged. In he went, with a surprised yelp.

He surfaced. Sucking in a deep breath, he glowered, then swam underneath her. She treaded water, feeling uneasy. Had she gone too far?

He roped one strong arm around her midsection. With a mighty heave, he tossed her up to the surface of the pool. Squealing, she flew halfway out of the water, then crashed back in. While she fought for control, he grabbed her around the waist and swam with her, backing her against the nearest wall of the pool. He pinned her there with his arms and body.

"Apologize!" he demanded.

She splashed him full in the face. He leaned closer to her.

"Apologize!" He came even closer.

Laughter bubbled inside her. She began to snicker. Where did that silly female giggle come from? "No way, coffee breath!"

His mouth was less than an inch away from hers. "Apologize." His voice, with its seductive southern accent, had become a low, sexy growl. He moved his hips into hers, the same way he'd ground against her in the elevator. His implacable, blue gaze bored into her.

She could emit only an agitated squawk. Colt's lips, shapely and firm, nibbled at her mouth. She became aware of his cock rising hot and thick, pressing against her mound. He wriggled, forcing her thighs apart so that he pushed against her clit.

Her body pulsed with desire while her brain wondered, *How does he do that?* Somehow, Colt turned her on faster and hotter than anyone she'd ever met.

She resented that.

Easing his mouth away from hers, he bent his head to kiss her neck. His beard scratched pleasantly as he nuzzled lower, going for her breast. She dropped her head back, arching her chest toward him.

Movement at the edge of the pool caught her eye. Her father. Shit. How long had he been there? What had he seen? Could someone really die of embarrassment?

Colt reached for her breast, and his grip on her loosened. She slid from his hold, dropping to the pool's bottom. After swimming over to the side, she climbed out.

"Hi, Dad." She struggled to keep her voice calm. She walked past her dad, picked up a towel and began drying her face. She noticed, almost objectively, that her hands shook.

"You should probably wash the pool water out of your hair, or the chlorine will turn it green." Tom's demeanor was serene. "Your mother doesn't want this wedding characterized by unusual hair colors." He went back into the house.

Sighing with relief, Dana headed over to the pool cabana to rinse her hair in the sink, grateful for an excuse to get away from Colt. As she turned off the water and stood, wrapping her head in a towel, she heard a soft male voice behind her ask, "May I have a towel, please?"

Colt leaned against the post of the open door. He raised one hand to push his wet, shaggy hair off his forehead. Muscles flexed in his sinuous frame. He smiled at her, his blue eyes twinkling. His moist eyelashes clung together in myriad starry points. Dammit, she still wanted to touch him.

"Y-yeah, sure," Dana said, disarmed by his gentleness. She wondered how long he'd been standing at the door, scrutinizing her. Then she realized he'd been checking out her butt, most of which had been hanging out of the skimpy bikini bottom as she bent over the sink.

She wondered if she'd shaved properly. If Colt was going to eyeball her pussy whenever he could, maybe she ought to get a Brazilian.

Mentally gathering the wisps of her shredded poise, she reached into a cupboard and pulled out a purple beach towel that yelled MAUI in giant black letters. She handed it to him. "I like this towel. It reminds me of Hawaii. Ever been there?"

"No, haven't had the pleasure."

"Great place." She scooted by him on her way out, her breast brushing his arm. Her skin sizzled from the erotic charge. The scientist in her visualized a mercury thermometer blowing its top.

Colt touched her naked shoulder. "I'll get that apology, toots, one way or another." Though his fingers were light, she feared third degree burns from their heat.

"Excuse me, cowboy, but…"

"What did you call me?" He backed away from her, eyes narrowed. He wagged a finger at her. "Don't you ever call me a cowboy."

"Huh? What about that hat you wear?"

Colt groaned. "Listen, toots. Call me anything you want. Pond scum, rat, creep, whatever—but don't ever call me a cowboy!"

"See ya later, cowboy," Dana said, in her sweetest tone of voice. She stepped around him to leave the cabana.

His arm shot out. His hand gripped the opposite doorpost, trapping her. "Just a minute, princess."

Dana's breath caught in her throat. Her heartbeat escalated. The mercury spurted, geyser-like, out of the top of the thermometer. "Wh—what do you want?"

"Oh, I think you know what I want. You owe me, and you're not leaving 'til I get that apology." He regarded her, his blue eyes glinting. "On second thought, that's not enough. An apology … and another kiss."

"You—you got a kiss, uh, before. In Boston. And a lot more!"

"That didn't count."

That intrigued her. "Why not?"

"That was months ago. Different situation, different intentions."

"Yeah, I know. You were trying to make a point. Point taken." Dana tried to push Colt's arm out of her way. The muscles tensed, stiff as an iron bar.

He smiled at her. That wicked smile, coupled with their near-nakedness, made her dizzy. He said, "That was just a quickie. You deserve better, and so do I." He slid one finger under her chin, lifting it.

For the first time in her life, six-foot-tall Dana had to look up at a man. Though Colt's tender, demanding gesture brought out the vulnerable woman in her, she didn't feel small. Instead, her nerves leaped with excitement. She swallowed, then jerked her chin away from his caressing fingers. "What about that scene last night with Nickie? If you'd rather be with my sister, I'm outta here."

"Forgive me, but your sister is a two-timing heartbreaker." His rough voice sent shivers up and down her spine.

"But what about me and Max? You could just as easily believe the same thing about me!"

He paused and rubbed his chin. "Dana, you really don't see it, do you?"

"See what?"

"You were set up, sweetheart. Nick set you up."

She pulled away, rubbing her hands over her chilled arms. "I can't believe that!" But in her heart, she did. She did. Nick always took whatever she wanted.

Lucky Dana hadn't really loved Max. But she'd cared, so—

"I don't want your sister." Colt interrupted Dana's mental tumult, shoving aside her confusion about Nick and Max. "I want you."

Again, he homed in on her lips. His eyes narrowed, seeming to darken. A breathless moment passed before Colt settled his mouth over hers. This time, Dana didn't argue or resist. Her flesh tingled from the delicious contact, her sensitive mouth responding to the softness of his lips, the gentle scratch of his beard.

He returned his fingers to her cheek. His free hand slid down to cup her breast, still damp from her swim. Although she wore a wet bikini, she didn't feel cold. But her nipple hardened where he touched it. When he rubbed his finger over the tight nub and pushed his tongue into her mouth, she thought she'd jump right out of her skin from the pleasure that zinged through her body.

"Dana!" Gabrielle's voice screamed from outside the cabana. "The U.P.S. has finally brought your dress. Come up to your room and try it on."

"Y-yes, Mother." Jerking away, Dana fled, trying to ignore Colt's pursuit.

Chapter Seven

Dana stared, horrified, at the bridesmaid's dress. The Nicole Newcombe Original made her look like a pregnant orca. The Empire-style outfit, in silk crepe, had a sleeveless white bodice and a full black skirt flowing from a high waistline, which was trimmed by a giant red satin bow. Its ridiculously long streamers fluttered down toward the floor-length hem.

The white bodice bleached her already pale coloring. Wonderful. She looked like a pregnant, *dead* orca. Despite several days in the California sun, her skin still had a scholarly pallor. With her platinum blonde hair, light brows, and hazel eyes, she looked ashen and ghostlike. What on earth had Nick been thinking? Dana wondered if their seamstress could re-cut the ample dress in the few hours remaining before the ceremony. However, correcting the effect the white and black had on her complexion might be beyond any tailor's best efforts.

She heard a tap on her door. "Come in!" she called.

Her worst nightmare became real when she looked up to see Colton Wilder, now attired in skintight jeans and a muscle-T, lounging in her doorway. When he looked at her in the tentlike dress, his brows slowly raised. "Holy parachute, Batgirl!"

"You're not kidding, cowboy."

He grimaced. "I guess I deserved that." Without an invitation, he entered and plucked at the voluminous skirt. "Nice silky fabric … and there sure is a lot of it!"

Gabrielle stepped through the door. Her mother raised her tweezed, dark eyebrows as she regarded Colt and Dana.

"Guess I'd better be going." Colt skedaddled.

Gabrielle turned her attention to the tentlike dress. "I don't understand. All of the gowns needed to be fitted, but none of them is so—so…"

"Gross? Hideous? Ghastly? Face it, Mother. This is deliberate. She wants me to look bad." Dana began to unzip the dress, her hands clumsy with rage.

"Dana, do not cause problems."

Dana glared at her mother. She'd had enough of the two of them—Nicole and Gabrielle. Was this a conspiracy to make her miserable? "I'm not letting her walk all over me anymore!"

"Calm down. Obviously zhere's been a mistake, and you will go to Alice and have the dress fitted properly. Don't worry about it. She expects to work on our clothes zis week." Gabrielle pulled a cellular phone from her pocket and punched one button. Dana watched, amazed. *Mother actually has her seamstress programmed into her speed-dialer. She's completely obsessed!*

After a brief conversation with Alice, Gabrielle clicked off the phone. "She expects you after lunch, with Sabrina. Change your clothes now." She gave her daughter a little shove, which was as close to a hug as Dana ever got from Gabrielle.

Nicole marched through the door. "Hi, everyone!" she called cheerily as she looked around. "My sweet Lord. She hasn't changed anything in here either."

Gabrielle stiffened. "What do you mean, dear?"

"I mean, Mom, it's pretty weird the way you've preserved our rooms. They're like shrines to our lost girlhood." Nick cast a glance around Dana's room, which featured a pink, canopied bed and a multitude of stuffed animals.

"It's worse than that," Dana said. "I never had stuffed animals, I had moon rocks and Hendrix posters. Mother replaced them." She winked at her mother. Gabrielle was rigid. "Mother re-decorated for the kids she *wished* she had."

"If the two of you are quite finished…" Gabrielle huffed.

The twins erupted in squeals of laughter.

"Quiet!" Gabrielle shouted. "Now, about this dress…"

Nicole, instantly serious, said, "What about the dress? It's perfect."

Dana gagged as she lifted up yards of fabric and swished them around at her sister. "Perfect? Perfect if you're a whale!"

"This is how the dress is supposed to fit!"

"This is how the dress is supposed to fit Free Willy," Dana snapped. "If you think I'm gonna let you make me look like crap warmed over…"

Gabrielle broke in. "Children, please! Change your clothes and go downstairs to lunch. We have guests, eh?"

~ * ~

Sabrina arrived, lending a note of needed sanity. Her older sister had been the calming element in the household for as long as Dana could remember. After lunch, Sabrina put Rose down for a nap, then took Dana over to the seamstress to have the preposterous bridesmaid's dress fitted.

With the Mustang's convertible top open, Dana clutched at her wide straw hat, carefully shielding her pale skin while the wind whipped through Sabrina's hair.

"You've been very quiet." Sabrina stopped at a red light. "What's up?"

Dana groaned. "I don't really know where to begin."

"Just head right into it." The green light flashed, and Sabrina resumed driving.

"Okay, I think Colt and Nick are still hung up on each other, and Nick is going to dump Max."

Sabrina's brows jerked. "What? Why?"

Dana told her big sister everything, starting from last November. "And I have to say, although he's slime, Colt … really is the, uh, more interesting of the two."

"Yes, and you should know." Sabrina cut Dana a keen glance.

Dana blushed. "Well, he certainly knows his way around a woman's body. But Max is a nice guy, and I feel sorry for him."

"Do you still have feelings for Max?"

"Umm ... Not really. He, uh, represented a lot of things I wanted in life, but I wasn't madly in love with him. I realize now that if I'd married him, it would have been wrong. And I think that Nickie feels the same way, down deep. She said that they'll give each other what they need, not that she couldn't live without him."

"Hmm." Sabrina pursed her lips.

"No one deserves to be dumped at the altar, and I'm scared that Nick will do just that."

"I must admit I haven't noticed Nick treating Max the way I expect a couple in love to behave. She's almost businesslike. I never see them touch or kiss. Remember how Steve and I were?"

Dana grinned. "Do I ever! You two were the most x-rated couple I ever saw. I got a whole education just watching you two at the dinner table."

Sabrina smiled reminiscently. "We were out of control, but we were very much in love. Still are. I don't see that in Nick and Max, but I don't see anything between Nick and Colt, either."

"You didn't see them holding hands."

"But Colt didn't kiss Nick in the pool, he kissed you. And he said flat out that he wants you, right?"

"Yes. Can you believe it?"

"Yes, I can believe it. You're a beautiful girl, but you've always let Nicole outshine you."

"Maybe he's hitting on me out of boredom, or he's on the rebound or something." Dana flung her arms wide. "Oh, I don't know! I just wish the whole thing wasn't happening."

Sabrina pulled into Alice's driveway and cut the Mustang's motor. "I think you're taking it all too seriously. If you want to help out Max, why don't you make sure that Colton is occupied with you, instead of with Nicole?" She got out of the Mustang and slammed the door.

"Isn't that a little manipulative?"

"So what? This way, the wedding goes off without a hitch, and you find out if Colt really likes you or not."

"Unless Nickie dumps Max." Dana followed Sabrina up the walkway to Alice's door.

"You can't do anything about that. At least you'll remove Colt as a factor." Sabrina rang the bell, then looked over and smiled at Dana. "What harm could it do? It's just a little flirtation. Plus, you'll also have a good time, especially if he's as hot as you say."

Dana blushed, remembering how Colt felt inside her. She'd actually come twice. She wasn't always orgasmic, and no other man had ever made her climax more than once. She'd thought that multiple orgasms were a myth. Now she knew better. "Oh, he is."

"Who's what?" Alice Johansen asked, as she opened the door. Both sisters burst into embarrassed laughter.

"Nothing—no one," Dana managed to gasp. After they stepped into Alice's sewing room she gasped again. Bridesmaid Leta Weller, a childhood friend, stood dressed in her gown. She looked terrific. The dress, minus the mass of fabric billowing the bodice and skirt, skimmed her waist and hips. The excess black silk had been stitched into an evening shawl, draped over her elbows. Redheaded Leta's coloring was flattered, rather than bleached, by the black and white ensemble.

"All right, Alice!" Dana said. "If you can do the same for my dress, we'll all look marvelous."

Alice grinned. "Just tell me I'm a genius."

"You're a genius," all three women chorused.

"Sabrina, I've finished yours also. Try it on. Dana, are you saying this dress just arrived?" Alice asked.

"Yeah, this morning."

"Strange," Sabrina said. "The others came weeks ago."

Dana shrugged. "I just got here a couple of days ago. Why should the dress arrive before me?"

"I can tell you," Leta said. "I went out with Nick and a couple of her buddies last Saturday night, and she had a few too many. I overheard Nick having a great big laugh about how your dress was gonna make you look like a dead cow, and she arranged to have it sent late so it couldn't be properly fitted."

"Really?" Alice's hands stilled. "We'll see about that."

"She's been pissy ever since your wedding, Sabrina." Leta folded her evening shawl.

"Oh, you must mean the Bozo episode," Dana said. "But as far as I'm concerned, she's been pissy all her life." She pulled off her T-shirt over her head.

"She's always been jealous of Dana." Reaching behind her, Leta unzipped her dress.

"What is this Bozo incident people keep talking about?" Sabrina asked.

Both Dana and Leta laughed. Dana said, "Don't you remember what happened at your wedding?"

"I remember the happiest day of my life, except perhaps when Rose was born." Sabrina smiled.

Leta hooted. "You were so wrapped up with Steve that you didn't notice anything else, like one of your sisters morphing into Bozo the clown."

"The hair problem Nicole had?" Sabrina asked. "What does that have to do with anything?"

"I love Nickie, but you know how obsessed she is with her appearance." Leta said. "She always has to be the center of attention. Why do you think she permed her hair and dyed it red for your wedding?"

"She wanted to look better?" Sabrina's brow crinkled.

Alice smiled. "You always think the best of others. Trust me, I've known the three of you since you were little kids. Nicole wants to make sure that her twin doesn't steal any of her thunder."

"Oh, that won't happen," Sabrina said. "The bride is always the most beautiful woman at her wedding. After all, she shines with an inner glow."

Dana rolled her eyes.

"Dana, please." Her sister faced Dana. "You know how important this wedding is to Mom. I know you and Nicole don't get along, but try to put up with her for another couple of days—for our parents' sake."

"What is it with the two of you, anyways?" Alice asked. "I know other sets of twins. Usually they're the best of friends."

"Not us. We're really different." Dana tugged off her shorts, preparing to put on the dress.

Leta raised her brows. "You're identical twins."

"So? Believe me, just because you share a womb with someone doesn't mean you share anything else. We're in the same species, but the similarities end there." Dana, trapped with the dress over her head, fought for freedom from the voluminous silk folds.

"The two of you have competed for attention since day one." Sabrina shrugged her shoulders, now clad in white silk. "I think that early on Nick became Mommy's girl, and you felt isolated from Mom. So you and Dad became close, and Nick felt left out. Things went on from there."

"Nick thinks I'm nerdy and boring and says so all the time." Dana couldn't help the bitter note infecting her voice. "How can I be close to someone who puts me down?"

"I'm not sure you can, but try to tolerate her, okay?" Sabrina tugged her gown over her head. "The dress looks good, Alice."

"Now you, Dana. Step up here. Hmmm," Alice murmured, circling Dana, who stepped onto a raised platform in Alice's large sewing room. "It looks like the entire dress has to be re-cut. Except for the shoulders, it's too big all over." Alice began jabbing pins into the sides, the waist, the hem of the awful gown. "Color doesn't do much for you, does it?"

"Not at all," Dana said. "I never wear black and white. It's such a strong combination. They'll wash me out since my skin and hair's so pale."

"Well, that can be changed." Alice tweaked the hem.

"What do you mean?"

"Get some more sun by your parents' pool and buy a darker shade of make-up. You getting a facial?" Alice asked.

"I hadn't planned on it."

"Have a facial tomorrow, and have the aesthetician dye your eyelashes and brows," Alice said. "And wear your green contacts."

"I have an idea." Leta pulled on her T-shirt. "You oughtta take the make-over one step further. What do you think about tinting your hair?"

"What's wrong with platinum blonde?" Dana began to feel that she was under attack. Skin, brows, eyes … was anything about her face and body acceptable?

"Nothing, except you're as colorless as an albino." Leta tugged on jeans.

"I don't want another Bozo incident," Sabrina said. "Mom will flip out."

"I'm not talking about anything extreme." Leta slipped her feet into sandals. "Just one of those temporary colorants in a golden or honey blonde. They rinse out after eight shampoos or so. If you don't like it, you just wash it out."

"Do it," Alice said. "You're not going to let Nick get away with this, are you?"

"No, I'm done with that. Why do you think I live hundreds of miles away from her?" Dana stared at the mirror. True, her platinum hair had been bleached even paler by the California sun. If she spent the next morning outside to tan, it would only get worse. Maybe Leta was right. "I'll try it."

"Okay," Alice said. "I'll bring the dress by tomorrow at about noon. You'll have plenty of time to get to the church for the photographs."

"Oh, joy." Dana climbed out of the yards of silk, then put on her shorts and T-shirt.

The doorbell rang, and Alice looked out of the window. "Uh-oh, here comes Ms. Trouble."

Dana peeked out. "Oh, no, it's Nicole."

"All right, put those dresses away." Alice went to answer the door.

Nicole entered the room behind the seamstress. "Hey, Leta! Good to see you. Aren't you going to model the dress for me?"

"Sorry, Nick, gotta run." Leta picked up her purse. "I'll see you at the church tomorrow at four for the photos, all right?"

"Aren't you coming to the rehearsal?" Nicole asked. "It's at five today, at the church. Then we're having dinner at Antonio's."

"Oh, yeah. Sure, I'll be there. With bells on." Leta hurried out of the fire zone.

Sabrina zipped her dress into a garment bag. "Nick, are we supposed to wear French twists, or what?"

"You know, I don't know," Nicole answered, sounding irrational. "I haven't decided. I may want to put my hair up, in which case, I would want everyone else to have theirs loose, you know?"

Sabrina and Dana exchanged glances. "Do, please, let us know when you decide, okay?" Dana said, sarcasm edging her voice.

"Get off my back, Dana," Nick snapped.

"What's your problem?" Dana asked. "Isn't this supposed to be the happiest time of your life?"

"Just shut up, all right?" Nicole turned to Alice. "Let's get this last fitting over with."

"Right away, ma'am," Alice said.

Nick stared at her. "What is it with everybody? Why is everyone so damn cranky today, anyhow?"

Sabrina asked quietly, "What do you mean, Nicole?"

Nick's eyes filled. "What I mean is Max and I haven't been getting along, and I don't know if I can go through with this!"

Sabrina took both of Nick's hands in hers, squeezing them gently. "Honey, what's going on?"

Nick burst into tears as Dana watched her, shocked. This wasn't the brash, brazen twin sister she knew.

But Sabrina seemed to understand the situation. She led Nick over to a couch, sat her down, and hugged her. "What's up, sweetie?"

"Max has been acting d-d-differently ever si-since we came to Los Angeles," Nick sobbed. "He's like another p-person—so d-d-distant and weird!"

"Maybe he has a touch of pre-wedding jitters," Sabrina said. "It's natural."

"And his family—I f-feel like everyone knows I had a relationship with C-Colt before I went with Max. And everyone's mad at me because of D-Dana." She cast a bitter glance at her twin.

Damn. Dana had thought that no one knew. If they did, they were sure doing a great job faking ignorance, at least to her face. It sounded as though Nicole wasn't as fortunate. "Hey, I didn't say anything to anyone. Don't look at me like that."

"It's n-not my fault if you and Max didn't make it. And it's no one else's business. What's done is done, and Max and I know what we're doing," Nick blubbered. "Alan and Judi are suspicious and critical because of C-Colt and Dana, and they don't like me at all."

"They'll get over it when they see that you and Max are happy," Sabrina said, in the same tone of voice she used when Rose threw a tantrum. "You can't worry about what either set of parents think. Remember what happened with me and Steve? Mom and Dad didn't like Steve at all. They were totally opposed to our marriage. But so what? We're happy, we have a good relationship, and they recognize that. Now dry your eyes." Sabrina reached into her pocket. Pulling out a tissue, she handed it to Nick, who blew her nose, then rubbed the reddened tip.

"You're right. I'm being stupid," Nick said. She sighed and stood up. "Okay, let's get the wedding gown on and hope I haven't put on any more weight." She unbuttoned the front of her summer sundress, letting it fall to the floor.

Dana couldn't help feeling anxious. Another snag on the road to true bliss! What would happen next?

Nicole laughed suddenly. "Look at you both!" she mocked, with some of her old spirit. "You look like two old ladies at a porn flick. Get going. I'll see you tonight."

Sabrina and Dana jetted out. As they left, Dana asked Sabrina, "Is her dress a big secret, or something?"

"I don't think so. I think it's just a traditional gown, puffed sleeves, full skirt, et cetera, et cetera. I guess her attitude is part of the pre-wedding jitters."

"Are you sure that's all this little scene was? Pre-wedding jitters?"

"Yes." Sabrina smiled faintly. "I know the situation is complicated by all the overlapping relationships, but I'm convinced her feelings for Max are real. Otherwise she wouldn't be so upset by a perceived change in his behavior."

"I hope you're right. Should we say anything to Max?"

"Oh, heck, no. Just steer clear of the whole mess," Sabrina said. "If you get bored, just amuse yourself with Colt."

Chapter Eight

A musing myself with Colt won't be so bad, Dana thought. Again impeccably dressed in his white linen suit, he stood at the opposite side of the crowded lounge in Antonio's, the site of the rehearsal dinner. An upscale restaurant specializing in the northern Italian cuisine, Antonio's was decorated for the occasion with massive bouquets of spring flowers.

Dana blinked to moisten her green contacts and watched him chat easily with her parents as though the scene her father witnessed in the swimming pool had never taken place. Rose toddled around the room, tugging at the grown-ups' clothes and demanding sips of their drinks. Dana moved to evade her niece's clutching hands, which invariably would be sticky.

When Rose neared Colt, she screeched, "Jafar! Bad, bad Jafar!"

He looked astounded. "Who's Jafar?"

"Jafar is the bad guy in the *Aladdin* movie she watched today." Sabrina picked up her daughter. "She thinks you look like him because of your beard."

He wrinkled his brow, stroking his beard with an obviously fond caress. He eyed Rosie. "How about if I shave it off? Maybe I'll look more normal to Rose, and the ceremony will be, uh, quiet."

"You are so nice, Colt," Gabrielle said, sounding grateful. "Thank you. I do not like to suggest it, but it would be best."

Even Mother likes him … this guy's slicker than snot! Dana shivered, recalling his demanding embrace in the cabana, to say nothing of the elevator scene. She wondered whether she should stick to her risky plan of distracting volatile Colt with flirtation. She'd never be able to keep him out of her bed; he was far too determined, and she was way too susceptible to his seductive charm. She already knew how great sex with him was, and she couldn't turn him down if he really wanted to get inside her. More of a man than anyone she'd ever met, he'd keep her on her toes or flat on her back.

Gabrielle left Colt to snag a canapé, and, shaking off her indecision, Dana swooped in. She sidled past Leta Weller, who gulped champagne. Dana frowned, then approached her father and Colton as they discussed the impending demise of Colt's beard.

"My barber is in downtown Glendale, near Newcombe Industries' first offices. I liked him so much I never changed barbers, even after the company moved." Tom chuckled.

"A man gets attached to his barber." Colt rubbed his chin. "Who knows, I might like yours so much I'll have to fly to Glendale every time I want a trim."

"It doesn't look as though you've found a stylist near that farm." Dana stared at his long, shaggy hair.

Colt grinned. "You're right. I've trimmed my beard, but haven't bothered to get a hair cut for awhile."

"When's your appointment?" she asked.

"I obviously haven't had an opportunity to make one, yet."

"Of course." Dana winced inwardly. If she stuck her foot in her mouth every time she talked with him, he'd run off with Nicole for sure. "But what I mean to say is that you'd best get your beard shaved off early in the day, and then get some sunshine. Otherwise, you'll have a tan line."

He speared Dana with his intent blue gaze. "You're so concerned. I'm flattered."

"She's right," Tom said. "It's happened to me after I went on a camping retreat to Yosemite. I didn't shave for a week. When I took my beard off, my face had an interesting two-tone effect."

Dana giggled. "I remember. Mother was appalled. She slathered your face with some indoor tanning stuff to even out your skin tone. It turned your skin two different shades of orange." She giggled again and shook her hair out of her face, hoping she looked flirty and cute. Damn, but flirty and cute was tough. She could do all kinds of things, from programming computers to decipher binary code, but flirty and cute eluded her.

"Sometimes your mother can be a bit over-zealous. Well, it's not too late to call to and see if Bill can fit you in early tomorrow." Tom reached into his pocket. "Must have left my phone in the car…" His voice trailed away as he hurried off.

Dana tossed her head and straightened her back, deliberately thrusting her chest toward Colt, who dropped his gaze from her face.

"Nice outfit." His eyes raked her body. "Did you buy it in Boston?"

"Thank you, but no," she said. "In Pasadena, when I went to school there."

"Pink silk, very feminine."

"Thank you." Her body heated as he overtly continued to check her out. She'd never been scrutinized so thoroughly by a male as virile as Colton Wilder. He looked at her as though she were on display, like a naked centerfold. She did feel attractive, though. Her silk dress caressed her body like a warm summer breeze. The matching jacket was hand-painted with a graceful flower. She wore the same strappy gold sandals as the previous night.

Both flattered and intimidated by his obvious admiration, she smiled and tried to meet his gaze with a flirty wink that which dropped one mascaraed lash into her right eye. She blinked furiously, attempting to dislodge the lash before it slipped beneath one of her green contact lenses. Unhappy experience told her that the tiniest hair would cause unbelievable agony if it became stuck under a lens.

Before she could embarrass herself further, Alan came by, tapping Colt on the shoulder. "Son, Dana, it's time to sit down for dinner."

"Ooh, good," she said, relieved. The eyelash had apparently floated away without inflicting further torture. Perhaps it had just been a bit of lint. "The food here is awesome."

"Maybe you'll help me order." Colt offered her his arm.

She took it, allowing him to escort her into an adjoining dining room. Leta stumbled behind them. "I don't know how I can help you," Dana said. "Didn't you travel to Europe?"

"Yes, and I went to Italy. But I went with a backpack on a shoestring. Believe me, the holes-in-the-wall I ate in were nothing like this restaurant."

Lined with rich wood paneling, Antonio's private dining room was dominated by a long table, dotted with low centerpieces of spring flowers and set with white linen, silver, and crystal. Colt sat Dana near one end of the table and placed himself on her right as the wedding party settled into their chairs.

She discreetly checked her eye make-up in a compact mirror she carried in her gold mesh evening bag, then looked around. Opposite her were Alan and Judi Wilder. Dana welcomed the opportunity to talk with them. She viewed the Wilders as scientists of another sort, involved in genetic manipulation rather than space exploration. Dana's parents sat to the right of the Wilders, and the Drakes took chairs beyond Colt.

Sabrina eyed Colt before settling Rose in a booster seat next to Steve Drake.

As waiters began to pour Chardonnay and distribute menus, Max and Nicole entered. Applause pattered through the room, and Dana saw her twin sister smile complacently. Bridesmaid Leta Weller, seated on Dana's left, whispered into her ear, "Princess Nicole graciously accepts the accolade of the adoring populace."

Dana put a hand to her mouth to stifle her chuckle. Leta, already several sheets to the wind, didn't bother. Her guffaw attracted the attention of Colt and his parents. Embarrassed for Leta, Dana elbowed her in the ribs, hissing at her. "Hush up, Alan's going to say something."

Colt's father tapped his fork against his glass to quiet the party as Max seated Nicole at the far end of the long table. Alan stood up, holding his glass. "Ladies and gentlemen, welcome to a very happy occasion. On behalf of the Wilder family, I'd like to take this opportunity to thank the Newcombes for their gracious hospitality."

Dana peeked at Colt and blushed when she discovered him staring at her. He leaned over to murmur in her ear, "How gracious is your hospitality, darlin'?" He sat back in his chair and palmed her thigh with his left hand. She'd skipped pantyhose—too hot— and now she realized her error as his work-roughened fingers slid toward her crotch. Her face flamed, but she didn't want to say anything and interrupt Alan's speech. Besides, Colt's touch felt too good. She didn't want him to stop, and since his exploring hands were hidden by the tablecloth, why should he?

He stroked up and down her thigh, then homed in on what was surely his target: her pussy. He pushed aside the thin strip of silk covering her mound, then parted her labia to caress the moist folds.

Pleasure raced through her, radiating in waves from her pelvis. Her hips jerked involuntarily, and she fought to control her breathing.

He fondled her clit, and she clamped her thighs together to keep him from moving away. *Yes. There.* Ecstasy rippled through her, and she bit her lip to keep from crying out. She bet she could come this way, but didn't dare. Not here, not now. With regret, she opened her thighs and let him go. His hand withdrew to her knee, giving her a pat. She leaned back in her seat and drew a deep breath.

She looked around the table to see if anyone had been watching them. Fortunately, everyone was focused on Alan. "The entire Wilder family is grateful that the Newcombes' hospitality includes giving their daughter's hand in marriage to my son Max."

Max called out, "Here, here!"

Leta said, "There, there!"

Colt and Dana exploded with laughter, which was lost amid another spatter of applause and the clink of glasses as everyone drank to the happy couple. Colt leaned toward Dana. "Where did you find *her*?" He gestured toward Leta Weller. He gave Dana's knee another friendly squeeze.

"We've all been friends since kindergarten." She chuckled. "Isn't she a kick?"

"I'll say. Is she as funny sober?"

"Nobody's as funny sober."

He smiled, opening his menu. "So, what do you recommend?" He leaned toward her, creating intimacy. His scent caressed her nostrils, a heady mix of a citrusy aftershave with an underlying hint of earth thrown in. Very masculine and potent. She closed her eyes and breathed to absorb his essence.

"Dana?" he prodded.

"Umm, the veal piccata is good, but if you prefer pasta, try the tortellini. The cream sauce has a touch of nutmeg. It's delicious."

"Not half as delicious as I bet you taste, darlin'." His hot blue gaze lazily perused her yet again, lingering on her breasts, then rising to her eyes. He smiled.

Ooh. She dropped her right hand below the table, placed it on his thigh, and eased it up toward his crotch. Colt, sipping his wine, choked slightly. *Oops.* Dana jerked away her hand and turned toward Leta, smiling to cover her chagrin.

Then he leaned toward her, so close that his breath feathered her ear. "Why'd you stop?" he whispered, squeezing her thigh.

She put her hand back, wondering if she should … yes, why not? She scooted her fingers up along his inseam until she encountered a bulge. Interesting that his cock lay in his left pant leg. That was an awfully intimate thing to know about a man, she thought. She sneaked a glance toward him, sure her face was on fire. He was smiling at her. "Nice," he said.

Emboldened, she leaned closer so she could get a really good feel.

Oh, my God. He was *huge*. She jerked her hand away.

Colt again choked on his wine, stifling laughter. He patted her on the thigh. "I guess that's enough for now, huh, honey?"

A waiter came by to take their orders before servers brought salads. Dana watched Leta drink Chardonnay as fast as she had guzzled champagne. Between big gulps, Leta regaled the groomsman seated to her left with a bawdy story about Nick's past.

When Dana heard Leta mention beaver shots in a skin mag, she turned back toward Colt. "Hey, if the waiter comes around, get me extra sauce on the veal, okay?" Without waiting for an answer, she hauled at Leta's arm. "Lee, come with me to the women's room."

"Okay," Leta mumbled.

Dana waited for Leta to get up, which she managed with difficulty. Leta stumbled out of the room with Dana's steadying hand on her back. Leta missed the door by about six inches, smacking into the decorative pillar adorning the right doorpost. Her trailing hand nailed a flower arrangement, almost knocking it from its pedestal. Dana grabbed it, managing to keep it in its place. She mangled only two or three gladiolus spears.

Grasping Leta's arm, Dana hurried her along the narrow, dark hall to the women's room. "What the hell are you thinking?" She pushed Leta through a swinging door. "I know you're not crazy about Nick, but if you didn't want to be a bridesmaid, why didn't you just say so? It's not like you're her sister!"

Leta moaned, clutching her stomach.

Dana marched her over to a sink. "Get rid of it!"

Leta's eyes rolled up into her forehead. She slid slowly down the counter to the floor. Dana grabbed her under the armpits. She could feel Leta perspiring heavily through her dress.

Dana hauled her upright and shoved her over to a stall. "Go on, put your finger down your throat."

Leta knelt to worship the porcelain divinity. "Oh God, oh God," she moaned.

Sabrina entered the room. "What's wrong?"

"Leta here has had at least five glasses of booze so far this evening," Dana said. "We just got rid of it. What I don't understand is why."

"I'll get her an iced coffee." Sabrina scurried out.

Dana helped Leta up, then over to a sink. Leta rinsed her mouth and groaned dully. She staggered to a chair, collapsing into it. "Honestly, Dana, I didn't intend to drink so much. It's been such a hot day, and I was really thirsty."

Sabrina returned with an iced mocha. Leta sipped it thankfully, then rolled the cup's surface over her forehead.

"All right," Dana said. "You can come back to the party when you've sobered up. If you can't behave yourself, call a cab and go home, okay?"

Sabrina and Dana left Leta to return to the dinner.

"She was getting pretty hostile," Sabrina said. "Was she talking about Nick's skin mag adventure?"

"Yes, that's when I decided to get her out. Leta's funny, but she has a mean streak."

"Nick sure doesn't need that old stuff dragged out." Sabrina went to her chair.

Sitting down, Dana asked Colt, "Did you order for me?"

"Coming right up," he said. "How's your friend?"

"She'll be fine. Nothing that coffee can't cure."

Gabrielle gave Dana an unusually approving look. "I must say, Dana, you took care of that situation very nicely."

Dana sat down to eat her salad at the very moment a waiter whisked away the untouched dish. However, the entrees were promptly served. The veal was so tender she could cut it with her fork. She closed her eyes as the buttery, lemony sauce filled her mouth, sending her into rapture. "Ummm."

"So, what was this beaver thing Leta was talking about?" Colt asked her.

She chewed her food. And chewed it and chewed it, until the bite of veal had liquefied. Maybe if she took her time, he'd forget his question.

"Dana?"

"Oh, it's just some old story."

"Was this in a national park?" Colt's voice was wry.

Across the table, Tom cleared his throat rather loudly. "Excuse me, Colton, could you pass me the salt?"

Colt complied. "The beavers?" He winked at Dana.

Based on the twinkle in his eye, she'd bet good money that he didn't mean four-footed beavers. He knew full well that Leta's story involved the other kind of beaver. The split kind.

She didn't like to be rude, but couldn't see an alternative. "I'm eating right now. Can't you wait?" She turned back to the remains of her dinner, watching out of a corner of her eye as Colt swirled his last bite of pasta around in the remaining sauce. He forked it to his mouth.

Her parents looked unaccountably anxious.

The gentleman who had been seated beside Leta Weller had disappeared, as had Leta.

Sabrina continued to feed Rose. Further away, Max tucked away his *taglialini al salmone* as though he didn't have a care in the world. Nick sat tensely, her eyes fixed on Dana, who enjoyed the power she wielded. Oh yes, she thought, karma exists in the universe. Maybe one day she could prove it by scientific means, but for now, here was the empirical evidence. She wondered how long she could torture Nicole. She swallowed a bite of veal and smiled at her twin.

A hush fell.

Dana lifted her eyes from her now-empty plate, saying to Alan and Judi, "I hear you have quite a horse breeding program out there in Kentucky."

There was a whoosh as someone let out a relieved sigh. Nicole, that 'ho. Dana couldn't help her smile stretching a bit wider. She winked at her twin.

"Yes," Judi said, "we've been at it for over twenty years now. We like to think we've achieved some degree of success."

Colt laughed. "Mom is just bein' modest. Wilder horses are known worldwide. They've run in all the big races, won a few, too."

"Really? What's your secret?" Dana asked.

Alan smiled. "There aren't any secrets, young lady. Just hard work and patience. Mostly we watch and wait."

"Watch and wait?" Dana picked up a spoon and dug into her chocolate mousse.

Judi explained, "We watch the races to see how the horses perform, even animals bred by other stables. We keep records and we chart all the top horses, whether or not they're competing. We select breeding stock very carefully, looking for traits we want in our horses, and then we wait. We wait out the eleven month gestation period for the birth of a foal, then wait another year or two, for the futurities, to find out if the trait we bred for has shown up in the horse."

"Have you ever considered a more direct approach?"

"What do you mean?" Alan pushed aside his dessert dish.

"How about genetic manipulation of the embryos?"

Alan frowned. "That's a little too high-tech for us. I realize that they've cloned sheep and monkeys, but that's a long way off from that kind of selective breeding of Thoroughbred racehorses. Maybe in the future." He stirred cream into his coffee. "Hopefully long after I've retired and passed the farm along to Colt."

Dana raised a brow. "So that's the plan?"

"Yep." Colt sipped his coffee. "Max is the money man. Me … I have a tradition to uphold."

"Colton Wilder, Mr. Tradition. Funny, I just can't see you as a tradition-bound person."

"Stick around, toots. I'm full of surprises."

~ * ~

After dinner was eaten, and toast after toast drunk to Max and Nick, Colton asked Dana if he could ride back to the Newcombes with her.

They walked to the old Mazda she'd borrowed from her parents for the evening. Across the parking lot, lit by pinkish street lights, Colt saw the Newcombes get into their Volvo, accompanied by Nicole and Max. Dana went around to the passenger side of the RX-7 to unlock the door, holding it open for Colt.

Her hands quivered slightly, and he was tempted to lick the exact spot where a pulse throbbed in her throat. However, his intuition told him that something was up, and he wanted to know what it was before going any further. Dana was like a prickly young filly, feeling her oats but a little nervous. What the hell was her game?

He settled into the big bucket seat with ease. Slightly toasted, he hoped that she'd enough to drink to relax her, but not so much as to make her an unsafe driver. "You all right to drive?"

"Oh, yeah. I quit drinking after one glass of champagne and had coffee with dessert. No Leta imitations for me."

"So what happened to her?"

"I told her it was okay to come back to the party if she wanted, or she could take a cab home. She was pretty ripped. I don't see her car in the lot, so she must have gone." Dana started the old sports car, then reversed it out of its parking space.

"The guy she was sitting with left. Maybe he took her home. So what was all this stuff about beaver shots and skin mags?"

"I'm sure you can figure it out. At least, part of it." Dana's posture was stiff, her voice cold. She turned left out of the parking lot onto a four-lane road.

"I want to know all of it. It was easy to see that it's a sore subject for your parents and Nick."

"I was pretty angry at the time."

"It must have been serious. You don't strike me as hot off the trigger."

"I'm not." She flashed him a quick smile, then turned her attention back to the road. "Scientists have to be patient."

"Especially astronomers. How often do breakthroughs come along?"

"Not often. And you have to wait your turn for time at the best telescopes. Studies can take years to complete."

"Beaver shots and skin mags?"

She hesitated. "Promise not to tell."

"Promise."

"Okay. Well, back in high school Nicole was very popular. I wasn't. Although we're identical twins, I have the eyestrain, the glasses, I'm the dweeb, you know? And that's all right. I like who I am."

Colt wanted to be reassuring. She'd opened up, and he liked the change from her prickly demeanor and her phony flirtatiousness. "I like who you are, too."

She heaved an exasperated sigh as she stopped for a red light. "You like who you think I am. Anyway, Nick had a lot of boyfriends, and some of them weren't, umm, too savory, if you know what I mean. Some sex pictures of her were published in our senior year, and I mean really raunchy ones. They'd just had sex, and, umm, they were very graphic. I'm not sure why she did it. It couldn't have been for the money, because our parents never shorted us. And she already knew she wanted a legitimate career as a model. Maybe she did it to be rebellious, or something … but the worst part is that she used another name. Mine." She accelerated away from the intersection.

"What?" Colt's mouth dropped open.

"You heard me. So I became very popular for the rest of the school year. I had loads of first dates, you know what I mean? Of course, my parents flipped when they found out."

"Whoa. Whatever happened to those photos? I bet that as Nicole became more famous, they became more valuable."

"Oh, they are. But one of the advantages to having money is that little problems like this can be suppressed. Dad bought all of them up, every one."

"I wonder if she's told my brother?"

"Colt, you promised not to tell!" Tires squealed as Dana pulled over to the side of the road, braked, then faced him.

"I won't tell. I won't. Calm down." He put a hand on one of hers where it was clenched on the steering wheel. "Hey, this wedding is really important to you, isn't it?"

"I just don't want to see anyone get hurt." Her voice was low and tense. "Max hasn't done anything wrong, and I'm trying to be mature about this mess."

He stroked her hand, then ran his fingers up to her elbow. He smugly watched the tiny blond hairs on her arm rise with his touch. He gentled his voice. "Darlin', this is nothing to freak out about. No one is going to get hurt."

"Give me your word that you'll do nothing to stop Nicole from marrying Max."

"Me? What could I do?"

"Judging from the handholding and the flirting, plenty."

He put his head down into his hands, buying time, then went for it, went for *her*. "Dana, I give you my solemn word of honor I will do nothing to prevent your sister from marrying my brother."

"So what was that conversation I overheard last night about?"

"I was upset when I heard about this wedding. Weren't you? Nicole hasn't treated you right."

"Me and everyone else she knows."

"Like I told you, your sister's manipulative and a heartbreaker. Why do you stick up for her so much? Why are you even here? If I were you, I wouldn't have shown up."

"You don't understand how my mother can be."

"Why do you let your mom and Nick push you around?"

"I generally don't. That's why I live a continent away from Mom. So she can't push me around. I'm here mostly for Dad."

"That's nice of you, but still…" How could he tactfully tell her that she needed to grow a backbone? "Look. Let's stop talking about anyone except me and you, okay? I don't want your sister. I want you."

Turning her head, she eyed him with blatant suspicion.

He leaned toward her, breathing in her flowery, intoxicating perfume. "All I know is that every time I see you I have an overwhelming urge to…" He broke off as he took her face in both of his hands, and kissed her.

He caressed her gently, reveling in the softness of her perfect skin and the sweetness of her mouth, which tasted of chocolate and coffee.

She pulled away after only a few seconds. "Didn't you feel the same overwhelming urge with my sister? And quite a few other women?"

"Well, yeah. After all, I am a twenty-seven year old red-blooded Kentucky male! I got hormones, you know," he drawled.

"Well, I'm mighty sorry, sir," she drawled right back at him, "but I don't feel obliged to fulfill your hormonal longings every second of every day!" She started the Mazda, and pulled away from the curb.

"Didn't say you had to, sweetheart. But you can't blame a man for tryin'."

Chapter Nine

For Nicole, the drive back to her parents' house in their Volvo was five miles of sheer agony. She had to get Max alone that night. She needed to find out whether his recent testy behavior was pre-wedding jitters, some deeper problem stemming from the senior Wilders' attitude, or even a concern due to everyone's former messy liaisons.

Worse was the thought that Max might harbor some lingering tenderness for Dana the dweeb.

And ever since the skin mag fiasco had been brought up at the rehearsal dinner, Nickie was terrified that Max would ask her about it. That fear overshadowed all her other worries, since the photos were not merely slutty, but humiliating. She'd been no more than a 'ho for doing the shoot. She hadn't the slightest idea what she'd say to her fiancé about it, and part of her wanted to avoid talking with Max entirely.

At the same time, she wanted to ensure her control over him. She fully intended to marry him the next day. As intriguing as Colton could be, Nickie was a person who craved command of her life. She would never release her autonomy to an impulsive, spontaneous husband she couldn't manipulate. Mild-mannered and predictable, Max filled the bill for her perfectly. He had the same erotic potential as Colton, but unlike Colt, Max's constancy had filled a previously undiscovered emotional void. Despite herself, she had become dependent upon Max in the past months and couldn't accept any threat to that precious security.

Fastened in her seat belt, Nick sat stiffly in the back seat behind Gabrielle. Her low cut, strapless dress had forced her to wear an uncomfortable underwired bustier, and the waistband of her tummy control pantyhose cut viciously into her belly. She couldn't wait to get home and strip.

She reached over and took Max's hand. She leaned toward him, whispering, "How about a midnight swim, just you and me?"

"Ummm," he growled into her ear. "Think we can get away with skinny-dippin'?" His narrowed blue eyes raked her body.

"We can try. I'll meet you out there about a half-hour after we get home. Everyone should be asleep by then." She gently nibbled on his earlobe.

"Good. We have a few things to discuss, you and me." He smiled at her as he turned away. Her eyes sprang open as the implications of his statement sank in. She swallowed hard.

~ * ~

As Dana pulled the Mazda into the garage, Colt noticed that the Volvo already occupied another space, which meant that Max, Nick, and the Newcombes had already returned from the restaurant. The house was dark and quiet, with only a few lights shining in the upper story.

He looked around. "I've never tried to find my way to the guest house from here. Will you point me in the right direction?"

"I'll do better than that. I'll walk you over." Taking his hand, she guided him out of the garage via a back door, which led onto a narrow path.

The flagstone walkway wound through the kitchen garden and out to the lawns. Moonlit and luminescent, Gabrielle's roses glowed in the back of the yard near the guest house. He sniffed the subtle fragrance of the flowers and herbs borne on the light breeze.

He laced his fingers through Dana's, then lifted their intertwined hands to kiss her knuckles. The moonlight gently lit her delicate features. He stroked her face with one hand, outlining her full lips as she smiled at him.

He replaced his finger with his mouth.

This time, she didn't pull away. He closed his eyes to explore her with his tongue, giving her a searching soul kiss that left her trembling delightfully in his embrace. Her vulnerability excited him, aroused him all the more. Her fingers, still twined with his, clenched when he found one stiff nipple and flicked the sensitive point. She moaned deep in her throat as he cradled her breast. Heavy and full in his hand, it seemed to swell as her sensuous purring increased in pitch.

So hard that he'd burst out of his pants in just a few more seconds, he pulled away, perhaps too abruptly. She opened her eyes with a dazed, startled look.

He touched her face. "You're so sexy." A few yards away, the swimming pool shimmered, its underwater light flickering through the turquoise water. A vision of Dana's naked breasts, slick with water and glistening in the moonlight, darted through his mind. "I think we both need to cool off. Wanna swim?"

"What a great idea. I'll meet you out there in five minutes." She walked back through the kitchen garden to the house.

Colt went to his room. After stripping off his linen suit, he hung it in the closet, then pawed through his belongings for his denim cut-offs, but couldn't find them. Mannering, he thought. The obnoxiously efficient butler had no doubt taken the cut-off shorts and sent them to the dry cleaners, or maybe he was ironing them.

Drawing an exasperated breath, he wondered if they were in the house, maybe in a laundry room. He wrapped a towel around his waist, then went back to the main house to hunt for the elusive shorts.

~ * ~

Dana, now in her red bikini with her hair covered by a cap, slipped into the water with a sense of relief. She always found her parents' heated pool soothing.

And after the tension of the rehearsal dinner, she'd truly enjoy a swim with Colt.

She rolled onto her back to float and closed her eyes, reliving their kiss in the moonlit herb garden. For the first time, she'd touched the magic that other women swore they felt when they fell in love.

But she didn't love Colt Wilder. This was lust, pure and simple. She liked it. A lot.

She'd always been methodical, a planner. Maybe even a little stodgy and boring. But with Colt, she didn't feel like dull-as-dirt Dana. Nope, not at all.

She wondered how far she'd let him go tonight. Why shouldn't she have him? Not only would it be hot, but it would totally distract him from Nicole.

Warm, strong male arms slid around her, supporting her in the water. *Ummm, yeah. Colt.* He squeezed her tight, kissing her deeply. She surrendered to the romance of the moment, delighting in the heated, intimate contact of his muscular body against hers. His erection, thick, hot, and hard, pressed against her bathing suit. He gripped her hips and rotated against her, sending his heat straight to her most sensitive parts.

She moaned as he growled deep in his throat. But when she caressed his face and kissed him back, she sensed that something wasn't quite right. Something was missing. What could it be? Had Colt shaved in so brief a time?

With a hoarse scream, Dana tore herself out of Max's grasp. "Max! What are you doing?"

"Dana? Oh, shit! Where's Nick?"

"I don't know. Where's Colt?"

Dana stared at Max, sure that the suspicion and dismay she saw on his face was mirrored in hers.

~ * ~

Colt opened the dryer door with one hand while he clutched a towel around his waist with the other. Because the dryer was a front-loader, he had to bend over pretty far to look through the contents.

Plucking out a generously-cupped bra, his imagination ran riot. He held it up to the light. Green silk, like the panties Dana had worn the night before… He grinned. Dana. He wondered how long she'd hold his attention and, more importantly, if he'd have her tonight.

After dropping the bra back into the dryer basket, he rooted around some more. He doubted he'd find his cut-offs. The contents seemed to be delicate washables, not heavy denims.

Someone seized him around the waist and yanked away the towel. Soft, sultry laughter echoed in his ears as his tender attacker lustily grabbed his buns before reaching between his legs.

Startled, he whacked his head on the rim of the dryer. "Jeez!"

Despite the blow, which made him see stars, risqué fantasies whipped through his head. His sexy little scientist was showing an unexpectedly seductive, playful side.

He turned and forcefully pulled her over for a passionate kiss. His eyes closed, he groped her squirming body and, tearing off her towel, stripped her naked. He didn't care about the pain in his head. The feel of her soft ass beneath his questing hand drove him wild. He sprang a rod in an instant.

"Ooh, baby. You are so hot!" He reached up her back and found a mane of long hair. "Hey!" His eyes popped open. "Nicole, what the hell are you doing?"

"What the hell am I doing? What the hell are you doing!" Nick pushed him away.

"What do you mean, what the hell am I doing?" he demanded. "Where's my towel?"

"How dare you kiss me like that!" She nailed his cheek with a noisy slap.

His mind reeled. "You—you seemed to want it."

"I thought you were Max!"

"You had a date with Max in the laundry room?"

Nicole threw the towel at his head and slammed out of the house.

With his towel tossed over his shoulder, he stumbled after her to the pool area, alternately rubbing his cheek and his head.

A man was already in the pool—with a woman. A naked man. His brother.

Well, fuck-a-duck. Max was skinny-dipping with Dana. Colt reminded himself that he had no claims on her at all. Nevertheless, he saw red, his jealous streak flaring to violent life. What was going on? If Dana was so all-fired hot for the wedding to take place, why was she in the pool with a naked Max?

"What the hell are you two doing?" Nick snarled. If looks could kill, both Dana and Max were on their way to the morgue.

"I have the same question. What were you two doing?" Max asked. "Nicole, I expected you out here some time ago. Where have you been? Why is Colt nude?"

"I heard a disturbance in the laundry room, and I went to check it out." Nicole sounded defensive.

"You have an interesting way of checking things out." Colt's head throbbed. "Why are you naked in the pool with Dana, Max?"

"What's all this supposed to mean?" Dana asked. "Look, I don't want to be involved with any of this. I'm going to bed." She swam to the side of the pool and climbed out.

Colt flinched as Dana targeted him with a glare that could scorch steel before she went into the house. "She's got the right idea. I'm outta here."

He'd better figure out a way to repair this breach, fast. He was hot for Dana and didn't want her to think badly of him, especially when there was no reason.

But what the hell was going on?

Nicole and Max were left facing each other. He continued to tread water as he looked up at his fiancée. "Want to swim with me, darling?" he invited, trying to resurrect the evening.

"I guess," she said. Nickie's long hair shone silvery in the moonlight. She twisted the molten mass high upon her head; pulling her towel off, she wrapped it around her hair. Her nude body glowed pearlescent as she slipped into the water using the steps at the shallow end of the pool.

He swam to her, then gripped her with one hand between her legs and the other around her waist. She pushed her cunt onto upon his forearm and sighed with pleasure as he pressed on her mound to arouse her. He bit one breast gently, watching her nipple pucker in response.

He maneuvered her back onto the steps, and rested her weight there, pulling his arm out from under her. He slipped one finger, then two, inside her. Her pussy was tighter than normal—from tension, he supposed—but after a stroke or two, she relaxed against his touch.

The muscles in Nicole's face slackened as she began to enjoy herself. "I'm glad we're able to spend some time together, darling," she said, twining her arms around his neck. "With all the wedding preparations, I feel we've grown apart a bit. How are you feeling?"

"I feel good. There's a lot of hustle and bustle, but that's to be expected." He massaged her internally, feeling her sheath cream with desire.

"I don't want to appear ungrateful, but I'll be happy when the wedding is over and we can get on with our lives."

He smiled at her. "We have decades to become an old married couple. It's time to enjoy this experience."

"You're right. We'll only get married once, you know!"

"What was this skin mag thing they were talking about at dinner?" he asked.

Nicole clenched around his fingers. Aha. Something definitely was fishy. He continued to caress her, deliberately keeping his voice calm. "Obviously, it's very important to you."

"It's something that happened with, umm, Leta, one of the bridesmaids," she said, twitching slightly. "It wouldn't be fair to her to tell you about it."

He considered. "Well, you're right about that." He withdrew his hand and stroked her inner thigh. Nevertheless, a tendril of suspicion twisted through his mind, and he made a mental note to ask Dana or Sabrina about the matter. There was also a good possibility that Colton had heard the gossip from Dana.

He rubbed the heel of his hand against her mound and delved into her pussy to find her G-spot. Nick's inner sheath clamped around his fingers. A husky moan escaped her lips before she kissed him deeply, breaking out into a light sweat.

With an ease born of practice, he rubbed her G-spot until she climaxed against his hand. When she opened her eyes, he noticed they looked silvery and cold in the moonlight.

Chapter Ten

Dana changed into a peach silk robe and a matching shortie nightgown, then stepped onto her balcony. Because her room faced the back of the house, she could hear murmurs and an occasional splash from the pool area, as well as see any action.

She chuckled. She'd give anything to be a water bug so she could hear the conversation below. Her brief make-out session with Max had been innocent, but she wondered how he'd explain the situation. And what on earth could her twin tell Max about the skin mag fiasco? Payback was sweet, all the more because Dana hadn't caused the situation that now trapped Nicole, that schemer.

Dana watched as her sister dropped her towel to expose her nude body. Nicole looked like a cold marble statue in the moonlight. Max swam toward Nick with an expression on his face that Dana couldn't identify and didn't understand.

Despite the warmth of the evening, she shivered, thinking, that's one relationship that's going down a black hole. She hoped against hope that they'd still marry. She didn't want to think about the pain and embarrassment her parents would endure if Nick and Max parted at the altar. Gabrielle, especially, had sweated every detail to make the demanding Nicole happy.

What on earth had Nick and Colt been doing in the laundry room, of all places? Dana knew that Nicole was loose and Colt a dog. But the laundry room?

She reminded herself of her purpose. She wouldn't see her parents hurt if she could stop it. She owed her father that much. Remember, any flirtation with Colt is just in the line of duty, she told herself. It's not real!

She forced Colt Wilder out of her mind, went inside, tossed her robe onto a bedpost, then slipped into bed. Cuddling into the soft, clean sheets, she let her body relax and her mind clear.

About to turn onto her side and go to sleep, she became aware of a dark presence in her room. Squinting without her glasses, she could see only a dim silhouette back-lit by the slight illumination cast by the few lights on outside.

Oh, dear God. Her heart chilled. The specter of kidnapping for ransom haunted all wealthy Americans, but her father was very careful. She knew she'd taken a risk by keeping her window open, but who could have gotten past the security fence? Tense in her bed, she prepared to make a break for the door.

She heard the intruder clear his throat. "Dana?"

"Colt, you moron, what are you doing here? I was about to get a gun, blow you away and phone 9-1-1 later." Relief made her crabby. She flopped back against her pillows.

He chuckled, a deep, rich sound in the darkness. "I didn't know you packed a piece. Guess I'd better stay on your good side." The bed creaked as he sat down, apparently making himself at home.

"What are you doing here?" she asked again, reminding herself of the reason for her flirtation with him. She didn't want her emotions to get out of hand. She had no intention of getting a broken heart from someone who seemed to have the morals of a jackrabbit and the roving habits of a migratory bird.

"I felt cheated." He shifted his weight, moving closer. "I kinda expected our evening to go on a while longer."

The warmth flooding her body had nothing to do with her flimsy bedclothes. She reached out a hesitant hand, encountering denim. "What are you wearing?"

"Disappointed, darlin'?" He chuckled again. "I found my cut-offs. They were in the closet in my room. That crazy man Mannering had ironed them and hung them up, for Lord's sake."

"Is that what you were doing in the laundry room?"

"Yep. Did you think your sister and I were fooling around?"

She was glad the darkness hid the warm blush creeping over her face. She'd wondered about that and felt sure that Max had, also. "Um, uh…"

"Nah. I told you. I'm not interested in your sister. But I'll admit I'm real worried about my brother."

She sat bolt upright in her bed. "Colt!"

"Shh, keep your voice down. You want your parents in here?"

"But you promised."

"So I did." He sounded reluctant. "Besides, everyone will think I'm just bein' petty if I say anything. So I'm keeping my mouth shut."

She calmed.

"I won't break my promises to you, sweetheart. But there is a price to be paid."

"A—a price?" She grinned. This sounded good. Her pussy clenching, she wondered what Colt would demand. With luck, they were on the same wavelength.

"Yeah, a price. What were you doing in the swimming pool with my brother?"

"I, uh, thought he was you."

"Yeah, right." Leaning over, Colt took her mouth with his.

When she wrapped her arms around his neck, Dana couldn't feel a shirt. She ran her hands down his smoothly muscled sides, discovering he wore only his cut-offs. As he kissed her more deeply, she let her lids flutter closed.

His firm, warm mouth receded. "No, baby. Open your eyes. Look at *me*. I bet a lot of men have kissed your pretty lips. I want you to know it's Colt Wilder makin' you feel so good."

He was close enough for her to see the shine of his blue eyes, each dusky lash, his sexy smile.

"Keep those beautiful eyes open, now. I want to look into your eyes when I make love to you."

He slid his mouth over hers again, nibbling at her lower lip. She opened her mouth, inviting his tongue inside. One hand fisted in her hair, controlling her head. His gentleness and strength were a heady combination, and she surrendered to the allure of domination by Colt, more demanding and potent than any other man she'd dared to possess.

He caressed her tongue with long, slow strokes. She touched his shoulders hesitantly, then gripped them with more confidence as the kiss deepened. He cupped one breast through her nightgown. One thumb rubbed over her taut nipple, back and forth, in a slow, sexual torture that drove her crazy for more. She lifted her chest, pressing her breast more firmly into his hand. The rough calluses on his palms stimulated her, excited her. She wanted that roughness, that hardness, all over her body.

His eyes stayed with hers, the look palpable as a touch, so intimate it was frightening. There was no reason to be scared, but their open eyes, their shared gaze, gave his kiss an impact she'd never felt before. He had become too close, too fast.

His eyes shifted. He released her mouth to whisper, "Yes, baby, yes." His breath feathered down her neck.

She stifled a moan. His hand tightened around her breast as she slid her hands into his hair, playing with the dark strands. She'd never found long hair sexy before. Now she couldn't keep her hands out of his unruly mane, which reminded her that she dared to tempt this elemental, savage male.

Fear retreated. She wanted more.

His mouth, hot and wet, found her nipple to suck it hard through her nightie. This time she couldn't stop the wild moan rising from her throat. His lips returned to hers, almost as though he wanted to drink in the sounds of her delight.

"Sssh, baby. Quiet."

"I c-c-can't…"

"You have to, or you'll wake up the house. Do you need help?"

"What do you mean?"

Even in the dim light, she could see that the expression in his eyes was intent, determined, more than a little hard.

A shiver ran down her spine. What had she started?

He drew away from her to pull the sash out of her robe. He ran the delicate, peach-colored silk between his fingers. It slid through his work-hardened hands, catching once or twice on his calluses.

She sat up, startled, but before she could react he'd wrapped the silk around her mouth.

She scrabbled for the gag, and he restrained her. "Don't worry," he whispered. "Nothing will happen that you don't want."

She tried to ask, *but how will you know what I want?* But he murmured, "I know what you want, Dana. Remember? Didn't I give it to you, back in that elevator?"

She had to nod. He had. He'd made her come more and harder than anyone, ever.

"Just lie back and relax, sweetheart, and let ol' Colt take you for a ride."

He pulled up the nightgown, and she cooperated by raising her arms, but he didn't take the nightgown off. Instead he slid it to her wrists, then twisted it, roping her hands.

She didn't resist, but found herself excited by this new, unusual game. She knew about bondage, of course, but none of her lovers had restrained her in any way. The gag was firmly tied but not uncomfortable, and she focused on breathing through her nose. It felt odd, since when she made love she usually panted, mouth open. Her breaths filled her diaphragm, heating her body, warmth dropping to her pussy.

Why was she so turned on? Was it the gag, the silk binding her wrists, or the thought of being restrained and in Colt's power? She didn't know; she only understood that she was so hot she could hardly wait for him to fuck her. Hard and long.

He eased her back onto the bed, then stood. He tossed a condom packet onto her bedside table before taking off his cut-offs. His cock sprang out. He was fully erect and so thick she feared for her tight pussy. He was big, and she didn't want him to tear her apart. Bound and at his mercy, there was nothing she could do except trust him.

She breathed, trying to control the quivering that shook her flesh. Her heart was pounding so hard she could see her left breast tremble.

He fastened his mouth around it, sucking until she writhed, tried to scream but couldn't.

His low laugh filled her ears. "That gag was definitely a good idea. You're so hot that most of L.A. would hear you come without it."

He scooted down the bed and pried apart her knees. His warm breath puffed over her pussy. Juices trickled out of her ready slit, but he was in no rush, instead looking, fingering, opening her.

He rubbed his face over her delta, and she moaned despite the gag. He toyed with her, penetrating her with a finger. Her slick channel opened to admit him, and the feeling of her tissues parting for his probing hand sent an erotic charge shooting through her. She shuddered, pleasure rippling through her in concentric waves, her pelvis the center.

He nipped her swelling clit, and she yelped with surprise.

"Shh!" He flipped her over and rapped his knuckles against her butt.

Once, then again, giving equal time to each ass-cheek. She squirmed to get away. She'd never been spanked and didn't know if she wanted it now.

He laughed again, pinning her to the bed with his lean, powerful body. She hadn't previously appreciated how strong Colt was, but now she realized that he was all whipcord and sinew, probably without a single fat gram anywhere. Solid muscle and bone, much stronger than she.

Wondering how he'd react, she tested his control, rolling over, squirming and pushing at him. With a soft chuckle, he readily moved, letting her climb on top. She relaxed. Despite the bondage, despite the spanking, he wasn't going to hurt her or abuse her. He just liked to play around.

But she'd already known that, if she'd thought about it. For her, the scene in the elevator had been humiliating. Colt being Colt, he probably thought of it as slap-and-tickle fun-and-games.

He sheathed himself, then pulled her hips forward so she could ride him. "Yeah, let's do it this way. So you won't get hurt." He winked at her.

He was so outrageous she had to giggle. Knees bent, she eased herself down onto his straining erection. When the round head opened her, she nearly came from the sheer joy of it.

She bore down so slowly that her thighs started to shake from the strain. She lifted herself up, then down again, giving her body time to adjust and her cream to flow around him, wetting her channel so she could take him in all the way. Hot and long, he filled her to her womb.

Closing her eyes to focus on the pleasure, she threw her head back and let herself go, rocking on his thick, hard cock. He bucked beneath her, driving slowly in and out. She opened her eyes to see him arch and bow before he let go of the headboard and reached for her, pulling her down so her body covered his. Her nipples rubbed against his chest, textured with dark curls and sleek with sweat. Waves of pleasure rolled through her. She caged his head with her elbows and rubbed her face against his, glorying in the touch of his beard, alternately soft and coarse, against her cheek.

She pushed her clit against his pubic bone, and he gripped her hips, his hands sinking into her buttocks. One finger wandered into the furrow between her butt-cheeks and pressed into her ass. She jerked with surprise, lust snapping through her. She arched and writhed, crying out beneath the gag. She came with a sharp burst of heat, then again as his finger circled in her snug back hole.

Limp, she lay on him, resting for a moment, shaking.

His finger left her butt, and he held her tight to roll her over, keeping her speared by his cock. Holding one of her knees, he opened her wide before pumping rhythmically into her. "So you're an ass chick, huh?" he breathed into her ear. "We'll do that too, but not right now…"

She wanted to tell him, *no, I'm not, I've never done that*, but couldn't. Her breath was stolen by a sudden burst of fierce, heavy thrusts. He banged in and out of her deep and fast, and dominating her so utterly that she could do nothing but take what he chose to give.

So wet that her pussy slurped and gushed around his cock, she lifted her hips to meet him again and again. He swelled inside her, pushing against her inner walls, hurling her into oblivion. Another orgasm stormed over her, matching his.

She heard laughter rise from the pool area, and a bumping noise from the bedroom next to hers.

He rolled off her, then pulled the gag off her and untwisted the nightgown from around her wrists. Her mattress squeaked as he shifted. He took her into his arms. "This is gonna be an awesome weekend." He brushed his lips against hers before giving her another of his mind-shattering soul kisses.

"Mmmm…" She snuggled close, letting the languorous afterglow lull her toward slumber.

After a few moments he groaned. "I'd better not go to sleep here. What would your mama say if she caught me here in the morning?"

They shared a brief chuckle before he whispered, "'Night, sweetheart." He brushed his lips across her forehead.

Colt left as quietly as he'd entered. Dana lay in her bed, wondering if she'd imagined the interlude. If she didn't feel so good, if her pussy weren't still tingling from his intensity, she would have thought it had been a fantasy arising from her most erotic dreams.

No wonder Nicole wavered. His kisses were magic, his lovemaking wild, knowing and demanding.

How did he do it? Dana sighed as she remembered that Colt had been the one to walk away from her twin. She hardened her heart. It was tough in the wake of the great sex, but she had to protect herself. She envisioned Colt the drifter, wandering through life leaving behind a trail of broken hearts.

Chapter Eleven

In the morning, Colt went with Max for his haircut and shave, then relaxed by the hotel pool after lunch with his brother. Although the weather was cloudy, Colt could even out his skin tone because ultraviolet rays pierced the thin overcast.

Sipping from a glass of iced tea, Colt glanced at Max, who occupied the lounge chair next to him reading a copy of *Forbes*. Contented as a cat, he seemed oblivious to the rumors swirling around his fiancée.

Maybe Max and Nicole would be all right. Colt hoped for his brother's sake that the marriage would be a happy one.

His thoughts shifted to Nicole's twin. He felt a lazy smile curl over his face as he stretched in the warmth of the day.

Dana.

Tying her up and ramrodding her good in that chaste little bed in her parents' house, just a few feet from her Mommy and Daddy's bedroom, had added zing to an already primo boink-fest. His smile faded as another realization struck him. Special in a way he couldn't define, Dana wouldn't be just another playmate. Her serious soul demanded more.

Max broke Colt's reverie. "So, what's with you and Dana?"

Colt tried not to look guilty. Apparently Max didn't know about the Four Seasons fuck. Did he still have feelings for her? If so, how would he feel about Colt shagging both twins in succession?

On the other hand, Max's own conduct had left much to be desired, depending upon one's perceptions and interpretation. Colt decided to play it safe. "Ah, nothing to talk about."

Max laughed. "Come on, Colt, this is your other half speaking. You expected to find her in the pool last night, hmm?"

"I expected to find her alone."

"Oh, absolutely nothing happened, I assure you."

Colt shot Max a sidelong glance. "Come on, Max, this is your other half speaking."

Both laughed.

"She's a sweetheart. I still care about her a lot." Max reached for his iced tea. "I don't want to see her hurt."

"It's a little late for that, dude," Colt said pointedly. Max wasn't in a position to criticize.

"I'm sure she wasn't really in love with me, so she wasn't really hurt."

"That's convenient."

"Come on, you know the effect you have on women. I'm wallpaper compared to you."

"Not in Nicole's eyes, and she's a pretty hot property. You ready for that kind of life?"

"Sure. Nickie and I have talked about it. Models have short careers, and once that's over, we'll settle down. Don't change the subject. We were talking about you and Dana, not me and Nickie."

Colt shrugged. "Dana's hot and available."

"Available? Not if I read you right."

"It's true that I don't like to share. But I have no claim on the lady."

"Yet."

"Yet."

"You have plans?" Max asked.

"I don't know. I'd like to see her again, but probably not. She lives in Boston. If I never go anywhere bigger than Lexington or Louisville, that'll be fine with me. And I wouldn't want to go to any city very often, large or small."

"What did you find to talk about with someone like Dana? She's … different, if you know what I mean."

Colt glared at him. "I like different."

"Not your type. She's scholarly and a little unworldly."

"Otherworldly, I'd say." Colt chuckled at his own joke.

Max joined him. "But seriously, what do you talk about with Dana?"

Colt glanced sharply at Max, whose voice had subtly changed. He wanted something, something he didn't want to reveal. Colt hesitated. He'd bet his favorite saddle Max was probing for gossip about Nicole's beaver shot adventure.

Damn. He hated to keep anything from his brother, but he'd given his word that he wouldn't tell. "What does anyone talk about with a woman?" he asked. "I mean, what do you discuss with Nicole? You flatter a girl, tell her how hot she is, and try to get into her pants."

Max grinned and sipped at his drink. "Well, did you?"

"Hey, I don't kiss and tell. What are you worried about? There's no future in it."

"Gone with the Wind Colt cares about a future with a woman?"

Colt frowned. Max painted a portrait of a man Colt didn't especially admire, but he didn't understand why. He didn't use or mislead girls. Hell, until he settled down, a serious relationship with someone like Dana Newcombe or anyone else was out of the question. In the meantime, he had fun with women, and they with him. "Probably not. Like I said, our lives are too different. This li'l dawgie stays wild."

~ * ~

Hot sun slanted into Dana's room at eight a.m., but as noon approached, clouds began to cover the sun and the weather took on an unpleasant sultriness. She knew that the humidity, as well as the inherent tensions of the day, would take their toll on her mother and her twin. She escaped most of the pre-wedding stress by napping poolside to deepen her tan.

After a light lunch, she left the house to shop. She took a few minutes to consider the relative merits of Ultress champagne blonde as opposed to Clairol honey blonde. She eventually went to an alternative health products store and purchased a golden shade of henna, figuring a natural product wouldn't damage her hair.

She breezed into the Newcombe mansion at three p.m. to find the estate peculiarly quiet. Though Sabrina and Rose were supposed to be waiting with Nicole, there was no hair stylist and no mother of the bride. She assumed their mother was checking last minute details at the church. Old-fashioned Gabrielle didn't employ a wedding consultant—she called them "Wedding Nazis"—since she believed she was equally capable of creating an appropriate occasion. In this she was correct, but only at the cost of tattered nerves and incredible stress.

Upstairs, Dana found Sabrina sprawled on the Battenburg lace counterpane of Nick's bed. Rose played with a stuffed toy, attempting to pull off Paddington's nose. All three females had bathed, and wore lingerie with their faces made up. Even little Rose had a lace petticoat and lip gloss. Their hair, however, was unstyled. Although Gabrielle had paid her hairdresser big bucks to arrive at two o'clock to fix the hair of the females in the wedding party, Madame Annika hadn't shown up yet.

And, of course, Nicole was frantic.

"Call 'em up," Sabrina suggested.

"I've tried. There's no answer from anyone."

"They're probably on their way," Dana said. "Just relax."

"I can't relax," whined Nick. "I'm all ready except for my hair. And where the hell have you been? You're supposed to be helping me. Isn't that the job of the maid of honor—helping the bride?"

Dana raised her brows. "There isn't much for me to do. The role is considered to be largely ceremonial, sort of like being Queen of England. So how's the blushing bride?"

"Cut the sentimental crap. Where have you been?"

"Shopping. I guess it's time for my shower, huh?" Dana whisked into the bathroom with her wrapped parcel of henna, shutting the door firmly. At this point, she didn't want Nicole checking on her activities.

As Dana's shower began to run, Gabrielle zipped into Nick's room. "But what is all this sloth?" she demanded. "And where is Madame Annika?"

"Your high-priced pal hasn't bothered to show up," bitched the blushing bride. "Any suggestions?"

Gabrielle pulled her cellular phone from her pocket and vigorously punched a number. Nicole watched, flabbergasted. *She actually has her hairdresser programmed into her speed-dialer. Mom's completely obsessed!*

"Annika," Gabrielle said. *"Comment allez-vous?"*

A gabble of French poured from the high-quality cellular. Gabrielle grimaced and held the phone away from her ear. She said, *"Où est-vous?"*

A shorter spate of babble ensued. *"Oui, oui, très bien, Anna. A bientôt."*

Gabrielle clicked off the phone. "Well, zhe is on her way. Zhe has had car trouble but will be here soon. Nicole, have you decided how to wear your hair?"

"Yeah, I'll have her put it up the way we discussed," she said, sliding a nervous glance at her mother.

Gabrielle frowned. "I zhink it is too elaborate, but you are the bride," she said. "Sabrina, perhaps you zhould do Rosie's hair. I do not zhink Annika will have time for the rest of us. I will bathe now. Do you want to borrow my curling iron?" Gabrielle left the room with Sabrina and Rose following her, leaving Nicole alone.

Nick had never before felt so bereft and ill-treated. This was supposed to be the happiest day of her life, and there was nobody around to share it with. By tradition, she would not see her bridegroom until the ceremony. She suddenly hated that idea. She sat down on the edge of her bed and fought to restrain an unforeseen weepiness that washed over her. She took several deep breaths, and calmed herself with the thought that in a few short hours, she and Max would be married and on their way to Cabo.

~ * ~

Dana struggled with the slippery, muddy henna. To begin with, the directions were lengthy and incomprehensible, and she was in a hurry. She saw that the henna needed to be mixed with water before it was applied, and eyed the immaculate white porcelain sink. Her mom would have a shitfit if it became stained or clogged, so she grabbed a nearby fern, yanked it out of its fancy brass flowerpot and set the fern, now clad in only a humble clay pot, on the counter. She rinsed the decorative brass pot clean, then dumped the henna powder into it and added water until the consistency seemed right.

She put on the plastic gloves provided in the package and hastily glopped the mud onto her head before she showered. She was careful to keep the henna on her hair, avoiding her skin. She was late and couldn't wait as long as the directions demanded, but she figured it would be okay, since she just wanted her hair a little darker. Her mother and her sister would freak out if she weren't ready to go to the church at four p.m. for photographs.

After she shaved her legs, she rinsed off the sticky color rinse and watched the exotic mud flow down the drain, praying it wouldn't clog or ruin the plumbing. As she rubbed her hair with a towel, she regarded its color. It looked kinda funny and dark, but she really couldn't tell with her hair so wet. She'd style her hair, get dressed, and have faith.

~ * ~

Madame Annika rushed in, full of French and excuses. She pressed a gift onto Nicole. "For the blushing bride," she gushed. Nicole thanked her graciously while thinking she was heartily sick of that ridiculous phrase. After Nick explained what she wanted, Madame began to dexterously plait Nick's hair into the elaborate coronet of braids Nicole demanded.

~ * ~

Dana stared with consternation at her head. After she had blown the hair dry, she could see that it was a delicate but definite shade of Titian. Titian, as in red. Red, as in Bozo incident. She shook her head slowly. It was not a radical color but it was certainly enough to give her neurotic mother a nervous breakdown. She groaned and headed back to the shower to try to rinse out the disastrous dye job.

~ * ~

At four-fifteen, Dana crept out of her room, hoping against hope she wouldn't be noticed alongside Nicole's magnificence. Even better was the possibility that she was so late that everyone else had gone. Then she could drive the Mazda to the church. Her sister surely wouldn't throw a tantrum on her special day in front of three hundred guests.

She slipped into an alcove at the top of the stairs. Darn. There she was. Her twin, attired in all her bridal splendor, descended the stairs to the middle landing.

Nick reflected the kind of attitude reserved for queens on Coronation Day. Her hands grasped the voluminous folds of her frothy silk gown, which was studded with tiny seed pearls. Even her hair had been braided and pinned to her head, crownlike, with scores of pearl-tipped hairpins. She wore a tiara and a smug smile.

Below, the rest of the family had gathered in the entry. Her father wore a shawl-collared black tuxedo. Her mother sported a long crimson skirt with a re-embroidered lace blouse and looked every inch the chic, French mother of the bride. Sabrina, dressed in a gown similar to Dana's, had curled her hair, which flowed below her shoulders; quite a concession for casual Sabrina. Flower girl Rosie wore a white lace dress and Shirley Temple ringlets.

As Nicole paused on the landing midway between the first and second stories, Dana hesitantly stepped out of the alcove. She hurried down the stairs, hoping to hide in Nick's train and lace-trimmed veil, floating behind. She expected to hear gasps of admiration for Nicole from her family, the response Nick merited. She did look gorgeous.

Instead, Dana's mother shrieked with dismay. "What have you done! Dana! You wretched, wretched child!" Gabrielle wailed. "I cannot believe this is happening again! We will be a laughingstock!" She hid her head on Tom's shoulder.

Nicole turned. Dana almost laughed at the sight of her model-perfect twin's mouth dropping open unattractively at the sight of Dana's new, red 'do. Rage flashed in Nick's eyes. She swung her right arm back and slapped Dana full in the face before she could duck. Then Nick erupted into a noisy fit of tears.

Dana grabbed her stinging cheek. "OW! It's not as though I did this on purpose! The package said it was golden henna! How was I to know it would turn red?" She retreated to the top of the stairs, well away from Nicole's swinging hand. Her twin had a mean right hook.

Tom patted her mother on the back as he regarded Dana through his tortoise-shell glasses. "Actually, she looks pretty good."

Gabrielle raised her head from his shoulder and hiccupped as she stared at Dana. Sabrina and Rose watched silently as Nicole searched in her old-fashioned reticule for a tissue and blotted her watery eyes.

"Tom, you are right," Gabrielle said. "It does not look so bad. It is just a shock, you know?" She glared at Dana, who fidgeted with the evening shawl draped over her elbows, guiltily avoiding Nick's accusatory gaze.

Dana knew that her twin had concluded that she'd deliberately dyed her hair red in order to mock Nick at her own wedding by this sly reference to the Bozo incident. Nick might also believe that this was Dana's revenge for stealing Max. Worse, nothing anyone could say would change Nick's mind; she tended to get attached to her ideas, sort of like a shoe fetishist with a new pair of spike heels.

"I think I better take the Mazda. See you later, everyone!" Dana bounced down the stairs.

When she tried to push past Nicole, the sculptured heel of Dana's evening pump caught on the wedding gown's lace-trimmed train, tripping Dana and tearing the dress near the bride's derriere. Clutching at her butt, Nick screamed at the awful sound of ripping silk, while a shriek burst from Dana's throat as she tumbled to the bottom of the stairs in a flurry of black crepe and red streamers.

"Dana!" Tom leaped to catch her, fast enough to prevent her from getting a nasty whack to the head on the marble tiled floor. Because the stairs were carpeted, she was bruised, but otherwise unhurt.

"OW!" Dana yelped again. She looked up at her father, managing a weak smile. "What a day! I can hardly wait for the ceremony."

~ * ~

Dana rode to the wedding chapel in the Volvo with her father. Sabrina, Rose, Gabrielle and Nickie went in the limousine, because Tom wisely concluded that the fragile family peace would be fortified by a cooling-off period.

Dosed with several ibuprofen and a glass of champagne, Dana pressed an icepack to her face. Nicole had hit her hard enough to cause swelling to her cheek. Her father glanced over at her as he drove, and Mannering occupied the back seat. As they neared the church, she dropped the icepack onto the floor of the Volvo, and searched through her black satin evening bag for blusher and powder. She used the wing mirror to repair her face, noting that her left cheek was only a little more swollen and red than her right.

The Volvo bumped over a pothole in the street, and Dana decided she'd freshen her lipstick at the church. Tom circled the building, driving around to its back parking lot. As they passed the front of the edifice, Dana saw Nicole and her gown arrayed on the front steps of the church. Seamstress Alice Johansen repaired and arranged her train while Annika fussed with the bride's make-up, hair and veil. Dana grimaced as she observed two video cameras recording the events.

After Tom parked the car, Dana sneaked into the small anteroom at the back of the church where the bride and her entourage were to wait for the processional. She again fiddled with her make-up, and wondered if there was any champagne available. Her cheek still stung. Her headache, the product of tension, the fall down the stairs, and her sister's slap, was growing like kudzu.

Alice entered. Grinning wryly at Dana, she said, "Well, you sure did a job on your sister's dress and your own hair."

"Please, don't remind me of how bad this day is already." Dana moaned and held her head. "I don't see how this wedding could get any worse. Did you manage to fix the train?"

"Oh, yeah. Your mother called me from the limo and I met them here. Luckily, only the buttons that hold the train onto the dress tore off," Alice said. "It's underneath a big bow. Easy to repair, probably sounded a lot worse than it was."

"Good." Dana leaned back on the lounge in the bride's anteroom. Upholstered in dull gold brocade, she imagined it had cradled generations of unhappy bridesmaids. "How angry is Nickie?"

"Oh, she's pretty pissy. But she won't show it because she's the bride, and there's too much attention focused on her. She wants to have a sweet smile for the pictures. So don't worry." Alice sat down next to Dana.

"At least this disaster distracted her from the alterations we made on our dresses."

"True. But how are you doing? Why are you hiding in here?"

"I'm hiding in here because I hate this entire thing and my head hurts. I'm hoping that the ibuprofen kicks in before the photographers find me."

"Good luck. Will you forgive me if I send them in here before they become too panicky?"

"Yeah, I guess so. Just give me some time, okay?"

Chapter Twelve

The Wilders, unlike the Newcombes, had arrived at the church on time and had their family pictures snapped long before the bride's limousine reached the church. Judi and Alan, attired similarly to the Newcombes, lingered in the whitewashed nave, admiring the decorations over which Gabrielle had agonized and numerous florists had labored.

Bouquets of red roses wrapped in oversized white satin bows adorned the central aisle of the church, one on each pew. Similar bouquets ornamented the vestibule and the altar. Gabrielle loved roses and hadn't skimped, so hundreds beautified the church. Their rich color picked up the glorious rose window that blazed high above the altar. The clouds had cleared, and the setting sun shone through the stained glass, enveloping the sanctuary in a ruddy glow.

Colt and Max, along with the other groomsman, kicked their heels in the chancel. For the first time since they had arrived in Los Angeles, the Wilder boys looked like brothers. Colt's beard had been shaved, and his long, shaggy hair trimmed into the same short cut as his brother's. It was parted neatly on the right side, just like Max's. The three men were dressed in the same shawl-collared tuxedos as the fathers. Instead of the traditional white carnations, each sported a red rosebud.

The groomsman, an accountant friend of Max's, was introduced to Colt as Frank Grayson. Frank pulled a silver flask from his pocket and offered the groom and the best man a shot of Scotch. The males began to gossip.

Colt asked Frank about the previous night. "I noticed you disappeared at about the same time that Leta left," Colt said. "Did you see her home?"

"You might say that." Frank smirked. "I saw a part of her home—the bedroom."

Colt whistled. "Party on, dude. Cool." He took another swig from the flask, and passed it to Max.

"Yeah," Frank said. "And those Newcombe sisters—whoa, there's a couple of hot chicks."

"Just what do you mean by that?" asked Max, his Kentucky drawl suddenly pronounced.

"The stories I heard from Leta didn't leave much of anything out. After all, she's known the Newcombe twins since they were all in kindergarten." Frank took the flask from Max's unresisting hand and gulped another swallow. "You're getting quite a hot mama, judging by the pictures I saw. But I'm sure you already know that, don't you?" He laughed coarsely. "I guess you both know that!"

Steve Drake entered and told them to relax. "They just finished the photos, and people are starting to enter the sanctuary. It'll be a few minutes yet." He took a swig of the Scotch Frank offered, then added, "I think you'll be charmingly surprised this evening."

"I'm not sure I want any more surprises," Max said. "What's going on?"

Steve grinned. "I don't want to tell you everything, but have any of you ever heard about the Bozo incident?"

~ * ~

As the guests began to filter into the church, Frank and Steve helped escort the elderly into pews.

The minister, bearing the marriage license, entered the chancel. "Congratulations, my son." The minister beamed at Max. He could be Harry Potter's Professor Dumbledore, with his corona of fluffy white hair topping a long white beard and robe. He held out the sheet of paper to Max and withdrew a pen from a pocket in his vestments.

Max took the license from the minister, regarding it solemnly for a few moments. Colt noticed Nicole had already signed the document. Max plopped into a chair in the corner of the chancel, staring at the marriage license without reaching for the pen.

Unease crawled up Colt's spine. "Max, what's up?"

"Do you know what the magazine and photo business is about? No one will tell me the truth, and it's bothering me. Why is Nicole keeping secrets from me?"

Damn. Colt tried to fake innocence. "I'm not quite sure, but apparently it was something that happened a long time ago." A horrible thought occurred to him. "Max, you love Nicole, don't you?"

Max leaned against the wall and rubbed his face.

Colt grabbed his brother's sleeve. "You're not marrying her for the Newcombe money, are you?"

Max snorted, pushing Colt's hand away. "Of course not. I'm doing fine. No, I'm marrying Nick for herself. But now I feel that I don't know who that person is! What if I'm making a big mistake?"

Shit. Colt's heart lurched. If Max dumped Nick now, Dana might think that he, Colt, had broken his promise. Dana had become important to Colt in the last two days, and he wanted her to believe in him. "Don't you trust yourself and your decisions? When you asked Nick to marry you, you had thought about it and knew what you were doing. Why are you second-guessing yourself now?"

"Actually, she proposed to me, not vice-versa. I don't like to feel I've been manipulated."

"I know it isn't traditional, but do you need to talk with Nicole? If you see her, I bet these doubts will all go away."

"Maybe." Max sounded dubious. "Maybe not."

Despite his shock, Colt figured he should have seen it coming. He swallowed hard. "All right. Are you going to tell Nicole you're having second thoughts?"

Max's shoulders slumped. "That's the problem. I can't hurt her like this. She'll be devastated."

Colt frowned. "Marry in haste, repent in leisure. She'll recover. Besides, if you don't want to marry her, why should you care about her feelings?"

"But I do care. Damn, but I'm confused!" In frustration, Max smacked his hand against the nearest wall.

"Excuse me, my son," said the minister. "May I offer some assistance at this time?"

Max raised his head. "Ye-es, sir. I guess."

"I've performed thousands of wedding ceremonies. Your feelings of fear are entirely natural, but are unfounded. Nicole Newcombe is a good woman, and she intends to be a good and loyal wife."

"I talked to her the other night and that was exactly what she told me," Colt said, glad to be of help. "Doesn't your reluctance to hurt her mean something?"

"She's my friend," Max said. "Of course I don't want to hurt her! I love her!"

"If you are founding your marriage upon loving friendship, I would say that you will have a happy life indeed." The minister handed Max a pen, then asked Colt, "Son, do you have the rings?"

"Yeah, right here." Colt held up his right hand. Max's wedding ring was on Colt's right ring finger, while Nickie's decorated his pinky.

"Good," said the minister briskly. "I'll cue the organist. I think we're all ready to go!"

~ * ~

From his position on the altar near his brother, Colt looked out over the sanctuary. As the organist played "Jesu, Joy of Man Desiring," he inhaled the heady scent of dozens of red roses. About three hundred people crowded the church, mostly business contacts of Tom's, he'd been told.

Leta Weller walked down the aisle toward him. Glad to see she isn't smashed today, he thought. Her measured tread matched the solemn music, setting the dignified tone of the wedding service.

Sabrina came in next. Colt was struck anew by the incredible beauty of the Newcombe women. Her lavish bouquet of red roses perfectly set off her formal black and white gown.

A striking redhead stepped into the sanctuary and Colt wondered who the voluptuous, Titian-tressed babe could be. Why hadn't he met her at the rehearsal dinner? He heard the audience gasp. Someone muttered, "Who is that woman? Where's Dana?"

As she approached the altar, his jaw dropped. As she paced up the aisle, he recognized her as Dana, whose face was redder than her hair. He winked at her, earning a glare from her green-tinted eyes. When she took her place, he couldn't resist whispering, "Hey, Gingertop! How you doin' today, darlin'?"

She stumbled, and he caught her arm. She dug her heel into his instep. He winced as he pulled her upright.

She smiled sweetly. "Sorry, *darlin'*."

Fortunately, everyone else's attention seemed focused on Rosie, dawdling up the aisle in her lace flower girl outfit. She tossed rose petals out of her basket as she headed toward her parents, who were on the altar

To Rose, the altar seemed as if it was a mile away. She plopped herself down on the white runner in the middle of the church, and announced, "I'm hungry. I want my mommy!"

Laughter rippled through the sanctuary as her dad sprinted down the aisle to her to pick her up. As he started tossing rose petals out of her basket, the assembled throng oohed and ahed at how cute they looked.

From her vantage point in her father's arms, Rose could see a bunch of people on the altar. She knew her mommy, of course, and sorta knew another lady, Leta. There was a strange looking red-headed woman there who was scary, 'coz she looked kinda like Auntie Dana, but not really. Rose looked away, shifting her gaze to Unka Max, then to this other guy, who … then back to Unka Max…

Rose shrieked in terror. Unka Max had a double! It was just like that in SpongeBob SquarePants, which she'd watched that morning, where bad Krabby put an evil double into poor SpongeBob's body. She burst into tears and buried her head in her father's shoulder. Her screams echoed through the nave as Steve rushed her out through the door of the chancel. Sabrina followed closely behind.

As the startled congregation calmed, the organist cranked up the volume on her instrument and started "Here Comes the Bride."

All distractions were forgotten as Nicole entered the church with Tom. Colt had to admit that Nick had never looked so good. Her bridal gown hugged her slim waist and flared gently at her hips. The lace-trimmed veil covered her lightly, front and back. She wore pearls, subtle and beautiful.

Colt glanced at Dana. As a redhead, she looked hot and spicy, good enough to eat. The bold act of tinting her hair showed her adventurous streak. He liked that.

Subtle and beautiful was nice, but he'd take hot and spicy any day. Yeah.

She met his eyes, a blush staining her cheeks. He wondered how Dana would look as a bride. Would she insist upon the conventional wedding her twin had demanded? Or would extraordinary Dana want a unique ceremony? If so, what kind of event would she choose?

He winked at her, envisioning her in a white lace minidress with a bouquet of exotic blooms, not the boring bunch of red roses Nicole held. Or maybe she'd wear white leather. Yeah.

Nick seemed to have eyes only for Max as she floated up the aisle. With relief, Colt concluded she truly loved his brother.

Max leaned toward Colt and whispered, "Remember that discussion we just had?"

"Yeah, I remember." Colt nodded, feeling wary.

"Forget about it." Max straightened his back and puffed out his chest, looking as though he were bursting with pride. Adjusting his cuffs, he squared his shoulders as Tom and Nicole neared.

Tom helped Nick with the steps up to the top,
ensuring that she didn't stumble over that crazy train.
She smiled brilliantly at Max through her veil. Colt's
brother smiled back as he shook Tom's hand. Tom went
to sit with his wife while Max tucked Nick's arm in his.
They turned to face the minister.

Dana left her appointed spot to see that her sister's
chapel train was properly arranged behind her,
spreading it over the carpeted steps up to the altar
where the bride and groom stood. As she heard the
photographer snap a few candid shots, she fluffed the
veil, then returned to her place as the organist wrapped
up "Here Comes the Bride."

The minister stepped forward. "Dearly beloved…"

As the minister went through the ceremony, Dana
tried hard to avoid the eyes of both Leta and Colt. The
stephanotis in her bouquet tickled her nose, and it
wouldn't take much to get her either laughing or
sneezing. Luckily, the ceremony would be short since
Nicole had told the minister to keep it brief on account
of her mega-high heels cramping her toes. For once,
Dana approved her twin's vanity. Only Nicole would
insist upon abbreviating her wedding ceremony so she
could wear the perfect pair of shoes.

While the minister droned through the ritual
phrases, Dana let her mind wander. How would it feel,
to love someone enough to marry? The awesome
commitment cowed her, just as it had at Sabrina's
wedding to Steve.

Marriage to the man of her dreams. She sneaked a
peek at Colt Wilder and caught him examining her with

more heat in his eyes than a wildfire. She didn't understand how his cool, cobalt eyes could look so hot, but they were steamier than Glendale in August. Her answering flush warmed her skin. Pressing a hand to her throat, she looked away.

She returned her gaze to the minister, who asked Colton, "The rings, son?"

Colt pulled Max's ring off his finger with a flourish and handed it to Nicole. The bride's ring was another matter entirely. Colt tugged at the gold band, jammed onto his pinky as though it had been affixed with Superglue.

"It's stuck," he whispered to the minister and Max.

The elderly minister cupped one hand behind his ear and asked him in a loud voice, "What is it, my son?"

"This ring is stuck on my finger," Colton hissed. "I can't get it off!"

Dana's decorum had been severely challenged by the entire spectacle. She put a hand over her mouth to stifle her giggles, but Leta joined her while Colt continued to yank at the offending band. Nicole glared at the trio as the entire congregation became restless, murmuring at the delay.

The photographer didn't stop shooting. *Click.* Looking desperate, Colt stuck his entire finger into his mouth and moistened his pinky. Nicole grimaced. *Click.* He pulled the ring off, but the slippery band flew out of his hands and sailed across the altar. *Click.* "Aw, jeez," grumbled Colt, sounding exasperated. "Sorry, sir," he said to the minister. "Didn't mean to take the Lord's name in vain, there."

The minister raised his brows as Dana joined the search for the missing ring. Guffaws echoed through the church as the groom, best man, and maid-of-honor knelt. *Click. Click.* Colt and Max both swept the floor around and underneath Nick's capacious skirt. Dana, kneeling near the minister's feet, could see Colt's hand whack her sister's ankle. Nick kicked at him. He yelped in pain as she stepped on his hand. Dana winced. *Click.* The video camera also whirred, immortalizing the moment.

"I've got it!" Max exclaimed. He picked it up at the edge of the altar near Frank's foot.

Dana and Colt leaped to their feet.

"With this ring, I thee wed," Max said hastily, shoving the ring onto Nick's finger.

Dana listened to her twin repeat the solemn words of commitment with somewhat more seriousness. The minister concluded, "You may now kiss the bride." Max flung off the veil that concealed Nick's face. He wrapped her in his arms, kissing her with obvious passion. After a few seconds, she drew away from him, gazing at him with an expression which left no doubt in Dana's mind about Nick's feelings.

"Let's get outta here," Max growled. "It's time to party!"

Applause and laughter broke out through the church as Max and Nick raced out of the church to the tune of "We've Only Just Begun."

The rest of the wedding party followed more decorously. As Colton took Dana's arm to lead her out

The Wilder Brother

of the church, he asked, "What were you thinking about when you looked at me?"

Cupping one hand to her ear, Dana pretended that she couldn't hear him over the music. She wouldn't discuss her deepest feelings and dreams with wham-bam-thank-you-ma'am Colt. What for?

When they left the church, she distracted him by waving at the bride and groom, who were climbing into a buggy drawn by two white horses. "They really went over the top, didn't they?"

"They sure did. I'm waiting for the doves."

"Doves?" she asked.

"Yeah, my mom said that they release a flock of white doves at fashionable weddings these days."

"If it's fashionable, Nicole and Mother will do it."

Guests poured out of the church. Colt kept his hold on Dana, keeping her by his side. "It sounds as though you aren't real enthusiastic about this wedding anymore. I thought you wanted your sister to marry my brother. It sounded that way last night."

"It's not the marriage. It's the wedding. I get bored with all this silliness."

"I see what you mean." Colt escorted her down the steps of the church, leading her over to a waiting limousine. "It's a lot of fuss and bother, but look at it as an opportunity to have fun."

He helped her into the limo, and joined her, sitting close. He kissed her hand in a romantic gesture, caressing her palm. "Finally, we're alone. I kinda missed you today."

Her body thrummed with sudden excitement before the door opened. Mannering herded Frank and Leta into the car with Dana and Colt. Dana stopped herself before she whined with frustration.

Just before the chauffeur closed the door, Mannering stuck his head back in. "Bye-the-bye, you'll find a little pick-me-up in the fridge." He gestured, indicating the small refrigerator built into the back-facing seat of the limo.

The driver slammed the door and prepared to leave. Frank pressed the button that raised the window separating the chauffeur's compartment from theirs.

Colt opened the fridge to withdraw a bottle of chilled Dom Perignon. "Very nice. I gotta say, Dana, your parents are first-class all the way." He popped the cork and filled four flutes.

"Yeah, they are." Leta took a glass. "Gabrielle and Tom have always been cool."

"I'm just glad that the ceremony is over," Dana said. "Hopefully Mother will calm down."

"Don't be so sure." Leta sipped. "I heard her talking about getting more group photos at the country club, 'cause they couldn't shoot any of the entire wedding party before the ceremony. Hey, there's the happy couple!" She rolled down her window down to hoot and whistle at the buggy carrying Max and Nicole.

The carriage, decorated with flowing white streamers, followed a van. The back of the van was open so a videographer and a photographer could record every smooch and cuddle of the newlyweds.

"Holy media event, Batman!" Dana said to Colt.

He grinned. "Not your taste, Dana?"

"Oh, not at all. If I ever get married, the only people who will know about it in advance will be me and my husband. My sisters' weddings have cured me of any desire for bridal madness."

"What if your fiancé disagrees?" Colton asked, his voice silken.

Dana frowned. Why would he care? "I don't know. I guess we'd somehow work it out. Maybe I'm idealistic, but I believe that if two people truly care about each other, they can resolve their issues."

Leta hooted again. "You're dreaming, Dana."

Warmth born of embarrassment heated Dana's face. "Hey, look at my parents. I've never met two people who are more different. But they get along fine, because they really love each other."

"Yeah," Leta said. "Nothing could be further from Tom's personality than this wedding. But Tom went for it, 'cause he knew it was important to Gabrielle and Nick."

"Pretty nice of him, considering that it must be hella expensive." Frank refilled his glass.

Dana ignored the tacky reference to her family's money. "Dad's a basically simple person. He'd rather be playing with his computer, and so would I, really." She sipped her champagne. "Why's this guy driving so fast?"

"I told you, Gabrielle wants more photographs before the other guests get to the reception," Leta said. "Everyone's milling around in the church, and when they get to GlenAllan they'll be greeted at the door with champagne and munchies. This way, Gabrielle creates time for more photos."

"What's GlenAllan?" Frank asked.

Dana pointed out of the window. A pillared portico, festooned with blooming purple bougainvillea, loomed as the driver stopped in front of giant, leaded glass double doors. A uniformed doorman opened the limo and the four tumbled out. Mannering advanced.

"How did you get here before us?" Colt asked. "I thought our driver was gonna get a speeding ticket!"

Mannering cracked a tiny smirk. "Ladies and gentlemen, if you will please proceed to the courtyard for additional photographs."

"This way." Dana sighed. She led them through the double doors of the main building of GlenAllan Country Club.

"You've been here before?" Colt asked.

"Oh yeah. Mother likes GlenAllan. Sabrina's reception was here, too. We've been members since we were kids."

"Nice lookin' tennis courts." Frank walked to a side window of the facility. "You play tennis, Dana?"

"Sure. Every summer, Mother enrolled us in every program they had: golf, tennis, swimming. In the winter, we played racquetball, took aerobics, or worked out. GlenAllan has it all." She walked to the back of the facility, painted peach with touches of cream. She stepped through wide glass doors to a courtyard with a large, circular fountain in the middle, where several tripods had already been set up.

Colt nudged Dana, jerking his shoulder toward a cage full of white doves set underneath the shade of the back portico. The birds twittered and cooed as he grinned at her, reminding her of the way he smiled down at her in bed the night before. Her pussy creamed anew, and she wondered if they'd be able to steal some more time together.

Unfortunately, a squeaky-voiced photographer had also preceded them to the country club. Dana tried to keep hold of her patience as the obnoxious broad herded them into a "casual" pose at the fountain. The fountain's tiled rim was wide enough for the women to sit on, and the males were arrayed near them. The photographer told Colt to put one foot upon the fountain's edge near Dana and to bend his head toward her as though they talked.

He blatantly stared down her bodice.

"Like what you see?" she asked.

"Oh, yeah. They tasted pretty good, too," he murmured.

She winked. "They still do."

Lust flared in his eyes as the rest of the wedding party arrived, the photographs became more complex, and the tension level in the courtyard increased. Finally, the entire wedding entourage, including parents, siblings, first and second cousins to the nth degree were guided into position with the golf course as a backdrop. It took only five takes before Rose would smile for the camera.

"Hey, Max!" Dana watched as Colt nudged his brother. "There's Aunt Julie and Uncle Ray!" Julie,

Judi's look-alike sister, hugged the groom and the best man while Ray, her husband, shook their hands.

"And who's this? Is this little cousin Patti?" Colt stood back and regarded the petite, attractive brunette, stroking her with his gaze, up and down. She wore a short silk sheath that clung to her slim figure, exposing her shapely legs. Stiletto heels lent her height.

Patti batted her lashes at Colt. "I'm not a little girl anymore, cousin Colt. I'm nineteen."

"Well, goodness gracious. Last time I saw you, you were just a kid! How's everything goin', cousin Patti?" Colt tucked Patti's arm into his and led her over to the shaded portico.

Dana was miffed. He had no business looking at another woman like that while he was boffing her. A horrible feeling invaded every cell with a sick sensation. Was it jealousy? No way. This awful feeling can't be jealousy, she told herself.

She didn't care about Colt, did she? The sex was amazing, but she had no reason to feel possessive about Colton Wilder. You don't own him, she admonished herself. And you were fooling around with him only to distract him from Nicole, remember?

She found herself comparing her looks to Patti's. If Colt preferred petite brunettes, Dana was sunk. She swallowed the bilious taste in her throat, suddenly feeling ten feet tall and very, very redheaded, as though her hair shone like a beacon.

From where had this emotion come? She told herself that she shouldn't feel this way and shoved Colton Wilder and his women firmly out of her mind, promising herself that she'd get through the rest of this wedding with dignity.

She pressed her hand to her forehead, then zipped out of the courtyard to find some restorative champagne and hors d'oeuvres. Colt and Patti remained to watch the photographers' activities together. As she left, Dana tried to persuade herself that she didn't care.

Chapter Thirteen

Dana tucked herself at the very end of the bar, wedged into a corner next to a potted plant. She guzzled champagne, glad for the respite.

Mannering advanced, trapping her. "Miss Dana, you're wanted in the receiving line."

"Aw, come on, Mannering." She kicked off her shoe and rubbed a squashed baby toe. "They'll never notice I'm gone. Mother's all involved with Nick."

"Now, Miss Dana, you know I'd like to keep my job."

"All right, only because it's you asking."

"Yes, ma'am."

"Why have you put up with all of us over the years, anyway?" She handed him a glass.

He sipped, looking startled by her question. "Miss Dana, I enjoy my job. Most days, the most serious problem I have is weeding the herb garden. Every once in a while Madame and I orchestrate a major event. I can't think of a more fulfilling existence."

"I guess it takes all kinds," she said, jamming her foot back into her shoe. She allowed him to guide her into her place in the receiving line, then squeezed his hand. "Thank you, Mannering."

The wide, pillared corridor in which she stood separated the two halves of GlenAllan's main building and was decorated with giant pots of bougainvillea. A videographer and a photographer recorded the moment as another assistant released the doves, which swirled around the wedding party, then obligingly flew away through the pillars into the sky. Dana guessed they returned to their cote.

She stood beside Sabrina in the line, greeting the hordes. Dana's roiling emotions were masked by the combined effects of ibuprofen and champagne. She didn't often drink, but she figured this was an unusual situation. Colt had disappeared with that pretty little brunette, and Dana didn't understand the war between anger and longing which tumbled inside her. She didn't want to acknowledge how insecure she'd become, even to herself. She hated how she felt.

She had to hand it to her mother, who managed the receiving line so it only took about a half-hour. Prior experience helped, as did the burgeoning hunger of the guests. The hors d'oeuvres served with the champagne had been savory but not filling. The time approached eight, and guests crowded toward their tables. Lemmings, thought Dana. Or perhaps ants.

The dining room had been decorated with the ubiquitous red roses, which adorned every available surface. The tables, draped in white linen, were ornamented with low rose centerpieces with two candles, white and red. From her mother's and her sister's blather, Dana knew they represented purity and passion. The dining room glowed with the setting sun and the candles' mellow light.

She found her seat between Colt and Frank, with Leta Weller on Frank's other side. Colt and Max flanked Nicole, creating an interesting threesome. Sabrina and Steve sat on Max's other side. A microphone was set up behind the bride's table, and a bank of ficus, decorated with myriad tiny white lights, hid the doors of the kitchen.

Guests found their places as Tom approached the microphone. He thanked the guests for their attendance and assured them that without their presence, the event would be empty and devoid of meaning. When he finished welcoming the guests, Mannering, who was acting as the master of ceremonies, intoned, "The bride and groom will now dance for the first time as husband and wife."

Nick slipped her feet back into her high, spiked heels and took Max's arm. They walked to the wood dance floor amid applause as the band played "Unforgettable." After a few moments, Tom and Gabrielle claimed Nick and Max as their partners.

As the band segued into "Love Me Tender," Colt took Dana into his arms. His lips brushed her temple.

"You look a tad down in the mouth, punkin'. What's up?"

Dana's anger took flight, like the doves. How did he make her feel so good? She smiled up at him. "That's what my dad calls me."

"Really? Oops."

"No, it's okay."

"Just as long as you don't start thinking of me in a fatherly way." He twirled her around.

"Oh, no."

Colt's arm tightened around her, and Dana's blood began to dance through her veins in time with the music. She relaxed against his strong chest, lifting her chin to cuddle her cheek against his.

She'd never felt this way with any other man. Everything—his scent, the smoothness of his skin against hers, the strength of his arms, romance of the setting—blended into a heady feeling of bliss that threatened to take over her mind, her heart and her body. His lips touched her temple again. The heat of his kiss curled around in her belly, reaching for her pussy with longing fingers.

God help her, she wanted him to tie her up again and make love to her.

Mannering announced that the best man would now dance with the bride, and Colt released Dana with a rueful smile when Max came to claim her as his partner.

Colt tried not to watch them, and wondered what they could be saying to each other. Then, with some misgivings, he took Nicole into his arms. She felt okay, he supposed, though not as good as her sister. At least she'd taken off that dang train. He'd been afraid he'd trip over it and the two of them would tumble into a humiliated heap right there on the dance floor.

Her sharp tones interrupted his musing. "I don't like the way you look at my sister."

"What?"

"You heard me. Dana does important work. She doesn't need a commitment-phobic jerk to mess up her life."

He grimaced. The picture that both Max and Nicole had drawn of him lately wasn't very attractive. "Do you mean the person you always described as 'the four-eyed bytehead'?"

Nick flushed. "Never mind that old stuff. Just stay away from my sister."

Colt briefly considered telling her off, but he reckoned that he shouldn't argue with the bride on her wedding day. Might even mean bad luck for his brother. "Whatever you say, babe."

"And don't 'babe' me."

Would this torture ever end? He sighed with relief as his cousin Patti—his step-cousin, really, but who cared?—tapped Nick on the shoulder. Beaming at Nicole, she asked, "May I cut in?" As Nicole stalked away from Colt, Dana saw Patti snuggle into his arms the same way Dana had moments before. She couldn't see Colt's facial expression, but assumed that his male ego adored the attention. She resolved to quit feeding that ego. She wasn't going to throw herself at this man or any other, no matter how good he made her feel.

Max asked, "What's wrong?"

"My feet are beginning to hurt. May I sit this one out?"

"Sure. It seems that the compulsory dance section of this event is over, since I see unsanctioned couples filling the floor."

Dana laughed. At last, Max showed that he had a sense of humor. She guessed he'd need it, married to Nicole. "Do you think we got a ten from the judges?"

"Oh, at least." He escorted her off the dance floor.

She found a chair and removed her shoes, unable to stifle her groan of relief. She wiggled her toes, glaring at Colton and Patti. Now the little brunette had wiggled her hips close to Colt's. *Hope she's using birth control. The way this dance is going, she could be pregnant before the last waltz.*

A touch at Dana's waist made her jerk in surprise. "Paul!"

Paul Doucette, Dana's French cousin, was dressed to the nines in full transvestite regalia: emerald silk from top to toe, a calf-length dress which hid his brawny knees and thighs, plus emerald silk heels and matching hat. The color flattered "Pauline," bringing out the chestnut highlights in his/her dark hair. Make-up cloaked any hint of beard.

"You look—you look—great," Dana said.

Paul smiled. Coral lipstick set off strong white teeth. "*Merci.* But you are sad underneath all your finery, Dana."

"Oh, I'm okay."

"*Non.* The petite brunette, she bothers you?"

Dana bit her lip. "Am I so obvious?"

"Only to your cousin who knows you. Let me help."

Dana's shoulders tensed. "What are you going to do?"

Paul, ignoring the question, sauntered off, all long legs and swinging hips. Dana watched him, dazed. Damn him, he had a sexier walk than she did.

Steve Drake slipped an arm around her. "Want to dance, Dana?"

As they circled, Dana noticed Tom dancing with Rose, who was standing on her grandpa's shoes. "I used to do that."

"With your dad?"

"Yes. In this very room."

"Getting maudlin?" Steve teased. "Sense of continuity, and all that?"

"Yeah, why not? Aren't weddings the corniest of corny occasions?"

"That they are. But this doesn't compare to ours. Remember when Gabrielle cried 'my baby, my baby' when we left for our honeymoon?"

"She acted as though your wedding to Sabrina was a funeral."

"It took having a grandchild for her to change her tune." His head jerked. "Oh, my God, look at that." His chest shook with repressed laughter.

"What?" She poked him with a finger. "Turn a little more so I can see, too."

Colton Wilder circled the floor with Paul Doucette in his arms. Paul, whose high heels made him inches taller than his partner, had Colt's head tucked under his chin and a smug smile on his face. Patti watched the two of them with a grimace that could make a baby cry.

Dana grinned. Paul had finally paid her back for his unauthorized exploration of her lingerie drawer.

~ * ~

After dinner and speeches, Max and Nicole left the reception in a shower of birdseed. To Dana's surprise, she found herself hugging an emotional, teary Nicole as her twin bid her good-bye at the entrance of GlenAllan.

"You'll feel the same way when you get married." Nicole sniffled and rubbed her nose with a lace hanky.

"As if." Dana rolled her eyes.

"Really, Dana, I know we've fought, but I love you and wish you all the best. You need to settle down with a nice computer geek and have a bunch of cute little byteheads."

"Th-thanks, Nickie." Yeah, right. After her sisters' wedding wackiness, the last thing Dana wanted was to follow in their footsteps.

She let Nick go and watched as Max urged her into the back of a big black limo. She knew the bride and groom planned to travel to Long Beach, where they'd board a cruise to Cabo San Lucas, Mexico. The party rolled on without them.

At midnight Tom, to Gabrielle's dismay, began displaying his juggling talent with five of the leftover bags of birdseed. Inspired, Colt and Frank organized a volleyball tournament on the dance floor using more of the tiny bags. Gabrielle closed down the party by instructing the band to play "The Party's Over." The chandeliers were taking too much damage.

Dana and the other stalwart partiers staggered into assorted limos and cars, and left GlenAllan. Colt sprawled on the seat opposite Dana, his blue eyes narrowed to slits. He'd taken off his jacket when Frank and Leta had left the limo, and tugged his bowtie loose. Crisp black hair curled in the V of his open tuxedo shirt, a brazen invitation her fingers had to resist.

She wondered if he'd have the gall to make a pass at her after his performances on the dance floor with Patti and Paul.

But if he opened his shirt just one more stud she'd be the one to jump his bones. She shoved her hands under her rear, controlling their impulse to wander in the direction of his chest. "You were pretty hot there, dancing with, uh, Pauline."

His brows lifted fractionally. "There's something strange about that woman, but I can't put my finger on it."

She giggled, wondering if she should tell.

"What's funny, babe?"

"You."

"Me? Li'l ol' me? What'd I do?"

She collapsed back against the seat in gales of laughter. She was certain that somewhere, sometime, Colt would learn the truth about Paul Doucette, but she wouldn't tell. Oh, no. She knew how to keep a secret.

"Aw, come on, babe! Share the joke."

"You're too far gone to appreciate it."

Colt had stretched out full length along one of the limo's long seats. His long, lean body was a temptation and a half, but Dana wasn't buying. Nope. Not after he'd practically conceived a child with little cousin Patti on the dance floor.

Chapter Fourteen

The next morning, Colt was abruptly awakened by Mannering as the butler invaded his bedroom and announced, "Rise and shine, Master Colt!"

Colt whined, "Mannering, why are you here?" Small, wicked imps had taken up an abode inside his brain, where they were busily trampling brain cells and playing tympani. His mouth tasted like the imps' trash heap. He couldn't open his eyes; the tribe of evil imps had cleverly sewn his lids shut, all the better to torture him. He clutched his head.

"News, Master Colt. Madame felt that you should see the Sunday paper post-haste."

He managed to sit up and wrench his eyes open. A blast of sunshine pierced his brain to the back of his skull; Mannering had opened the curtains. The imps squealed and shook tiny spears in triumph as Colt fell back onto his pillow. "Later, please," he groaned.

Mannering bore a silver salver upon which rested a glass of orange juice, a pot of coffee, and a newspaper. "Come now, Master Colt! There's nothing wrong with you that coffee and aspirin won't fix. Here." Mannering waved a cup of hot, fragrant French roast past Colt's nose.

He sat up again, and opening only one eye to a tiny slit, reached for the cup. He sipped and swallowed carefully. The imps stamped tiny, booted feet as they jeered and booed. Mannering handed him two aspirin, which Colt took with the orange juice.

After two cups of coffee the imps had been routed. Colt examined the newspaper as Mannering tidied his room. A banner headline blazed across the first page of the Sunday Los Angeles *Times*. STRIKE CLOSES LAX.

Colt's tired brain initially failed to process the information. "Lax? What is lax, and why should I care about it?"

"L.A.X. is the local international airport, Master Colt." Mannering shook out Colton's tuxedo jacket, pursing his lips with disapproval. Colt had dropped his formal wear in a heap on the floor before falling onto his bed. "We suspect that many of our guests will be having trouble with their return flights."

"Oh, no! How long is this strike supposed to go on for?" Colt demanded ungrammatically. "I have to get back to the farm before the fourth of July weekend." He scrambled out of bed and hastened toward the shower.

"Unknown, Master Colt," called Mannering above the running water. "Apparently the workers are prepared for a lengthy walk-out."

~ * ~

Later, as Colt sat at lunch with the Newcombes and the Wilders in Tom and Gabrielle's dining room, he learned that the news was worse than he imagined. The strike was predicted to halt all international and local flights from the Los Angeles area for at least two weeks.

Alan proposed that his son drive with them to Rancho Santa Fe, near San Diego, and visit with Patti, Julie and Ray before boarding a plane in San Diego for Louisville. Patti thought that was a great idea, and said so. "We could spend a little more time together, cousin Colt," she said pertly.

Dana raised her brows and silently munched her fruit salad.

"Impossible!" said Gabrielle. "Zhe airport workers around zhe state are walking out in sympathy with zhe people in L.A. You can try to get a flight, but I doubt one will be available."

A phone call to her travel agent proved her assessment correct. The option of driving with his parents was out also, since they had planned to take their time meandering across the country.

"Perhaps you can call the farm and work it out," Tom said. "Clearly the situation is unavoidable."

"I dunno. The Fourth of July weekend is coming up, and we'll be short-staffed just when more hands need to be there. Everyone seems to want to ride out for a picnic on the fourth," Colt explained. He turned to Dana, who seemed unperturbed at the news of the strike. "Dana, you're very mellow about the situation. How are you getting home?"

"Oh, I'm traveling by train. I always do if I have the time."

Colt blinked. "By train?"

"Yeah. I hate planes. They're crowded and stuffy. There's at least one whiny kid on every flight, and I always seem to pick up some new virus. Train travel is much more fun."

Patti stiffened as he stroked his chin, appraising the alternative. "That's an interesting idea," he said. "How long does it take?"

"Depends on your route. I'm leaving on Tuesday night and arriving on Friday, in time to see the Fourth of July fireworks over Boston Harbor."

"How hard is it to make arrangements?"

"Oh, it's easy. Want me to show you?" Dana left the rest of her lunch and headed for Tom's den with Colt following.

"Dana, you did not ask to be excused!" her mother called after her.

"Oh!" He stopped and asked for the both of them. "Gabrielle, can we please be excused?"

"Yes, you may," Gabrielle responded, obviously gratified. As he left the room he heard her compliment his parents on his nice manners.

When he entered the den, Dana was already seated at Tom's computer, busily clicking the mouse. "Do you surf the net?" she asked.

"I'm afraid not, since my computer's old and has a really slow modem. I only use it for word processing, spreadsheets and so on. I guess I'm just roadkill on the information highway."

"It's easy with the right equipment. Watch."

When the homepage of Tom's server emerged on the oversized screen, she typed in *http://www.amtrak.com*, which denoted Amtrak's location on the Internet. A few clicks of the mouse later, and Colt filled in his destination, route and credit card number. His route would take him across the country from Los Angeles to Louisville via Albuquerque, Topeka and Chicago.

After a short wait, she said, "Hmmm. Looks like a lot of people have had the same idea." She clicked and typed. "I can only find you a coach seat, but you can share my room if you leave the same time I do."

"Did you book a sleeper?"

"Oh, yeah. Like I said, I love train travel and I planned this trip a month ago. You'll dig it, Colt," she said. "Train travel is one big, cross-country party."

~ * ~

Dana hadn't exaggerated. As Colton and Dana settled themselves into her compartment, they could hear other travelers shouting cheerfully at each other as they wandered up and down the corridors, finding their sleepers and their seats as their train left Los Angeles' Union Station two days later. "This train stops at the Nevada border," she said. "People get off and bus to a nearby gambling resort called Laughlin. Everyone who goes there is in a partying mood."

"They must arrive pretty early in the morning," he said.

"Yeah, but that doesn't bother them. They'll hang out in the club car all night drinking. Or, they'll watch a movie or something."

Colt watched Dana as she bustled about the tiny compartment. She wore black capris and an oversized tuxedo shirt, complete with onyx studs down the front, with cufflinks securing the starched French cuffs. The shirt barely covered her hips, and the tight pants limned her excellent legs. He jealously speculated about the identity of the original owner of the shirt. *Frank??*

She wore her shoulder-length red hair in a straight unadorned bob, and tortoise-shell glasses perched on the end of her nose. Colt thought she was adorable, except for the damn shirt. *Maybe it's Tom's.*

The First Class Superliner Service of the Southwest Chief consisted of a small, upper level private room, a bathroom that included a shower, plus a sofa and an armchair. The furniture converted to two bunks. Dana promptly opened out the beds, and stowed their gear underneath them. "It's easier to just leave the bunks open rather than keep rearranging the room. Are you comfortable with the sleeping accommodations?" she inquired politely.

"Oh, you know it, baby." His grin flashed through his dark stubble; Colt hadn't shaved since the wedding, since he wanted to regrow his beard. He pulled off his chambray workshirt, exposing a white muscle-T with a red and green Italian flag on the front. The back of the shirt read *Milano.* He tucked his shirt back into his snug blue jeans, and said, "Wanna go exploring?"

"Yeah!" She strapped her fanny pack around her waist, locked the door of her sleeper, and followed him down the corridor.

Dana herself wasn't entirely serene about the situation. She had offered to share her room with Colt on the spur of the moment, and had forgotten the erotic charge that threatened to overtake her when she was alone with him.

Neither his snug T-shirt nor his tight jeans left much to the imagination. She firmly suppressed her growing arousal, believing the presence of cousin Patti had destroyed any burgeoning relationship she might have had with Colt. He'd spent most of the time since the wedding at the Marriott where his parents were staying with Julie and Ray. Dana assumed that he had seen a lot of little cousin Patti, because Colt had paid no attention at all to Dana since she had made the train reservations for him. She'd been annoyed, but reminded herself that the purpose of her affair with him had been fulfilled, and at this point, she merely had to endure his company for a couple more days. Once she returned home and immersed herself in her work, she wouldn't miss him.

Much.

Colt pulled out his ticket from the pocket of his tight jeans, focusing her attention on his hips. The memory of those hips grinding into hers shot through her mind before she squelched it, along with the useless feelings the sensual image engendered. She lifted her hair off her nape, feeling warm.

"Let's check out the seat I'm supposed to be in," he said.

"Why?"

"I don't know. Maybe just to see. It gives us additional options. You might get sick of my company and kick me out."

She raised her eyebrows. "As though I'd be so rude," she said. "Besides, there's plenty of room."

They walked through the club car, the lounge, and the dining car before finding Colt's coach seat. When they arrived, they saw a tot asleep in a baby carrier, which was securely strapped into the chair. A heavily pregnant teenager sat next to the child.

"Oh!" she gasped, in a flat Midwestern twang. "Is Lindy in your seat?"

Colt nodded, but said, "Don't worry about it. I'm staying with my friend, here. She has a sleeper." He gestured at Dana, who blushed, figuring that this stranger would promptly make the obvious deduction: that Dana and Colt were lovers. They were, sort of, but … she flushed even more redly as he turned and smiled at her. Wanton longing shot through her body, a solar flare of desire, which overheated like an old car radiator in the California sun. She took a deep breath and attempted to calm herself.

"Oh! Thank you. There was a mix-up with the tickets, you see," the teen explained. "My daughter is supposed to be sitting next to me, of course. It seems that the travel agent made a mistake, and her seat is across the aisle."

"Is this your baby?" asked Dana. The woman seemed quite young for someone who had one child and another on the way.

"Yes, she's all mine," said the girl proudly, twisting a plain gold band on her left hand. "Mine and her daddy's, of course. We're going to see him in Leavenworth."

"Oh!" Dana gasped. Was this poor kid hitched to a con?

"It's not what you think," the woman said quickly. "Mike is an M.P. stationed at Fort Leavenworth. I've been visiting his parents in Long Beach."

"I'm sorry, Mrs...." started Dana.

"I'm Jenna Norton, and this is my daughter Lindy."

"Colt Wilder, and this is Dana Newcombe," said Colton. "I'm going to Kentucky, and Dana is on her way home to Boston."

"Ooh, all the way across the country, that's exciting," said Jenna. Her curly auburn hair framed a round face dotted with freckles and a couple of zits.

"Hey, are the two of y'all alone?" he asked.

Jenna looked embarrassed. "Yeah. Mike will pick us up in Kansas City in a day and a half. But until then, we're on our own, Lindy and me."

After a short pause, during which Dana wondered quite what to say, he said, "Well, if you need anything, just let us know. Maybe we can have breakfast together tomorrow morning when your daughter is awake."

"Okay," the girl timidly agreed. "I'll see you in the dining car tomorrow."

Neither Dana nor Colt said anything until they had reached the next car. Dana remarked, "I'm really sorry for her."

"Why?"

"She can't be any more than nineteen. She's got one baby and she's about to drop another, and she's alone taking a train halfway across the country."

"So? She seemed all right to me. Her baby was clean and happy. Heck, Lindy has a better disposition than Rose. Rose would be howling."

Dana blushed for her niece. "It's true, Rosie is pretty temperamental and neurotic. I don't know why. Sabrina and Steve are such calm people."

"Maybe too much contact with your mother."

"What about my mother?" Dana opened the door to the club car. A sign on the door read, "WELCOME ABOARD, FIRST CLASS PASSENGERS!" The car was decorated in soothing tones of taupe and beige. Tables of food and drink were available for the first class passengers. She walked over to a tray of appetizers and selected one. He followed her to take a bottle of Bud.

"Don't get me wrong, I like your mom. She's charming and intelligent, if a little, um, managing. But I noticed that you don't have much to say to her." He opened the bottle and took a swig.

"We have plenty to talk about," lied Dana, after she had swallowed her canapé. She picked a bottle of fizzy Calistoga water and tried to open it, her hand slipping around its wet neck.

Colt took the bottle from her, wiped it on his jeans, unscrewed the top, and returned it to her. "You have exactly two words to say to Gabrielle. '*Yes, Mother.*' It's as though she reduces you to a child."

She stared at him, a little shocked by the truth in his observation. She recaptured her sense of self and said, shrugging, "It's true, we don't have very much in common. But Mother and I love each other in our own way. Anyway, you're changing the subject."

"There's nothing wrong with Jenna's life. Everyone doesn't have to be like you and your family, you know."

"What do you mean?" Dana sipped her Calistoga.

"You seem to feel sorry for Jenna because she's decided to become a mother instead of a scientist or a, uh, supermodel. She looks happy with her life. Who are you to judge her?"

Dana was taken aback. "Maybe you're right. But that seems to be such a waste. Anyone can have kids. What's so special about parenthood?"

"Nothing. But not everyone is special. You're a remarkable woman, but you don't seem capable of understanding someone who lacks your abilities." Colt drank more of his beer and took a crab canapé from a nearby tray.

"Who says she lacks abilities?"

"I don't know that she does. The point I'm trying to make is that no life path is better than any other except to the extent that it makes someone happier or more productive. We have no reason to think that Jenna is unhappy." He grinned. "She's obviously productive."

"Yeah, of children."

"How about you, darlin'? Are you entirely happy and fulfilled by the choices you've made?" Colt's intense blue gaze seemed to penetrate the secret, untried places of Dana's heart.

She fiddled with her water bottle, tearing at its damp label. "Well, yeah. I have great work, I like the place I live, and I'm very happy."

"But are you fulfilled? Do you have a boyfriend back in Boston?"

"Of course I don't!" she said furiously. "We wouldn't have done what we did if I had!"

"Aha, so you remember."

"What a stupid statement. I don't sleep with so many men that I'd forget. What kind of person do you think I am? You're the one who seems to have forgotten."

"Oh, I remember. I remember everything we've done, darlin'." Colt's voice carried a warm, sexy note.

Dana's pulse bounced, but she managed to control herself. "I thought maybe your cousin Patti had made you forget."

"Cousin Patti? What does Patti have to do with you and me?"

"There is no you and me."

"Are you jealous of that little girl?"

"Little girl? Cousin Patti is no little girl," Dana said, remembering slinky Patti's mini-dress.

Colt snorted. "Patti is a nineteen-year-old bubbleheaded lamebrain. She lives with her parents in Rancho Santa Fe, reads *People* magazine and *The National Inquirer*, and thinks of nothing more serious than shopping at the mall. Patti is not my type."

"So what's your type?"

"Boy, you really want your ego fed tonight."

Dana wanted to christen him with her Calistoga. "What's that supposed to mean? First I'm judgmental, now I'm an egomaniac. Why are we having this conversation?" She stalked away, heading for her compartment.

~ * ~

Colt spent several nervous minutes trying to figure out a strategy for placating Dana. Despite the great sex they'd shared, the damn woman was more and more like a nervous filly, temperamental and jumpy. Besides, he was sharing her room, and; if she continued to be angry, not only would he have to give up his fantasies of hot train sex with her, but it would be a mighty uncomfortable trip for them both.

He then spent another hour drinking beers in the club car with a group of other young male passengers. The company of men was his antidote to unreasonable feminine moodiness.

He was in a difficult position in regard to Dana, and keenly felt the lack of a florist, a candy store, or even a jeweler.

The train pulled into San Bernardino, California, at 10:15 p.m. Colton peered out. The train station was sizable, so he took a chance.

Chapter Fifteen

At ten-thirty, Colt tapped hesitantly at Dana's compartment door. After a few moments, she opened it and stared at him, hazel eyes wide behind her tortoise-shell glasses. She held a sheaf of computer printouts in one hand. Sheryl Crow softly sounded from a portable CD player in the corner.

Dana in relaxation mode ... she'd lit a little candle in a jar, and its sweet, vanilla fragrance scented the compartment's air. Even better, she'd taken off her shoes and her bra. He could discern her full breasts, swinging gently and enticingly beneath the starched cotton of the tuxedo shirt.

Trying not to ogle her distracting chest, he pulled a bouquet out from behind his back with a flourish. "Happy anniversary," he said.

"Huh?"

"We met each other again about a week ago," he explained inaccurately. "So, happy anniversary."

"I'm not sure I want to remember that meeting. Didn't you dump a drink down my front?"

"I know I did. Peace?"

She shook her head with obvious disbelief, then smiled. She opened the door wider. "Peace," she agreed. "Colt, you're a genius. Where did you find these?" She buried her face into the flowers.

"Oh, I'm very clever when it comes to pleasing the lady in my life." He entered the small room, and closed the door with a click.

"I'm the lady in your life?"

"Dana, I don't know what kind of person you think I am, but I don't screw around indiscriminately."

She raised her brows.

"Well, not much. And not lately. Okay, so we've had great, wild monkey sex. Beyond that, we've shared secrets, an important family celebration, and now we're related, sort of. I don't know what that means to you, but to me it means that we're not just a guy and a girl."

"What kind of relationship do we have, in your view?" Her voice was still chilly, but did he detect a thaw?

"I told you. You're the lady in my life, if you want to be." He was aware of his heavy breathing, and wondered why this woman got him so hot and bothered. His glance shifted to her breasts. Okay, he knew why she got him hot, but why bothered?

"This seems rather sudden. We don't really know each other very well." She went to the bathroom, flowers in hand.

Curious, he followed. She put the flowers in the sink and filled the small ice bucket with water.

"We have lots of time to get to know each other better." He took the bucket from her so she could arrange the flowers in it. When she was done, he set it on the ledge near the window. "For example, what are you working on?"

"Oh, you don't want to know about my work. As Mother says, 'no one's interested in Dana's silly planet.' " Dana's voice squeaked into an imitation of Gabrielle's accent.

"*I* am interested in Dana's planet. In fact, I am interested in everything about Dana. So tell me, what is this?" He pulled out one page of the sheaf she held. The paper was covered with columns of numbers, which appeared to be arbitrary.

"*This* is raw material for *that*." She gestured at her laptop computer, which rested on the bed. It was plugged into a nearby wall outlet. The screen of the computer showed an irregular network of cracks, a jagged pattern of lines and rough, black and white terrain.

"What is that?"

"That is a picture of the surface of the moon Europa, taken by the Juno project."

Colt sat on the bed and stared at the screen. The twisted surface of the satellite resembled a blurred photograph of the North Pole. "Looks like icebergs, all squashed together."

Dana nodded. "Good guess. That's exactly what it is. Europa is covered by a field of water ice." She sat down behind him.

"How do you and your colleagues know it's water? Couldn't it be anything, methane, ammonia or whatever?"

"All are good assumptions," she said. "Many of the outer planets and their satellites have high concentrations of both methane and ammonia. We know that Europa is covered with water ice because of tests called spectroscopy. In essence, the light that bounces off the moon is analyzed, and its wave pattern tells us about its chemical composition. I helped write a paper on the subject."

"That's totally cool. Do you have a copy?"

"Not with me, but it's up on the Internet."

"Let me see." Colt moved over to give her room to use the laptop. Dana cuddled between him and the computer, her warm, curvy body nestling against his as she tapped on her keyboard. The position sent his temperature rocketing as far as Europa. Progress, he thought, casually circling her waist with one arm.

She tapped a few more buttons, and he realized she must have connected to the Internet via satellite or by some other arcane method he didn't understand. She clicked into Google and typed in: *D.T. Newcombe.*

After a few seconds, the program indicated that there were nearly 800 entries with the name Newcombe, but she quickly found a paper called "Spectroscopic Analysis of Europa, New Findings," which had appeared in the *Journal of Astronomy*

Letters. One of the five co-authors was D.T. Newcombe.

"This is astounding," he said. "What does this part over here mean?" He pointed to a series of chemical formulae.

"That is a description of Europa's atmosphere."

"Atmosphere?"

"Why, yes." She peered at him, pushing her tortoise-shell glasses further up her nose. "Europa is one of four moons in our system with an atmosphere. Got a lot of oxygen, too."

He sat back. "So, your father wasn't joking when he said that Europa has colonization potential."

"Oh, no. That is absolutely not a joke. Europa appears to consist of ice fields floating on a water ocean, with a rocky, dense core. It has a thin atmosphere containing oxygen. Some of my colleagues theorize that it may support life forms, microbial stuff, obviously." She smiled placidly at Colt. "No L.G.M.'s, though."

"What's an L.G.M.?"

"Little green men. Like on *X-Files.*"

Colt regarded her. Dana sat, cross-legged next to him on the bed, dressed in capris and a shirt, chatting about aliens and space colonization as though the subjects were the most ordinary in the world. "You are really a remarkable girl."

"Aw, come on."

"No, really." He leaned closer to her. "You're easily the most intelligent woman ... no, make that the most intelligent person I've ever met. You are absolutely the most beautiful."

"What about my sister?"

He shrugged. "I thought we already talked about that, got that out of the way. Nick's a great girl, but with me, she always had, umm, how can I explain it? She never really let me in, I think. She was always so involved with how she looked, dressing in the coolest clothes, being at the right restaurants and gallery openings. And flirting with every man she met, too," he added with an edge on his voice.

"I'm not saying I have any regrets. I don't. I just want more. I want to be like, like Romeo and Juliet." His smile was challenging.

"Ooh, depressing. Didn't they die at the end?"

"Well, then, like strawberries and cream."

She chuckled. "Dessert and coffee."

"Tweedledum and Tweedledee." They laughed harder.

"Laurel and Hardy."

"Besides, you're prettier than she is."

"What a ridiculous statement. We're identical twins." Dana clicked off her laptop, unplugged it, and started to put it away on a luggage rack above the window.

"Not right now, you aren't."

She turned, dismayed. "Please don't tell me you like the red hair."

"It's not the hair, it's the style. I mean, like, what about that dress she wore to the party on Thursday? Shades of Morticia Addams." He chuckled.

"Actually, I thought of Dracula's Daughter."

"Bride of Frankenstein." They continued laughing as the train chugged to a stop. "So you see, it's you, not her. Does this close the subject?"

"I guess it does," she said.

"Seal it with a kiss?"

"Weeellll … a little one, if you insist."

"I do." He leaned forward and gently brushed her lips with his. Dana shivered as his stubbly mouth scratched hers pleasantly. Her pussy throbbed to life.

Colton smiled at her. "Where are we?" he asked.

She breathed deeply, recovering her poise. She consulted her watch and her schedule. "It's midnight? Barstow, California. Our next stop is Needles, where all the partiers will get off. It'll be pretty noisy until then. It's probably not worth trying to get to sleep now." She was pleased to note her voice was steady, and didn't reflect the odd quivery feeling in her stomach, which felt like unset Jell-O.

He stretched and yawned. "Midnight. Boy, the evening went by fast." He winked at her. "Well, I guess time flies when you're chillin' with a rising star in the space business."

"Oh, you!" Dana threw a pillow at him, and he promptly retaliated, then wrestled her down onto the bed.

He stretched out full length upon her, and trapped her head with one corded forearm on each side of her face. He gripped both of her hands in one of his, and pinned them down on the bed above their heads.

"Darlin'," he murmured huskily, just before he took her mouth with his.

He leisurely plundered her lips, sweetly savaging them with his stubbly mouth. Pleasure flowed through Dana's limbs and body, pounding hot and wild in her delta. Tingling deliciously, she rubbed against his torso, her body arching up toward his, her breasts seeking his whipcord chest.

She'd set up this sex-charged scenario when she asked Colton to share her room, but when they'd argued, second thoughts had intervened. Colt, being a horndog, would seize on any invitation to get physical with her. But why had she done it? What exactly did all of this mean? She hadn't seriously considered continuing their relationship, so she hadn't thought about the emotional and practical implications of Colt in her life. And could they share the same train compartment for four days without arguing?

But their affair would probably end when he got off the train. Not to worry! she told herself.

He slid one hand underneath her shirt, searching for her breasts. She'd taken off her bra after returning to her room, since she wore underwiring and was far more comfortable without it. She hadn't known if Colt would choose to visit her again.

Now his restless hands sought and found her breasts. Already they prickled with longing, the nipples hard and ready for his touch.

"Very sexy, you wearing a man's shirt," he murmured, cupping and squeezing. "Did you intend to drive me crazy with jealousy?"

"Jealous?" She managed to gasp, though his sensual caress was more than a little distracting. "What kind of man is jealous of his lady friend's father?"

"A very silly man. I thought perhaps that you got the shirt from someone else. I tolerate no rivals." His voice deepened into a growl.

"There aren't any, sweetie. I'm afraid you overestimate my charms."

"No, I don't." He pinched and rolled her nipple. "I'm just one of the few men around who's seen you without those glasses."

"What about my glasses?" she asked frostily, as he pulled them off her nose.

"Now, don't get all chilly on me, darlin'. You have beautiful eyes, and most people haven't seen them. I have. As far as I'm concerned, you can keep the glasses on with everyone but me."

He kissed her throat as he attempted to tug loose the onyx studs that secured the shirt. The first stud stubbornly resisted his efforts, and she started to giggle. Her chuckles increased to unflattering whoops as Colt tried the second, the third, and the fourth. He finally gave up and, resting himself on his elbows above her head, glared down at her. "For goodness' sake, woman," he thundered, "can't you help?"

"Goodness has very little to do with this."

"I thought I was very good. You certainly seemed to like what was happening."

"Well, yeah, but what's the point of rushing everything?" Teasing Colt was fun. He'd ignored her for days, so he deserved it.

Standing, he adjusted his jeans over his crotch. "Mutual enjoyment, I suppose."

"I'm enjoying myself just fine with my shirt on."

"Oh, really?" He chuckled. He pulled his T-shirt off slowly, continuing to rake her with his laser-hot, intent gaze. He dropped it on the floor. He stalked away from the bed, turning his head over his shoulder to give her a blatantly seductive come-hither look.

She couldn't take her eyes off him, but couldn't decide which part of him she wanted to look at the most: his handsome face, chiseled pecs or … oh my goodness… He peeled his jeans off, leaving his red silk boxers, which showed an interesting tent in the middle. He tossed his pants onto the other bed.

She licked her lips, then reached for him, stroking his erection. He groaned. She deliberately ran her fingers up and down the rigid shaft, the round head of which was plainly visible through his boxers. She looked up at him to gauge his reaction, then pressed gently with the heel of her hand.

He grabbed her wrist. "I'm warning you, Dana…"

"Warning me of what?" she asked, her tone oozing phony innocence.

"Don't tease the tiger unless you want to get bit."

"In that case…" She reached into the boxers' enticing slit.

He dove for her, ready to sink in his teeth. He tore her collar loose and went for her throat, sucking at the tender flesh.

Was he going to mark her, give her a hickey that would settle any doubts about whose woman she was? The thought excited her, turned her on even more.

His cock jumped into her searching fingers. Thick and raging red, his flesh exuded a sweet male musk that was irresistible. She opened her mouth and took him in all the way to the root.

He let go of her neck and fell back against the pillows with a feral cry. Cupping his balls, she pulled away, letting his rod slip out of her mouth but retaining the rounded head. She closed her teeth over him, very gently.

With another shout, Colt dug his hands into her hair. She wanted to show him what she could do, draw out the blow job, keep him on the edge for an hour, but he'd have none of that. Gripping her head, he pushed deeply, asking her to take all of him.

She responded to his need, relaxing her tongue so she could deep-throat him. To her surprise, he jerked out of her mouth so fast that her teeth scraped his cock harder than she intended.

He pushed her down onto the bed. "Now, baby, now."

She grabbed his shoulders. I've unleashed the tiger, she thought, but she wasn't scared. Her pussy was creaming to the point that the crotch of her pants was moist.

Colt opened her zipper and tore down the capris. She writhed, her legs trapped. He slowed, smoothing his fingers over the marks the waistband had left. "What a shame," he murmured. Sliding down the bed so his knees hung over the bottom, he laid a ring of kisses across the red line on her belly.

She quivered, his gentleness affecting her far more than his prior intensity. The combination was heady, addicting, like no other lover she'd ever had. Don't tell yourself that, she reminded herself. This is Mr. Here-today-and-gone-tomorrow. Don't get attached!

His kisses trailed down, down, down until his nose nested in her muff. She moaned and lifted her hips so he could lick her clit. He responded, then raised his head and said, "What a sweet little pussy you've got, darlin', but you're awfully furry. Will you let me trim you up a bit?"

That dumped a bucket of ice all over her growing arousal. She grimaced, thinking of Nicole, who'd gotten a Brazilian wax once and complained about how painful it had been. "Umm, how?" Dana asked.

"Oh, nothing radical. I don't want you to look like a little girl. I'll use an electric razor." Colt leaned back and picked one of her pubic hairs out of his teeth. "I just don't enjoy nature's dental floss."

When she looked hesitant, he said, "Trust me. I promise to make this train trip unforgettable."

She took a deep breath and said, "Okay."

Standing, he went to his luggage and hunted around inside it until he found his electric razor. He switched it on.

The razor's hum vibrated along her nerves. "Uh, Colt, I don't know how this is going to feel."

"You didn't know how what we did the other night was going to feel, but it was okay, wasn't it?"

"Umm, yeah." She grinned, thinking of how great she'd gotten off after he'd bound her hands.

"Okay, then. Get naked and step into my laboratory."

She obeyed, realizing that he wanted her shirt off because its long tails could get in his way. In the bathroom, she saw he'd spread a towel onto the small patch of floor.

"Open your legs and push your hips forward." After she obeyed, he applied the razor to the side of the thick patch of curls covering her mound, running it along the crease between her abdomen and her left leg.

Hot but not uncomfortable, she thought, and said, "That feels okay."

"This is a really good razor. I've never gotten razor burn or pinching from it." He shaved along each side of her muff, then used a different attachment to thin the triangle of blond curls that remained.

She closed her eyes. The razor's vibration was sort of like an electric dildo. She bet she could come like this if he'd just keep it up.

He stopped. "Put your foot on the side of the sink."

She did, and watched him as he carefully shaved around her clit. It was a little scary, but his brow was furrowed with total concentration, and she knew he wouldn't hurt her. Because he was naked except for his red boxers, she could admire the way his corded muscles bunched and flexed as he worked.

With one hand on her buttock, he opened her crack while shaving inside her furrow with the other. The sensation was incredibly erotic, unlike anything she'd ever felt. She'd never used a vibrator around her ass, and now she discovered, just as she had when he'd put in his finger, that her back hole was exquisitely sensitive.

She threw back her head, panting.

"Hold still," he commanded. "I don't want to hurt you."

She tried not to writhe, but her legs had started to quiver. She grabbed the side of the sink for support.

A sudden silence enveloped them when he clicked off the razor and set it onto the counter. "Now I can lick you all over without anything in the way." He took a washcloth, wet it and wiped away all the stray bits of hair.

The cloth's gentle rasp against her newly naked sex took her higher. He tossed it into the sink, and she gasped, "Don't stop, don't stop."

He laughed, his chuckle replete with male satisfaction. Then he replaced the cloth with his tongue, lapping at the tender flesh until she moaned. He rose, his cock peeking out of the boxer's slit and impaled her, driving his hard shaft through the lips of her wet, waiting pussy.

With one long thrust, he found the entrance of her womb, and she felt herself yielding to his masculine potency, his power, his strength. A wail escaped her lips. He picked her up and set her bottom onto the counter's edge and draped her legs over his arms, spreading her wide for his enjoyment. He held her hips steady as he bucked in and out of her.

She closed her eyes and luxuriated in sensation. She was close, so close, but not quite there ... what did she need? She didn't know, but Colt was driving her steadily, inexorably, to an erotic frenzy.

He pulled out until only his cockhead remained inside her and reached for her breasts, lifting them to his mouth. He kissed one after the other, then picked the left one to suckle hard, stretching out her nipple with his lips before he released it with a tiny pop. "Touch yourself," he demanded.

Her eyes sprang open. "Wh-what?"

"Play with your clitty." His voice lowered to a dark drawl. "I want to watch you."

She sucked in a nervous breath. Surely the men she'd been with had watched her come, but she didn't really know because her eyes were usually closed. Colt tended to watch and to want her to be aware he was watching her, too ... this new game freaked her out a little bit, but excited her, too. No one else had commanded her to put on a show.

She stared into his intent blue eyes. He leaned forward and kissed her. "Play with yourself. For me. Please."

She lowered a hand to her pussy and found her clit. It was slick with their juices and swollen from his tongue-lashing. She stroked it just as he slid his cock back into her. She cried out.

"Yeah, baby, yeah..." Colt fucked her harder.

She took her clit between finger and thumb to give it a pinch. That sent her over the edge, and she screamed. He planted his mouth onto hers and swallowed the wail of her completion. His hands clamped onto her hips and he surged deeply into her, banging hard and fast three, four, five times until he also came, spurting into her wet recesses.

Chapter Sixteen

Dana was awakened by the early morning light gleaming through their window. Propping herself up on one elbow, she contemplated Colt. They'd started to sleep together in one of the narrow bunks, but later he'd moved to the other bed, claiming he couldn't sleep and didn't want to disturb her. She'd appreciated his thoughtfulness, but due to the smallness of the room, his head still was only a few inches from hers.

His straight, dark hair fell over an unlined brow. Except for his rakishly unshaven cheeks and chin, Colt asleep was the essence of untroubled innocence. She wondered if he would retain his serenity through the vagaries and stresses of adulthood. She wanted to find out, but questioned whether Colt was what or who she needed in her life on a permanent basis. Though he'd labeled her the lady in his life, was he really just an amusing vacation fling?

If so, that was okay. Actually, she was grateful. Her sister's wedding to her ex-boyfriend could have been nothing short of one humiliation after another. Instead, Colt's antics had provided a never-ending show, from the ring incident through his dance with Paul Doucette.

She slipped into his bed, snuggled close and nuzzled his neck, enjoying his masculine, musky scent. He opened one blue eye. He rolled her in his arms and kissed her on her forehead. She cuddled against him, feeling deliciously complete.

"You hungry?"

"Yeah, I guess I am." He yawned and stretched.

"What do you want for breakfast? The dining car has everything."

"What I want is right here, baby." He sought to kiss her mouth, but she resisted. "What's wrong?"

"I'm sorry, but my mouth tastes like a garbage pail. I have major morning breath. I need to brush my teeth, shower and do all that stuff."

"Oh." Disappointed, Colt watched Dana leave his bed and head into the bathroom.

Colt had spent most of the night troubled by another aching erection. He'd tried not to toss and turn. He hadn't wanted to disturb Dana since she'd given him enough already and no doubt needed her rest.

He grinned, thinking of the awesome bathroom sex. So far, they'd made it in an elevator, a bed, and a bathroom … what would be next? On the platform between train cars? On top of the train?

Despite the great sex, he'd known that if he so much as touched Dana's hair, rich with her vanilla fragrance, he'd explode. He'd lain stiff and rigid in their narrow bunk, listening to her even breathing for hours. He finally moved to the other bed, hoping sleep would come without the disturbance of Dana slumbering next to him. He was wrong. He had eventually fallen into a restless sleep after envisioning the trail of her scent following him wherever he went.

When he followed her into the crowded dining car, he admired her fine ass, gorgeously displayed in tight white shorts, and became entranced by the flashing beauty of her tanned legs as she strode through the train. He wanted to lick the smooth limbs from thigh to toe and back again. He imagined proceeding further, remembering her sweet, shaved pussy. He tried not to spring a rod at the thought and adjusted his jeans.

What was happening to him? He'd never wanted anyone quite like Dana Newcombe. Only a few days ago he'd declared *this li'l dawgie stays wild,* but Dana, already a family member, couldn't be just another fuck-buddy.

She was everything any sane man could ever want in a woman … more, really, since she was so very special. Unique. Beyond her obvious smarts, she was sweet and giving. She'd wanted the wedding to take place without a hitch even though watching her sister marry her ex couldn't have been pleasant. Still, she'd participated, because it was important to the people she loved.

Stunning, sweet, sexy and smart, he mused. I love this girl!

Dana stopped near Jenna Norton's booth as the full impact of his feelings and thoughts struck Colton. Dazed, he regarded Dana in a new, more serious light as she greeted Jenna and Lindy. The young mother was feeding her tot strained peaches.

"Good morning!" said Dana cheerily. "Looks like you beat us into here. Have you eaten yet?"

"Actually, we just got here. I haven't even looked at a menu, since I wanted to get Lindy squared away. She's cranky when she's hungry."

Colt recovered himself and asked, "Can we to take you to breakfast?"

Jenna looked flustered and stared from Dana to Colt. "Well, okay, I mean, thank you. If it's not a hassle."

"No problem," he said. "You'd be doing us a favor, since the dining car is pretty full. Besides, I enjoy watching you with your baby." He smiled at Dana. She smiled back, but narrowed her hazel eyes. He wondered if she always squinted slightly when wary or suspicious. He wondered if she wanted children. He broadened his grin and tried to regard Lindy in a paternal manner. The baby had strained peaches—an orange colored slop—covering her chin and bib.

"Umm! I'm really hungry this morning." Dana sat opposite Jenna and her baby, and picked up a menu.

"Well, you've been expending a lot of energy." Colt grinned, sitting next to her. "On that laptop, I mean."

"And how about you, sir? It seems to me you should be ready for a four course meal." Her thigh rubbed against his, and she wound her sneakered foot around his ankle.

"Oh, not really. I've hardly been exerting myself," he said, squirming in his seat.

Dana's head jerked up as a waiter came by and took their orders. When Jenna took Lindy to a nearby lavatory to wash her face after the baby's meal, Colton regarded Dana.

His blue eyes sparkled as he addressed her; she noticed that when he flirted, his accent became more pronounced. "Y'know, young lady, your teasin' is goading me beyond endurance. I might just have to take you back to that sleeper and teach you a lesson or two."

"Lessons? You think you can teach me anything I need to know?"

"Oh, yeah. Many, many lessons, of the nicest kind." He flirted with his eyes.

"Even though I've been a tease?" She winked.

"Especially because you're a tease."

"What if I say no?"

"Why would you ever say no to new knowledge? Isn't that what being a scientist is all about?"

"Hmmm. Maybe you're right. Maybe you have information I could use."

"My best guess is that you do need it, darlin'."

"Let's make a deal," she said. "How about if I work in the mornings for the Juno project, and in the afternoons…" She broke off when Jenna returned with a clean, dry tot.

After they finished breakfast, Dana went to her compartment and set up her laptop on a table beside the window, planning to look at the passing scenery while she worked between Colton's "lessons." But he wouldn't let her alone. He seemed to enjoy rubbing her shoulders while he peeked at the screen, asking her a million questions. Ahead of schedule with her portion of the Juno project, Dana didn't mind. Though distracting, she liked the shoulder rubs. A lot.

The tight quarters and close contact between Dana and Colt had a powerful effect on her emotions. Strangely, she was not cramped or impatient with his nearness, but missed him when he left to fetch sodas or take a walk. As a result, she was constantly in an irritating state of emotional turmoil as well as sexual arousal.

She tried not to let it get to her, but she was as randy as a cageful of rabbits and needier than she liked to admit.

The countryside through which the train passed that morning consisted mainly of the high deserts of Arizona and New Mexico. After lunch, the train stopped for about a half-hour in Albuquerque, New Mexico. The Albuquerque train station wasn't interesting, but Dana liked the opportunity to get off the train and move around more freely than the railway cars allowed. She and Colt jogged, evading Jenna, who'd put Lindy into a collapsible stroller for a walk.

After lunch, Dana returned alone to her compartment, lit another couple of candles and turned on the C.D. player, preparing to work while wondering where Colton was. Hadn't he promised her lessons?

And from the tone of his voice, wouldn't they involve wild monkey sex?

Interrupted by a knock at the door, she opened it to find Colt lounging in the doorway, with a small glass flask in his hand.

"Time for your lessons, darlin'."

A shiver ran up her spine. She nodded at the object he held. "What's that?"

He held up a cruet of golden liquid, letting it dangle from his long fingers. She remembered how those fingers could make her feel, and another sexy shiver ran riot through her body.

She squinted. "Salad oil?"

He came into the small room, dominating it with his size, his scent, and his sheer maleness. "Oil is oil, darlin'. Where's that wonderful perfume you wear?"

"What on earth for?"

"Consider it part of your education."

She brought him the perfume. "Where did you get the oil?"

"Liberated it from the dining car at lunchtime. They'll never miss it." Opening both bottles, Colt poured several drops of the perfume into the oil, then shook the cruet.

"What are you going to do with that?" Dana asked.

He smiled at her, his blue eyes twinkling. "Take off your clothes."

She twinkled back. "There's only one way this is gonna end."

"Dana Newcombe, you bad, bad girl. As if I'd ever think of doing such a thing. Get your mind out of the gutter." He started taking off his clothes.

"What? Colt Wilder, you dog! All you ever think about are your hormonal urges."

"Take some of that nice massage oil I made and rub my back." Naked, he lay on his stomach on the bed, then turned his head to stare at her. "What did you think I meant?"

"What do you think?" She laughed, eyeing his lean buttocks. "Give me a second…" She stripped down to a T-shirt and panties. Picking up the cruet, she straddled his body and poured a puddle of oil into her hand. Rubbing it up and down Colt's back, she enjoyed his happy, appreciative moan.

She liked the mastery and control she had while seated on top of him. She worked the fragrant oil into every muscle of his long, lean body, kneading and exploring his whipcord physique.

Colt was even more thorough. As he massaged, he waited until she was completely relaxed to remove every remaining shred of her clothing. The variation of strokes he used seduced her … she had never been pleasured by feathery scratches as well as deep tissue massage and everything in between. Her skin rippled when he ran his stubbly chin over the backs of her knees, up to the cleft of her backside, over to the underside of her breasts. Somehow he raised cool quivers at the same time she was approaching meltdown.

She was close to peaking when he stroked the satiny skin of her inner thighs with the backs of his knuckles. Her flesh leaped with awareness. She had never before felt so open or so alive as she writhed with passion on the sheets.

She was completely trusting as well as aroused, though a small part of her mind wondered how Colton would use his control. He was damned unpredictable.

He ran a gentle finger over her moist lower lips, and she bucked involuntarily. She pushed herself against his hand, purring like a cat.

Colt cradled her head with his other hand, pulling her close for a more demanding kiss. His tongue, hot and needy, invaded her mouth as two fingers took her, sliding inside her wetness.

Dana's hips gyrated in a frenzied spasm of pleasure as she came. She wrenched her mouth away from Colt's, completely losing control with an orgasmic cry of ecstasy. Her passionate scream was lost in the swelling music. He continued to stroke her as the train rocked over the rails. Sharp, jolting spasms wracked her body as he kissed her.

He flicked his tongue tantalizingly over her mouth and massaged her pussy, maintaining her incredible erotic high. She wrapped her arms around him and ecstatically rubbed her body against his.

He smiled down at her. "You're great."

"What do you mean? You're the one doing all the work."

"You're so hot, so responsive."

"I'm hot?"

"Oh, baby, you're steaming." He continued to tenderly stroke her mound. "Remember the elevator?"

"God, that was embarrassing."

"Not for me. It was great. And now for something completely different." Flashing her a wicked grin, he knelt between her spread thighs and reached for the candle, which she'd set next to her laptop on the tiny table.

"You've got the greatest rack in this world or any other," he told her in a husky voice. "I love your tight little nipples. They're so great that one deserves to be immortalized."

She tensed. "You'll burn me!" She imagined the sensitive skin of her breasts blistered by the melted wax.

"No way. These are unscented, right?"

"Yeah."

"Then no problem." He set the candle aside and rubbed his hands over her oil-slicked breasts, then played with her nipples until they grew hard and red. He leaned down and whispered into her ear. "Trust me. I've done this before. It won't hurt you."

She closed her eyes and breathed deeply. "Okay."

"Eyes open, now." He stroked his cock, ensuring it was well-lubed with oil, and pushed it between her pussy lips, anchoring himself inside, watching her react.

She gasped and squeezed him, and he closed his eyes with a low groan.

"Eyes open, now," she said.

Opening his lids, he managed a chuckle. "Push your breasts together for me."

She tried to relax as she did as he asked, but she was scared.

"Cup them, baby, for me … ohhh, you look so hot." Picking up the candle, he said, "Remember, everything else we've done has been good, hasn't it?"

"Yeah."

She fearfully watched as, from a height of about a foot, Colt turned the jar holding the candle, letting a drop of molten wax fall. It glittered in the dim light, then hit her right nipple.

It scorched, and she gasped, peeking at her breast. Its nipple was tipped with a pale halo of hardening wax.

"Okay, baby?"

"Yeah." Her other nipple tightened in response.

He dripped another bead onto her nipple, next to the first drop but not right on it.

"Aahhhh…" The burn was maddening. Her entire consciousness was now focused on her breast.

He dribbled three drops onto her nipple in rapid succession. At the same time, he thrust fully into her cunt, burying himself to the balls.

The heat on her breast matched the liquid fire in her pussy, and she screamed and writhed. He set his forearms onto her shoulders, pinning her torso as her pelvis jerked and bucked. He let the wax set for a minute or so, then peeled it carefully away from her nipple and placed on the table.

He blew on the stinging flesh. The sensations were unlike anything else she'd experienced. The intense sensuality edged with a slight trim of fear combined to rocket her into the stars.

How much more of this could she take before she fell in love with Colt?

Chapter Seventeen

After they made love, Dana dropped into an exhausted, satiated sleep. As they slept, the afternoon darkened into evening. The train turned northward; the route taking them through the southern Rocky Mountains. At dinnertime, it passed from New Mexico into Colorado. Even in midsummer, night fell early in the mountains when the sun dropped behind the high granite peaks to their west. It was dusk by seven p.m. as they left Trinidad, Colorado, for La Junta.

After they showered, Colt took Dana to dinner. The tables in the dining car had been set with fresh linens and small bouquets in glass vases. With the lights dim and a menu full of treats, dinner turned out to be a lovely occasion. After they ate, she went to their compartment and put on comfortable sweats while he left for the club car to drink a beer or two with the dudes he'd met the evening before

Truth to tell, she needed some space away from him to examine her feelings. Not that she was bored. Far from it. But she needed to think about what had happened in her life. The past few days had tossed her into an emotional maelstrom she didn't understand. She'd experienced too many emotions, too close together, since the moment he'd dumped champagne over her breasts ... had that only been a week before?

She stared out the window at the deepening night, seeing nothing but her redheaded reflection and a few lights. She turned them off and lit a candle, smiling at the memories it engendered.

If she were honest with herself, she had to admit that the tumult dated from the moment he'd walked into her apartment the previous November.

She was a scientist, dammit, and she'd approach this phenomenon like the logical person she knew herself to be. First she'd analyze the stimulus: Colton Wilder. Height: six-two. Hair: black. Eyes: the most vivid shade of blue Dana had ever seen. Physique: oh, baby! Age: twenty-seven, two years older than she.

But what do I really know about this man? she wondered, as logic deserted her. *Okay, he's handsome and smart and everything I've ever dreamed about... He's even interested in my work!*

So I'm the lady in his life, I guess. But can we really make a life together? And is that truly what he wants? And what do I want?

She forced her mind back into its usual rational track. Since they met, their mutual attraction had intensified rather than diminished. At this point, the passion between them roared and flamed like a wildfire. But was it enough?

What about the past? She still worried about Colt's prior relationship with her twin, especially about the speed at which he'd dumped Nickie. Then came the Four Seasons fiasco, followed by a seven-month-long silence. Only last week, Colton seemed like a creep who wanted to disrupt his brother's marriage.

Now she feared he was shallow and superficial. Her passion for him was over the top and out of control, but she didn't want to become more involved unless she was sure he felt the same way. But walking away would leave her with nothing at all, so she'd just have to see how life with Colton would turn out.

She wasn't a slut, but she figured she'd had an average number of relationships. Colt's lovemaking burned away every memory she had of other lovers. No one compared to him. He could be tender. He could be forceful. And inventive didn't come close to describing his tastes.

She touched the wax mold of her nipple he'd made that afternoon. He'd set it on the little table in their compartment and had decorated it with a red rose from the bouquet he'd bought for her.

Good sex—okay, mind-bending, unbelievably great and awesome sex—couldn't be enough. There was more between them, wasn't there? He'd promised not to disrupt his brother's wedding, and had kept that promise even though he had wanted to warn Max away from Nicole.

She blew out the candle and watched a thin stream of smoke curl up from the blackened wick. Colt could be trusted to keep his word. That was important. Better, he had held back solely because Dana had asked. He'd held back for *her*.

But the mess with Max had taught her something: that the most attentive, loving man might not truly know who she was. Max had done everything right, but still hadn't been able to tell her apart from her twin. He should have known, Dana told herself. He should have known the minute Nicole opened her mouth and started to talk. After all, Colt had, and they'd had much less contact.

The most important question still remained: Would she, Dana Thomasina Newcombe, scholar, scientist and woman, get the kind of acceptance and support she needed from Colt?

Metal screamed on metal. The train shuddered and bucked. A horrified shriek burst from her throat, and everything went black.

~ * ~

Dana came to awareness in the darkness, in a pain-filled, dizzy haze. She was lying on her side, curled into a ball, clutching her belly, which was tender and sore. She moved, and her world lurched and swayed.

The train … the train must have crashed and lost power. She blinked. Her glasses had fallen off and could be anywhere in the pitch-black compartment. Shit. She reached out with one arm, sweeping the floor with her hand. She felt an edge … the table? A chair? She gripped it and tried to stand.

Again, her world wobbled, and her stomach roiled with nausea. When her eyes adjusted to the darkness, she realized that the train had fallen over onto one side. The floor on which she rested was actually the train's wall, slightly curved. Whenever she moved, so did it.

Not good.

Colt, she thought desperately, where are you? Screams and moans of the injured filled her ears as she waited for her head to clear. *Oh, God, Colt! Please, God, not him!* A baby wailed in the distance: a desolate, awful sound. *Lindy?*

She crawled, hoping slight movements wouldn't set the train rocking and her belly heaving. Her compartment was a mess, with everything thrown around. The crash must have done that. How could she get out? Where was the door?

Telling herself that her weakness wouldn't help herself or Colt, she pulled herself together. She fumbled in the absolute darkness for her glasses. She found her fanny pack and clipped it to her waist, but had no luck with her glasses. Damn. She had no alternative but to find a way out, half-blind. Grabbing deep, trembling breaths, she struggled for control. Hideously afraid for herself and for Colt, she had to get to the club car to look for him.

She guessed that the door of the compartment was now above her head, and she had to climb up the furniture to get to it. Taking a deep breath, she firmed her resolve and stood on the window frame, afraid to test the strength of the glass. So far, so good. She leaned over to her right and groped for the bedstead, which had shifted in the crash.

Searching with her foot, she found the bottom of their bed, then stepped over to it. Her feet became entangled in sheets and blankets. She kicked the bedclothes away. But they stuck on something … what was it?

Her laptop. Yes, she'd left it on the bed. She scrabbled in the darkness for the flash drive storing her last week's work. She tugged, and it popped into her hand. She put it into her fanny pack and dropped the laptop with only slight regret for the two-thousand-dollar machine packed with her programming.

Standing on the bottom of the bedstead, she stretched her hands high. Could she reach the top of the bed? Yes … she clutched the frame, hoisting herself up, praying that the metal frame wouldn't collapse or fall over onto her. She flailed with her sneakered feet for purchase on the slippery bed, digging her toes into the mattress. Luckily, the rubbery soles gripped the cotton fabric.

She reached out to touch the "ceiling" of the compartment with her left hand. This was formerly the wall in which the door was located, so she began to search for the door latch, gasping as the air in the closed compartment became thick with her heavy breaths. Frantic after several minutes of pawing the wall in the darkness, she finally snared the latch and pulled the door open.

The cries of the injured had softened to whimpers and groans of pain, interspersed with shouts from the unhurt as they worked to help their fellow passengers. It was still very dark, though shafts of light intermittently bobbed and wove above her head. She guessed that some people had flashlights.

"Help me!" She tried to shout, but only a wheezing gasp squeaked out of her dry, sore throat. She gulped, ran a dry tongue around her mouth, and tried again.

Nothing. No help came. She'd have to help herself.

Gripping the rim of the door with both hands, Dana began to haul her body up to the level of the door. She couldn't climb very fast, since her head and her stomach still hurt like the dickens. What had she hit? She'd been sitting at the table when the crash happened, so maybe the table's edge jammed into her belly. Maybe she whacked her head on the window frame or the floor when she fell. Who knew? Who cared?

The car lurched. Her sweaty hands slipped. With a startled cry, she fell heavily to the bottom of the car, hitting her shin on the bottom of the bed. She squeezed her eyes shut, ordering her tears back into their ducts. She curled up into a ball against the pain for a few moments, then took a deep breath and steeled herself for the climb back up the bed, figuring that since she'd done it once, she could do it again.

Suddenly, a shaft of light invaded her prison. "Ma'am? Ma'am?" A conductor knelt at the open door, wielding a flashlight.

"Yes, I'm down here." Her steady voice surprised her, since a quivering mass of fear had replaced her insides.

He set the flash down. With light, it was easier for her to jump and grab the edge of the door. The conductor reached down to seize her arms above the elbows. Pulling hard, he hauled her out of the compartment while she kicked, trying to push off the wall of the shuddering train. He reached in and somehow managed to close the door, locking it so that no one would fall through it as other passengers left.

"Go to the end of this car and get off the train," he said. "There will be somebody there to assist you."

"But—the friend I was traveling with…"

"Don't worry," he said. "So far, no one's been seriously hurt, just a few bruises and scrapes."

Dana sagged with relief. Chances were that Colt was okay.

He continued, "We're evacuating the train. Please, proceed to the end of the car and get off. There will be further instructions soon."

Shivering, she complied. She could see by the light of the lantern that the train was tilted at a ninety-degree angle. Without her glasses, the world was a blur. Few people had been in her car at the time of the derailment, since most had been dining or drinking in the club car. She shuddered to think of the chaos in those cars. With broken glass, flying cutlery, and bodies flung everywhere, it was a miracle that no one had been killed.

She crept down the hall, walking on the flimsy walls rather than the floor. They creaked with every step. When she reached the end of the car, the pneumatic doors were ajar. She wrenched them open further and peered into the space between the cars.

Below her, she could vaguely see the ground, covered by railroad ties and tracks. She climbed feet first through the opening, grasping the top of the door to lever herself safely to the ground. Her hands, slick with sweat, slipped on the metal surface. She fell onto her elbows and knees. Pain stabbed, and she gasped with renewed agony. Sobbing softly, she rolled onto her side on the tracks.

She rubbed her knees, then stumbled to her feet. The ambient light from outside of the train dimly lit the small space. Ahead of her, a few faint lights illuminated the tumult inside the club car. Broken glass from myriad bottles and glasses glinted through the clouded panes set into the car's doors. She pulled the doors open and called, "Colt? Colt? Where are you?"

There was no answer but the moans of the wounded. A uniformed figure, indistinct in the gloom, snapped at her, "Lady, get off this train right now! Your friend is probably outside." He straightened up from bending over a supine passenger. The body on the floor groaned. A female voice, she noted with relief, then damned herself for her lack of sensitivity. Still, she couldn't help being glad that the injured passenger wasn't Colt. But where was he?

"Dana? Dana? Is that you?" A hand reached into the space between the cars and tugged at her.

"Colt?"

"Yeah, it's me. Come on out here." He reached out for her with both hands, pulling her through the opening between the steel wheels of the car.

"Dear God, I thought I'd lost you," choked Dana, hugging Colt tightly. She clung to him as tears spilled down her face.

"Oh, darlin'. It's all right, I'm here. Just hold me tight." He kissed her cheeks, her eyes, her hair, her mouth, and squeezed her until her ribs creaked.

She leaned against him and breathed in deep gusts of the cool evening air. She hadn't realized she'd been sweating with fear. She shook in his arms. She ran quivering hands over his body and his face to satisfy herself that he was okay, and as she touched his forehead, her fingers came away sticky. "Colt, you're hurt!"

"It's not bad. Just some flying glass. Believe me, I was lucky. Two inches southward, and it would have been my eye."

"I hope everyone was as lucky."

"I doubt it. The train was pretty full. Chances are a few people are seriously injured. I'm just grateful you're okay."

"But what about Jenna and Lindy? I thought I heard a baby cry."

His lips tightened. "I don't know. They both should've been strapped into their seats when the crash happened, but I haven't seen them yet."

"I think her car is two down from here. Let's go see."

They wrapped their arms around each other as they walked. Loose gravel crunched under their shoes.

"What happened? Did you hear anything?" she asked.

"There's a rumor that a landslide closed the track ahead of the train. They didn't know about it, so we crashed into it."

They sidestepped a group of people climbing out of the gap between the dining car and the lounge, then traversed the length of that car. Dana felt a strange sense of displacement and disorientation as they moved down the train, walking along the graveled verge of the tracks as if they were taking a stroll through Gabrielle's roses after lunching on salads and iced tea.

Colt peered through the gap between the next two cars. "Looks like Jenna's coach. There's still a lot of people inside."

"How can we help?"

"I don't know. Let's find out."

Frantic hands beat at the windows of the coach. No one was helping the panicky passengers to evacuate. He squirmed into the opening between cars to tug at the door's latch. "I can't pull it free. I think it's stuck. Stay here. I'll get a conductor or someone who knows how to open it."

Dana watched as Colt, a darker mass in the night, went back to the club car and returned with an older man in a rumpled uniform. He carried an emergency lantern, which he handed to Colt. The fellow fumbled for the lever securing the doors of the coach car. After a few strong yanks, the doors opened. They heard a babble of voices and the scream of a baby.

"Everyone all right in there?" he hollered into the darkness.

"Yeah! We're all right!" came the answer. "But there's a pregnant girl here with a baby, and they need to get out."

"Jenna!" exclaimed Colt and Dana together.

"Yeah, it's me," came Jenna's wavering voice. "Can you please take my baby's carrier first?"

Colt gave the lantern to Dana, then helped the conductor as he hauled the wailing Lindy out of the coach. Dana set the lantern down and took the handle of the carrier. "I have her, Jenna!"

"Okay! I'm gonna try to climb out now!"

"Plucky girl," murmured the conductor. He reached down to grab Jenna's forearms.

Jenna kicked at the doorway, pushing against it with one foot as she was hauled out of the car. She squeezed out, demanding, "Where's my baby?" She grabbed the carrier and pulled her child out, hugging her crying baby fiercely. Lindy took a deep, choking breath and calmed. Her hysterical screams mellowed to soft sobs, then stopped as Jenna rocked and crooned to her.

"She's okay, we're all okay," Dana babbled. "Jenna, are you all right?"

"I don't know. I guess so. But my water broke. I'm getting contractions," she said, sounding helpless. "I can't have this baby now!"

"You may not have a choice. Hey, let's get away from here. They're still trying to get people out." Dana picked up the carrier and took Jenna by her free arm.

Colored lights and sirens rent the night as rescue vehicles arrived. Fortunately, the railroad track paralleled a road. Dana could see several ambulances and paramedic vehicles arriving to care for the injured. She jumped up and down. "Help! Over here!"

Several figures in fluorescent yellow suits detached from the main group of rescuers and ran over to her. "What's your situation?" one asked.

"This woman thinks she's going into labor! She also has a baby with her!"

"Okay, let's get 'em!"

The rescuers were quick and efficient. Within seconds, they'd packed both Jenna and Lindy into an ambulance and left, probably for the nearest hospital.

Dana rejoined Colt at the opening to the coach and did what she could to help fellow travelers escape the swaying, dangerous train. However, she felt shaky and ill.

A paramedic came by, flashed a light into her eyes and felt her pulse. "Shock and a possible concussion," she commented to a co-worker. "C'mon down, hon, let's go take care of you."

Dana pulled away. "I'm traveling with someone…"

"It's all right, Dana," Colt said. "I'll come with you."

Her mind seemed entirely disconnected from her body as she looked at him. His wild dark hair was matted with dried blood. His clothes were covered with

dirt and broken glass. He'd never looked better. He put
his arm around her and helped her into an ambulance.
She lay down on a stretcher, still clutching Colt's hand.

Chapter Eighteen

Dana awakened to see pale light in a beige room. She smelled ammonia. A hospital? Colt slumbered in a chair beside her, his chin slumped into his chest. His wound had been cleaned and stitched. The stiff suturing stuck out from his forehead in tiny spikes. His closed lids nestled in darkened pockets of flesh, slack with fatigue.

She stretched and moaned. Every centimeter of her body ached. Her head throbbed where it had hit the window frame. Her knees felt bruised and tender, as did her hands and elbows.

He stirred. "Sweetheart, how are ya feelin'?"

"Sore, but that must mean you're a sight for sore eyes."

He chuckled gently. "You must be all right, to crack a joke. Let's tell them you're awake." He pressed a button on her bedrail.

"Colt, where are we? And, when is it?"

"We are in a hospital in Pueblo, Colorado." He turned his head to check a clock on the wall. "It's noon on July third."

"Thursday? Wow." Dana sat up abruptly, then leaned back as dizziness assailed her. "I was out for a long time."

"Close on to twelve hours, darlin'."

"Gosh." She stirred restlessly in the bed, noticing the intravenous tube in her wrist. She rubbed her temple. "Any chance of getting some ibuprofen? My head is killing me."

"Yeah, me too. And I hope we can leave soon, since you're awake."

"Is there anything wrong with me?"

"Nope, nothin' at all. They took x-rays of both of us when we came in. No fractures, just my cuts and your bruises."

A petite, white-coated brunette bustled into the room. "Hi, I'm Dr. Casares."

"Hi. I'm Dana Newcombe." Dana extended a limp hand.

"Oh, I know who you are. Your father's company makes most of the machines in this place. He's been calling every hour on the hour. He'll be pleased to hear you're awake."

"I hope he hasn't been any trouble."

"Oh, no. We were sure after the x-rays that your sleep was natural, the product of shock and exhaustion. Good morning, Mr. Wilder. Now let's see how your fiancée is doing today."

Dana's mouth dropped open.

"You can close your mouth, dear. I don't need to check your throat." The doctor took Dana's pulse, then checked the rest of her vital signs as Dana turned her head to glare at Colton.

He waved his hands at her behind the doctor's back, and put his finger vertically over his lips, signaling *shh!*

"I'll recommend discharge and advise you to purchase some over-the-counter painkillers. You'll feel sore for the next week or so. Drink plenty of fluids." Dr. Casares poured Dana a cup of water from a plastic carafe on the bedside table.

Dana noticed her fanny pack next to the pitcher. She rubbed her face, wincing at her sticky, grubby skin. "What do I do now?"

The doctor plucked the i.v. from Dana's arm, then dabbed the area with an alcohol-soaked pad. "Your father gave us your insurance information, so you're free to go." She whisked out.

"What on earth was that fiancée thing about?" Dana eyed Colt.

He blinked. "I wanted to stay with you, honey. You seemed so scared last night about being alone, and the only way they'd let me stay was if I was a family member. I wasn't sure that 'brother-in-law' was good enough, so I said we were gonna get married."

The phone beside the bed rang. He picked up the receiver as she attempted to sit up and take charge of her life.

"Oh, good morning, Tom. How are you today?"

"Yes, thank you. And she's fine." He paused, as if allowing Dana's father to speak. "Oh, the doctor told you?" His eyes shifted to her. He covered the mouthpiece with one hand to whisper, "Your father thinks we're engaged!"

"Oh no!" She felt her eyes round with horror. "We have to tell him!"

"Tell him what? He's very happy for us."

"Give me that phone!" She snatched the handset from Colt. "Hi, Dad."

"Hi, punkin! Hey, honey, are you all right?"

"I'm fine, Dad, really." She didn't want her parents to worry about her.

"I'm glad to hear you sounding so well," Tom said. "Your mother and I were quite anxious when the news of the derailment came on C.N.N. this morning."

"Hey, Dad, about Colt and I…"

"Sweetheart, we are so very happy for you. He's a fine young man."

"Dana? You are all right?" Gabrielle came onto the phone.

"Yes, Mother."

"I'm so pleased for you, dear. Colton is such a nice boy, and obviously he's taking good care of you."

"Yes, Mother." Dana's brain was numb.

"You let us know when you pick a date."

"Yes, Mother."

"*Au revoir*, Dana!"

"Bye-bye, punkin!"

The line went to a flat dial tone. Dana replaced the receiver and stared blankly at Colton. "Boy, are we ever in trouble."

"What trouble?"

"Are you kidding? They think we're getting married! They'll probably tell your parents, and then what will we do?"

"So why didn't you tell them we're not engaged?"

"I didn't have a chance. You know how my mother is. She wanted to know about dates!" She sagged against the pillow. Her head swam. "I can't deal with this now. I'm taking a nap, and then I'm going to shower, get dressed, and leave this place."

"Get dressed in what? You have no clothes."

"I have no clothes?"

"Nope, not a stitch, except for your shoes. They cut your clothes off of you so they could check you out. Stay here and shower. I'll go out and buy some new stuff for you. I think I noticed a K-Mart down the street, if you don't mind the ol' blue light special."

"I'm not a clothes snob. K-Mart will be fine."

"Don't need Nicole Newcombe Designs originals?"

"Heck, no. But I'm a 32-38 in Levi's and I prefer oversized T-shirts."

~ * ~

Dana's silly dream had to do with marrying—of all people—Colton Wilder. But the minister was Elvis Presley in a black leather jacket! Colt wore his cowboy boots, and when she looked down, she was attired in a miniskirt and sandals.

A slight, sweet pressure on her forehead brought her out of the freaky dreamland. Had to be Colt's lips. Nothing else in the universe felt so right.

"Hi, honey," she said. "Where are we?"

He looked at her with an odd expression, she thought. "We're still in the hospital in Colorado, darlin'. Are you feelin' okay?"

"Yes, much better. Can we leave now?"

"Sure. You ready for a shower?"

"Oh, more than ready. I'm really yucky. Will you help me?"

"Sure I will. I might even sneak a shower here myself."

She'd been placed in a semi-private, three-bed room with a full bathroom, including a shower. Fortunately, no one else occupied the room.

"Take your time, and don't move too fast. Try sitting up first." He went to the bathroom, and after a few moments, she could hear water begin to run. He returned and reached into a bag, removing a bottle of over-the-counter ibuprofen. He shook out four pills, two for each of them. He handed Dana's to her with a cup of water.

She shifted her legs to the side of the bed and dangled them over, then tried to sit up. Dizziness assailed her. She stopped to breathe deeply, waiting for it to pass.

"I'm gonna shower. Stay right there until I'm done, all right?" Colt stripped rapidly, tossing his dirty clothes into a corner. The devil in Dana made her peek at his naked buns. Nice and tight, she thought, still feeling woozy.

When he exited the bathroom, a towel wrapped around his waist, she made it to her feet, clinging to the bedstead. He rubbed his head with another towel.

"Did you track down Jenna and Lindy?" she asked.

"Yeah. Actually, you missed all the excitement. She had her new baby on the ambulance ride, and her husband arrived from Leavenworth to pick her up this morning." He dabbed carefully at his forehead around the stitches.

"Boy or girl?" Swaying slightly, she released the bed frame, hoping she'd be all right.

"A boy. So now they have a set."

"Is he nice?"

"Too young to tell." Dry, he opened one of the plastic K-Mart bags, and took out a new pair of jeans and a blue workshirt.

"The father, not the baby."

"Oh, he seemed pleased as punch with his son. Maybe they'll stop having kids now that he has a boy. You know the type?"

"Oh yeah." She wandered across the room in the general direction of the bathroom. The room spun, so she stopped until the universe had settled down again. He made a grab for her arm. "Sweetie, I'll be fine," she told him. "Just get me a towel, okay?"

~ * ~

Dressed in stiff new jeans and workshirts, they ate at a cafe that served breakfasts at all hours of the day and night. Still queasy, Dana stuck to fruit salad and stolen bites of Colt's meal. He ate heartily, as usual.

"I'm not going to wait until Amtrak gets around to giving me my travel voucher." He dug into a breakfast burrito loaded with eggs, beans and salsa. "I feel as though a truck ran over me. You were in shock last night and you still look like a wreck."

"Gee, thanks." She sipped her coffee.

"Cut me a break, babe. You know what I mean."

She tried to smile at him. "Yes, I guess so. What do you want to do?" She leaned over the table and stabbed a portion of his breakfast with her fork. "Umm, good sauce."

"I wanna go home."

"Well, me too."

"I want to take you to the farm. Let's rent a car, drive to an airport and get on a plane and go to Kentucky for a few days to relax. We deserve it."

She waved her hands around, indecisive. "Okay, I guess."

"You could sound more enthusiastic."

"Hey, I'm a mess. You're right. My mind is one great big blank page. I know I slept, but I don't feel as though I did. I'm not sure I want to get into a car right now, either. Why don't we spend another night here and start in the morning?"

He rubbed his head near the stitches. "I hate to waste the time. How 'bout if we get a nice big car and you can just go to sleep? You'll be unconscious either way."

They took a taxi to the nearest car rental, where they found a Camry, not the largest car in the world but good enough. The next stop was a small shopping mall, where Dana located an outfit that gave eye exams and produced prescription glasses in one hour. Exhausted by five o'clock, she tilted the front passenger seat all the way back and settled in for the night.

~ * ~

Colt glanced over at Dana, sleeping like a bear cub in winter. The dim light from the car's interior fixtures lent a soft, ruddy glow to her hair. He couldn't help grinning as he remembered Steve Drake's story of the Bozo incident.

Dana. How had he fallen in love with her so quickly?

Their romance had moved along better than he'd dared to plan. In Los Angeles, he'd been reconciled to the differences in their lives, and he would have boarded a plane to Louisville and flown away from her without a backward glance if it hadn't been for the airport strike. He made a mental note to contribute some money to the airport workers' union. He owed them one. A big one.

Sharing the train trip and even that awful wreck had given their relationship a boost and a half. He'd seen her in the worst possible situation. She'd come through like a superstar, a real heroine. Though she'd been in shock, she'd even helped with Jenna's rescue. What a great gal!

He had to figure out how to keep her in his life. He could never ask her to give up her career, though. His Dana was brilliant. He didn't want to hide her light, but wanted her to glow with additional radiance. He knew he could make her happy.

But he didn't want to leave the farm. He'd always known what he wanted in life. His fate lay in Kentucky's bluegrass, not Jupiter's moons.

Chapter Nineteen

They stepped out of the Louisville airport terminal at about three p.m., with Dana holding onto Colt's elbow, just in case. The fuzziness infecting her brain still hadn't receded entirely. The driver of a battered red pick-up truck honked from the curbside.

"Hey, Jim!" With a big grin, Colt bounded forward and yanked the door of the truck open with a creak. Behind the wheel sat a grizzled black gentleman dressed in blue jeans and a workshirt with "Wilder Farms" embroidered in red on the pocket. He wore a faded red baseball cap with the same logo on the front in blue.

Pulling her by the hand, Colt shoved her into the cab, then crammed himself into the passenger seat beside her. He slammed the creaky door closed, reaching across her to slap the driver's shoulder. "Jim, this is Dana."

"Hey, Dana, pleased to meet you. I heard the good news. Congratulations to both of you. When's the happy day?"

She tipped her head to one side, and Jim winked at her. She smiled at him although she was really confused. Why would he congratulate her? What happy day? She turned to eye Colt, who put his arm around her to give her a cheerful hug. Jim switched gears and gunned the engine of the ancient pick-up.

"Er, thanks. Who did you talk to? You don't seem too surprised by Dana and me," Colt shouted over the noisy engine and the wind coming through the open windows of the truck.

"No, Al and Judi called last night, and I got the drift of what was going on," Jim yelled back. "I figured you two would end up comin' in, what with that train crash and all."

She shuddered. Although two days had passed since the derailment, she still felt bruised and battered.

Jim turned to her. "So you were in the hospital overnight? How you feelin'?"

"I'm okay," she replied. "Still tired and sore."

"Well, we'll put you into the hot tub when we get home and then into a nice soft bed," Colt said. "I know it's not the Fourth of July you planned, but we'll get you fixed up right quick."

"It's the Fourth, that's right. I'd forgotten." She looked at Jim. "Thank you for picking us up. Is this your day off?"

"Not a problem, happy to help." Jim downshifted, and the truck lurched. "And today isn't a holiday at the farm. Plenty of boarders are there riding."

She must have looked puzzled, because Colt said, "One of the services Wilder Farms provides is boarding. Folks from Louisville and Frankfort keep their horses at the farm and come out to ride on holidays and weekends. Staff days off will be next week."

The route Jim picked was crowded with vacationers, but the drive wasn't long. "Here we are," Colt said as white painted fences enclosing views of green, rolling hills came into sight. "We're now on Wilder Farms property."

"Wow." Dana craned her head to see beyond Colt. "Gorgeous. How big is the farm?"

""We own over two thousand prime acres of Kentucky bluegrass country," Colt said. "It's one of the premier thoroughbred farms in the world."

"Huh. We're the best." Jim's posture was confident and erect.

The truck rolled through elaborate iron gates. In the distance, smartly dressed equestrians galloped over wide fields on their mounts. The more sedate walked or trotted their horses on manicured trails over the hills or down by a small lake. Split-rail fences and numerous buildings dotted the land. Surrounded by corrals, a cluster of white-painted barns and stables sat about three acres from the main gates.

A minute later, Jim stopped the truck outside a gabled house, painted pale yellow with white trim.

Colt smiled at her. "Welcome home." He climbed out of the truck and stretched, then helped her down. She pressed her hands to her low back and arched, hearing the pop of taut tendons. She twisted back and forth, finishing her stretch, then took stock of her surroundings as Jim left, driving toward the stables.

The Wilder home was set back from the public areas of the farm, several acres from the gates. Stands of evergreen, oak and hickory clumped around the house provided more privacy. The sprawling, single-story residence seemed quiet, and she guessed that neither staff nor family were present, since Judi and Alan were still on the road.

Colt dug his keys from his pocket. ""It's a miracle we got out of the crash with my wallet and my keys on me. Can you imagine what a hassle everything would have been if we didn't have my wallet and your fanny pack?"

Carrying their one bag, he opened the door to the house and nudged Dana inside. Polished wood floors were covered by braided rugs, and handmade quilts hung on the whitewashed walls. The furniture also appeared to be handmade, products of the Appalachian craftman's art.

Walking over to the fireplace, she touched the worn back of a wooden rocker and set the chair moving. "Your house is beautiful. Did you grow up here?"

"Yeah. I'm glad you like it, honey. We're gonna spend lots of time here." Taking her by the hand, he led her through the house, showing her the kitchen, bathrooms, and bedrooms.

"Here's my—our—bedroom." He opened a door. The simple, white painted room was like all the others, with a wood dresser, an adjoining bathroom, and soft, handmade quilts on the double bed.

Overcome with weariness, she sat down, leaned back, and closed her eyes. He pulled off her shirt, caressing her breasts in passing. She pushed his hand away. Apparently undeterred, he tugged down her jeans and unlaced her sneakers. Still clothed, he picked her up with ease and walked into a hall. His new clothes felt pleasantly scratchy against her nude flesh.

She managed to wrench open one lid. "What are you doing?"

"You'll sleep better if you get into the spa for awhile. It's the best thing for sore muscles. Then we'll take some more ibuprofen, eat some soup, and go to bed."

"What was Jim talking about when he congratulated us?"

"Um, well, he thinks we're getting married."

"What?" She involuntarily lurched in his arms.

He almost dropped her. "I think you can walk now." He set her on her feet and reached into a linen cupboard for towels.

"Yes, I can walk. Why does Jim think we're getting married?"

"My parents apparently heard from your parents that we're engaged." Again leading her by the hand, he took her out onto a wood veranda at the back of the house, then into a nook. Lattice fencing covered by flowering honeysuckles concealed the area from prying eyes.

"Why would they think that we're getting married?" She sniffed. The honeysuckle's scent invaded her nose, a sweet flood. Bees hummed through the fragrant vines.

"From the hospital." He pulled off a padded cover from the top of a round, redwood hot tub, sunk into the deck. Inviting steam billowed out of the spa.

He stripped off his clothes. As usual, his nude body was unbelievably distracting, but she took a deep breath to steady herself. She tried to focus on this latest mystery. "Why would someone at the hospital say that?"

"Don't you remember? It's just a little mistake. Don't worry about it. I told the people at the hospital that we were engaged because you wanted me to stay with you. You refused to let go of me." Stepping into the hot tub, he extended a hand to help her in.

"I did?" *How embarrassing.* She clung to his proffered arm and lowered herself into the comfortably hot water. She sighed. "How come everything is suddenly so complicated?"

"Darlin', nothing's wrong. We're in a wonderful, peaceful place and in two or three days, you'll feel good as new."

How could he be so calm? When she opened her mouth to continue her protests, he covered it with his until she responded, matching her movements to his. Their tongues played and explored, wrestled and made peace.

Dana knelt on the seat in the tub and wrapped her arms around his lean, muscular shoulders, drawing him close. She gently scratched a sensitive spot she'd discovered at his nape. He groaned as he cupped her breast with one hand and sought her pussy with the other. Desire gathered in her pelvis in a hot, flowing mass of arousal. As he delved into her depths, seeking her sensitive core, she rocked wildly against his fingers.

"Easy now, babe, let's not go too fast." He withdrew his fingers to caress her.

"Why n-not?" She quivered with her approaching climax.

He stood up, with her arms still clutching his shoulders, lifting her out of the spa. The water flowed off his slick body in sheets as the summer sun reflected off every muscular plane. He lay her down on the sun-warmed deck and gazed at her as he massaged her torso, outlining the curves with loving fingers. He bent his head to brush his lips, then his stubbly chin, on her nipples.

She closed her eyes, watching the patterns of light and shadow the arbor made on her lids. Flowery perfume filled her nostrils. She shivered, savoring the sensations as excitement thrilled through her body.

Playing with her breasts, he gently pinched the nipples until she moaned. She twined her arms around his neck and kissed him. Opening her eyes so she could avoid his stitches, she ran her hands through his hair, down his shoulders, and across his muscular chest. She found his nipples and plucked them, imitating Colt. He immediately reacted, placing one of her hands on his rod.

She explored his erection, warm in her palm as she caressed his hard shaft. His responsive moans delighted her. She loved to pleasure her man.

He stopped her, saying, "Let's not do that too much unless we're ready for me to use it. Do you feel okay?"

"Oh, I'm fine. Really. Please, Colt."

"Are you sure?" He stroked her belly. "You still have a little bruising here."

"I hit the table when we crashed, I think."

"Ouch." He slid down her slick body to stroke the sweetest spot with his tongue. Exquisite excitement shot through her. She breathed deeply, relaxing into the rapture that only Colt could create. His practiced mouth, fuzzy with stubble, took her higher, but not high enough.

Thrashing her limbs, she cried out. "Please, please."

"What, baby?" Sitting up, he held her on his lap.

She put her feet flat on the deck, lifted her body, then lowered herself onto his cock. His length throbbed deliciously in her sheath. He ground his hips into hers and gave her a slow, sexy smile that warmed her right down to her toes and heightened the ache in her needy pussy. He took her breasts, one in each hand. He squeezed them gently, watching her with a narrowed blue gaze, then tugged at the sensitive tips. Panting, she closed her eyes and rolled her clit against him, welcoming the pleasure that shafted through her.

She looked up at him. His eyes were filled with a peculiar intensity, one she didn't understand. She nibbled on his neck, and he gasped. She pressed her breasts against his furred chest and rubbed back and forth, reveling in the pleasantly scratchy sensation.

Pulling herself off of him, she rubbed her hungry clit against his nice, hot cock. He bucked, groaning, "Oh, God, Dana, I'm gonna come…"

He impaled her again, gripping her hips so he could embed his entire length in her. He spurted into her, hot and wet, then reached between them to pluck her clit, hurling her into a maelstrom of pleasure.

~ * ~

Dana woke when the digital clock on Colt's dresser indicated that it was shortly after four a.m. The lace-trimmed curtains, oddly feminine in this man's bedroom, were open, letting starlight stream through the window. She slid out of bed, careful not to disturb Colt, whose low, regular breathing told her he was deeply asleep. His face wore the same serenity she'd seen the first time she had awakened near him, in the train. She smiled slightly, then pattered over to the window to peer out.

No lights disturbed the rural night, and the star-watcher in her saw an opportunity. She put on her new glasses before she slipped out of the room. Naked, she was a bit chilled, but she assumed she wouldn't be out of bed for very long. She found her way through the dark house to the nearest door and stepped outside.

The splendor of the starry sky awaited her. She reveled in the radiance of a clear, country summer

night, astounded at what she'd missed living in cities.
The stars, their light unimpaired by any urban glow,
glittered in myriad profusion, diamonds scattered by a
careless jeweler throughout the black velvet of infinite
space. *This is it. This is why I do what I do. To know
this glory.*

A shooting star overlaid a narrow silvery trail across
the arching Milky Way, a diamond necklace worn by
the Queen of Heaven. Dana's vision blurred with tears.
She blinked them away.

The bright starlight let her see dim outlines of trees,
outbuildings, and rolling hills. The night was quiet,
broken only by the chirp of crickets and the breeze
sweeping softly through the trees.

She understood the look of serenity and calm she'd
seen on Colton's sleeping face.

The screen door banged as he joined her. "Dana,
honey? What'cha doin'?"

"Just looking at the stars."

"Yeah, they're beautiful out here. Nothin' quite like
a country night." He slipped his arm around her and
tipped his head back to stare at the sky. "I'm surprised
you study astronomy in places like Pasadena and
Boston. Can't really see the sky."

"We observe space using instruments like the
Hubble telescope. Not too much more to discover just
by looking. The era of the backyard astronomer is
pretty much over."

"Maybe not. What about those people who find new
meteors?"

"True."

"Wait here." Colt scurried back into the house to re-emerge a few moments later, carrying a pair of binoculars.

She thanked him with a kiss, then put the binoculars to her eyes and adjusted them. "These are really quality binocs." Familiar with the summer night sky, she located the planets Venus and Mars, hovering at the eastern horizon. "Look at this."

He took them and peered through the lenses at the patch of sky she indicated. "Hey, Mars really is reddish!"

"Sure it is. That's not a legend, that's a fact." Her attention was drawn by something unexpected. "Whoa, what's this?" She showed him a tiny smudge in the sky.

"I dunno. You're the astronomer. You tell me."

"I can't. I don't know what that is."

"Is it something new?"

"Maybe. There isn't supposed to be anything in that position. May I use your phone to make a couple of calls?"

"To whom?"

"Palomar," she said. "That's where my CalTech buddies star-gaze."

He handed her the cordless handset. Still a little mystified, he watched while she punched in a string of numbers and connected with one of her former colleagues from CalTech. "Yes," she said into the phone. "Central Kentucky, just a few degrees above the east-northeastern horizon. Any new comets recently?" She grinned at him as she heard the news, then completed the call.

Her grin spread wider. "So, how does the Comet Newcombe-Wilder sound to you?"

He stared at her. "You're kidding."

"Nope. We're the first to spot and report an apparently undiscovered new comet. That means it's named after us."

"How come no one else saw it before?"

"Lucky, I guess. Plus, a lot of astronomers and observatories are near enough to cities that dim objects can't be seen. In addition, we're usually working on some kind of grant or project. Very few grants for just looking at the sky at four-thirty a.m."

~ * ~

Too excited to go back to sleep, Colt suggested an early morning ride. Dana didn't have the nerve to refuse. What would he think if he learned she was frightened of horses?

Large beasts, horses had disproportionately small brains. They were unintelligent and unpredictable. Why should she ride when she had perfectly good legs?

After they dressed, Colt led Dana to the stables. She tried to find the words to back out, but she couldn't figure out what to say.

The eastern sky grew pink with the approaching dawn. Drawing in a deep, invigorating breath, she smelled the fragrances of dew and bluegrass borne on the fresh breeze.

Following Colt, she nervously entered the stable, filled with the aromas of dry hay, leather tack, and clean horse. He stalked up and down the row of stalls, greeting each horse by name. "This here's Silver Shadow. She's a two-year old, daughter of a great mare, Silver Cloud." The filly, a distinctive silvery color, whickered as Colt stroked her nose. "Cloud just got sold for a bundle. She's a proven breeder, already produced two good colts."

"Er, v-very nice," stuttered Dana.

He proceeded down the stalls. "This is Wilder's Choice." Choice was a huge black stallion. He seemed to look down his long nose at Dana before snorting and turning away. "He'll do fine."

"For what?" she squeaked.

He turned to her with a searching glance. "What's wrong?"

"N-nothing."

"When was the last time you rode a horse?"

"Never. B-but how hard can it be?"

"Jeez. Didn't you go to camp in the summer?"

"Yes, of course. Computer camp and space camp."

He rolled his eyes and snorted, sounding remarkably like his horse. He expertly lifted a blanket and a saddle from the door of Choice's stall and placed them on the back of the very large stallion, who danced restlessly. Colt led him out of the stable, then tied him to a post in the adjoining corral.

Colt re-entered the stable, with Dana practically treading on his heels. "Colt! You don't mean I have to ride that—that…" Words failed her. She didn't want to insult Wilder's Choice, but she also wanted to live the day through.

He grinned. "No, sweetheart, I wouldn't do that to him. I'll ride Choice, and you'll ride Seven."

Seven was a placid dapple-gray who stood calmly in his stall as Colt urged Dana to make friends. Bringing some carrots from a bag in the back of the stable, he handed them to her. "Hold 'em on your palm. Don't curl your fingers, he'll try to eat them."

She squealed, but managed to keep still while the soft, moist lips of the elderly Seven stroked her palm, removing the carrots. He munched while regarding her with approval … or so she hoped.

"All right, Seven ol' boy, let's go for a ride." Colt positioned a blanket, then heaved Seven's saddle off the side of his stall and onto the horse's back and led him out of the stable. In the corral, Colt fiddled with the horses' tack as she watched from her perch on a split rail fence. He tightened girths, checked bridles and bits, then said, "Here's your moment of truth, darlin'. Hop on!"

She walked over to the right side of the horse. Seven snorted and sidled away.

"No, honey. Never get on a horse on the right side. They don't expect that. Walk around him. Not so close to his heels, okay? Come around his head." Colt held Seven's bridle as she stepped fearfully around the gelding to the horse's left side.

"Now, put your foot in the stirrup. No, your *left* foot," he said. "Now, just push down and get yourself on."

She obeyed, though she was about to have a nervous breakdown. Sitting on a large, living, moving creature, which might not cooperate, made her insides quake. But she had to try, though the last thing she wanted was to look like a fool in front of Colt. Fortunately, Seven appeared to be unaffected by her state of mind.

Colt seemed to spring onto Choice's back in a single easy movement. "Wow, this feels good! Let's go."

She kicked the sides of the horse to get him moving, just like she'd seen in movies. She sucked in a relieved breath. The films hadn't lied.

After just a few paces, she began to grasp why so many people loved to ride. The perspective from horseback was unique and ever-changing. She smelled the pungent scent of the animal and the freshness of the early morning air. She enjoyed the pleasant rocking motion of the horse beneath her. It was … sexy.

And there was Colton. Colt on horseback was even hotter than Colt in a tux or Colt in cutoffs. In fact, he was hotter than Colt any other way except naked with his cock inside her. Back straight and head high, he controlled the restive stallion with expertise and grace. Her flesh prickled with awareness. She'd never felt so vital and alive.

Following Colt, Dana headed out of the corral toward the small lake, walking her horse but occasionally breaking into a trot. She quickly learned to post by copying him. It was simply a matter of self-preservation. They dismounted at the lake to let the horses drink.

"Colt, why do you ever leave this place? I love the farm."

He was silent for a very long time, then said, "It gets old, for a young person. But I'm happy here, now. So you like it?"

Aware she was closer to making a major life decision, she paused. "Yes, I do. Anywhere you can see the stars like this is a good place."

"What about your work? Don't you have to be at some sort of academic institution to explore Europa via computer?"

She shook her head. "I can get data from the net or electronically and analyze it anywhere. We like to work in groups because it's more fun. Plus, other scientists are available to check and recheck results, and to help if anyone gets stuck or sidetracked. But I can do all that by phone, e-mail, or occasional meetings."

"What are you saying to me, babe?" He sounded a little stilted, even nervous.

"Umm, nothing yet. Just … thinking out loud, really."

"Oh." She didn't miss the disappointed note in his voice and wondered what that meant. He hadn't said a word about commitment, but they'd grown so close … what would happen next?

Choice, finished with his refreshments, nudged Colt's shoulder. "Dana, I'm going to gallop back to the stable. He needs a workout. See you there!"

He cantered off, leaving her with Seven. She eyed the horse. The horse eyed her. "Well, I better learn how to do this alone, if I'm gonna be around here for awhile."

She went around to the gelding's left side, and, grasping the pommel, mounted. Then she realized she had forgotten to pick up the reins before climbing onto Seven. She reached over the horse's head, trying to grab them without getting off. Apparently mystified by the procedure, Seven tossed his head, narrowly missing hers.

Sighing, she dismounted to gather the reins in her left hand. She pulled them into what she hoped was the correct position over the horse's curved neck before climbing back onto Seven, who showed an unexpected streak of hastiness as he trotted back to the stable. She remembered to post and clung onto the horse for her life as he speeded up into a gallop. She hauled back on the reins as he dashed through the open corral gate.

She saw Colt's startled face as she and Seven raced into the pen. Seven stopped abruptly in front of the stable with a jerk. She somehow avoided falling off his back and slid off the horse with, she hoped, some semblance of grace.

"I think he might want his breakfast," she said to Colt, who was talking to Jim and another of the hands.

"You got that old boy goin' pretty well, Miss Dana," Jim said, grinning. "How d'yoo like him?"

"Oh, er, he's a very nice horse. Nice horsie," she said. She heard Colt, that wretch, laughing as he led Seven to his stall.

Chapter Twenty

Hungry, they raided the big refrigerator in the kitchen. "Not a thing." Dana let the door close with a thump.

"Not surprisin'," Colt said. "Mom and Dad planned to be away for three weeks. Mom wouldn't leave anything in the 'fridge to spoil. I bet there isn't anything in this kitchen that isn't canned or frozen."

"I'm starved."

"Good. You haven't eaten properly since before the train cr…" He was interrupted by the front door chime. His brow wrinkled. "Who could that be?"

She followed him to the entry. "Maybe one of the hands needs something."

"They would have phoned." He yanked open the door.

On the doorstep stood Max and Nicole.

Neither looked particularly happy.

Uncharacteristically grim, Max wore an ancient gray T-shirt and grubby white pants. He had a black eye. A third of Nicole's face was hidden by huge sunglasses, and the visible two-thirds was twisted into a grimace. She appeared equally travel-worn, in a wrinkled green blouse and jeans. Behind them, a taxi idled, its driver unloading luggage.

"Wh-what's up?" Colt sputtered.

"Everything's fine," Nicole and Max chorused. Identical phony smiles spread over their faces.

"We just got tired of Mexico and decided to come home." Max pushed past Colt and strode through the door toward his bedroom, not sparing a glance back to see if his wife followed.

While Colt followed Max, Dana helped Nick bring the luggage inside. "What's going on?" Dana hissed to her twin.

"Sshhhh!" Nick put her finger vertically over her lips. "Max has just gone a little crazy. Nothing that a few peaceful days won't fix … I hope." Her voice wobbled.

"Crazy? Max? The man you labeled a dullard and called Mr. Meticulous?" Dana stared at her twin.

"The very same." Nick's mouth drew into a tight line. She pulled Dana away from the entry and said, "Is there somewhere we can talk privately?"

"Sure, almost anywhere." Dana led Nicole to the Wilders' kitchen and closed the door. "What's going on? What are you and Max doing here? Aren't you supposed to be on a cruise in Mexico?"

"It … it was impossible. Things have really gone wrong, faster than I could have believed." Leaning closer to Dana, she whispered, "He got so mad, he … I think he's going to leave me."

"Max? No way."

"Way. Look at this." Nick took a rolled-up magazine out of her Mexican straw satchel. The copy of *American Stud,* a men's magazine, sported the headline, NICOLE NEWCOMBE REVEALED … TO THE PINK and the photo on the cover was of a much younger Nickie. A high school age Nickie.

Dana sucked in a breath. "Oh, my God. The beaver shots. They finally surfaced. How did this happen? I thought we tracked all of them down."

"Apparently not. The asshole who took Dad's money cheated him, and us. He held onto the negatives and released them on our wedding day. We found out on our honeymoon. People on the cruise ship…" Nicole's voice broke. She gulped air and regained her composure. "People on the cruise ship had them. They were selling it in the ship's store, damn it. Men were walking up to me in the dining room and asking me to autograph pictures of my pussy. In front of Max."

"Oh, my God. No wonder he's upset. He got into a fight, didn't he? Is that how he got a black eye?"

"Yep, sure is." Nicole's voice dropped to a whisper. "He's really angry with me. For what I did, and for not telling him about it."

"Nick, I'm really sorry." Dana twisted her hands together.

"I think I'm going to lose my husband." Nickie's voice broke, and this time she didn't try to stem the tears. She sank to the floor and buried her face in her hands.

Colt and Max came to the door. "Pull yourself together," Max said brusquely. "We're going out for something to eat."

"I'm not hungry." Nicole's voice was muffled.

"Come on, Nick, quit being such a prima donna."

"Prima donna! How dare you!" Nick jumped to her feet, face flushed and blotchy. "Who's been freaking out for days? Who's gotten into fights over something that happened years ago? Huh? Who?" She got right into Max's face. "Max the Drama King, that's who."

He grabbed her upper arms to hold her back. "It's not the pictures, though having every man on earth gawk at my wife's snatch doesn't turn me on. It's the fact that you didn't tell me." He cast a bitter look at Dana. "Neither did you."

She tried to control her temper. "I had forgotten about it, to be honest. It's old news to us. I only remembered when Leta brought it up at the rehearsal dinner, and I didn't think it was appropriate dinner table conversation."

"You could have told me later."

"Why?" Dana asked. "Look, anything I could have said to discourage you from marrying Nickie would have looked like sour grapes. And the same goes for Colt."

"Did you know?" Max asked his brother.

Colt crossed his arms over his torso. "Not until later, after that dinner."

Max rubbed his face. "You could have told me. Now I feel as though three people I thought I could trust kept something from me. Thanks a lot."

"For God's sake, Max, the tabloids will care about this only until the next scandal comes along. In a week, we'll be old news. Or we could hurry the process along." Nicole took a flat plastic pack out of her satchel.

"What's that?" Colt asked.

"Contraceptive pills." Nicole flung them into the wastebasket.

"What are you doing?" Max dashed to the pail and bent to retrieve the pills.

"If I get pregnant, that'll knock the skin mag fiasco right off the front page," Nicole said. "Everyone loves a baby."

"That's about the world's worst reason to have a child." Dana grabbed Colt's hand and started to haul him out the door. "We don't belong in here. You two need to talk this out."

Alone with his sort-of wife, Max asked Nicole, "Are you nuts? I can't even decide if I want to stay married to you, let alone have a baby."

Her face starkly white, Nicole sank to the floor and started to sob. "Please don't say that. You can't mean that!"

"I don't see how I can stay married to someone so deceptive. And why would you throw away your pills without talking to me about it?"

"Isn't it a woman's choice?"

"I get no say at all? We're married!"

"Not if you walk out on me."

"I don't know what I want to do yet." Max stalked out of the room, and Nick followed him into the stable.

The place had an unpredicted calming effect, at least on Nicole. The late morning sun slanted through cracks in the wooden walls, casting slivers of light on the golden hay and the horses' shining coats. The dusty air was filled with the aromas of clean horse and straw. Nickie sneezed and rubbed the tip of her already damp nose with a shaky finger.

Max cast her a dispassionate glance. "Better take a Benadryl if you're sensitive to dust or animal fur. I'll get you some." He went to the stable office and fetched the medicine and a paper cup of water from a cooler.

She took them and looked up into his unsmiling, cold eyes. For a moment she faltered, then said, "So you do care … a little bit?"

"Oh, I care. Perhaps too much." He stepped away from her and said, "I believe that women should be independent, but I also believe that marriage is a partnership. I thought you did, also. At least you said you did. But you're running the entire show. You plunge us into scandal before we're married for a week. Now you want to get pregnant without my agreement. This can't go on. It's not fair. It's not right."

"So what are you going to do about it?" Nicole set a cocky hand on her hip.

His eyes slid to one side of her. "Reclaim my power."

"How?"

He strode past her to where a short whip hung from the wooden wall. Yanking it off its nail, he slid his fingers up and down its length.

Swallowing, Nicole eyed it. It consisted of a braided leather handle ending in two long leather straps. "Wha-what's that for?"

"It's for you." He advanced on her. He hadn't shaved for a couple of days, and his dark visage had a savage, raw edge. "It's a quirt. It's normally used to train horses, but in this case…" He ran a considering glance over her.

"You want to … you're kidding!"

"No, I'm not. This situation sucks. What you did was horrible, and you need a lesson. There are some acts you can't get away with. I love you, but I won't be led around by my heart or my cock by a deceptive, manipulative woman."

She stared at the quirt, her mind blank with shock. "You can't … you can't mean that."

"I mean it. Do you want to stay married or not? Look, I saw the way you interacted with your parents. You've wrapped Mommy and Daddy around your pretty little finger all your life. That's not me, babe. I'm not a tyrant, and I *don't* have to be the boss, but I … we … need to balance the power in this relationship."

She swallowed, her gaze fixed on the quirt. "I've read about … I've read about some women who, who, like that."

Max smiled. "Are you afraid you might be one of those women?"

"Yes," she managed to whisper.

"That's an even better reason to try this."

~ * ~

In the adjoining stall, Dana whispered to Colt, "This is weird. We shouldn't be watching this!" She dragged him away, toward the stall door.

He resisted. "Hey, we were here before they were. First you drag me out of my house, now you want to haul me out of my own stable. What gives?"

"This is private, between Max and Nickie. We have no right…"

"To hell with right. This could be a mega-hot scene."

She glared at him. She had thought that, despite the hassles Max and Nick were experiencing, she was on her way to becoming reconciled to the phony engagement and had been considering a real one. She'd been close, damned close to proposing. She'd just needed a little more time.

Only one qualm had stopped her. She felt sure she could merge her life with Colt's, but they hadn't been together very long, and that gave her pause. But if she had proof that he really understood her and could support her in the ways she needed, well… And now, here was an additional factor. Colt was showing a streak of wildness she wasn't sure she could take.

She heard a slapping sound and a yelp, followed by a sigh. "Max!" Her sister's voice. Nickie didn't sound distressed, just surprised.

Colt tugged on Dana's hand and took her close to the stable wall. He peeked through a crack between the boards. In spite of her misgivings, she was unable to resist. She imitated him.

Nicole was bent forward over a saddle on a stand, her denim-clad rear in the air. Max stood nearby. Dana watched as he raised the quirt and swished it down over Nick's butt. It landed with a decisive rap.

Dana gasped, desire snapping through her. No, she thought, this can't be!

Nick moaned and writhed, but didn't scream no, didn't get up, didn't run away. Clearly, this was what she wanted.

Max lashed her again and again. Nickie's body jerked with each strike. She lifted her rear up and down, groaning his name, begging, "Oh, Max, oh, Max."

To her shock and surprise, Dana's arousal heightened with each crack of the quirt. Not because the man wielding the quirt was Max and the woman getting spanked was Nicole, but the act itself … Nickie sure didn't seem to be in distress. Quite the opposite.

"Please please please…" Nicole lifted her hips up and down, banging the saddle. Through her growing erotic haze, Dana wondered if the whipping would have its desired disciplinary effect.

"Please what, sweetheart?" Max's voice was tender, not mocking or cold.

"Please let me come. I'll never do anything like this again! I promise."

After one last slash drew a scream, Max dropped the whip, lifted Nick up off the saddle and took her into his arms. Nicole curled into his embrace, and they sank to the stable floor, tearing off each other's clothes.

Hot and a little shaky, Dana held onto Colt's elbow as they left. She said, "I never knew ol' Max had it in him."

"She pushed him pretty hard. Me, I don't need to be pushed."

Dana stopped walking. "To do what?"

Smiling, he reached under her shirt and caressed her breasts. The nipples had shrunk to hard points. "Admit it, darlin'. You're turned on."

She was sure her face was now the color of a stop sign. "I, uh, uh…"

"It's okay, babe, you don't have to say anything. Just come with me." He yanked her by the hand back into his house, down the hall, then into his bedroom.

She stuttered, "Colt, umm, Colt, I'm not sure I…"

He kicked the door closed and took her into his arms. "Haven't you learned by now that I'd never hurt you?"

"Ye-es. But a whipping?"

"Oh, no." His smile was the essence of seduction. His embrace tightened. "Too impersonal."

"What d-do you mean?" She squirmed, aware that her pants were too tight for her swelling pussy.

"My hand and your sweet ass have a date, and that time is … now." He ran a hand over her butt and squeezed.

He wanted to spank her.

He wanted to *spank* her?

Her hips jolted, and her cunt hit his erection. Their flesh sizzled through two layers of denim. Not only was her pussy throbbing, but she was wet, creaming at the thought of the sensual discipline that Colt wanted to deliver.

Letting her go, he walked over to the messy bed. He stacked the pillows in the center and said, "Take off your pants."

"J-just my pants?"

"Hell, take it all off, baby. Just take it off fast." He unzipped his jeans, and his cock, already aroused to its fullest extent, leapt out of the confining denim. He was big, hard, red, and ready.

She gulped. "I'm not sure about this."

"Take it off, babe. Every stitch." He eased his pants over his lean hips, and they fell to his ankles.

"I'm not saying I don't want to. It's just … it's just…"

"What?" He kicked the jeans away. His body was flagrantly eager for sex. His cock twitched, as though looking for somewhere to nest.

"I—I've never done that before."

"All the more reason for you to try something new." He flung himself down onto his bed and leaned against his headboard. "Strip for me. Please." His tone deepened into a growl. "Now."

"I'm not sure how to start."

The glint in his eyes was devilish, lustful. "Follow your instincts. Do it for me, baby."

She stood in the middle of the room. Now what was she supposed to do? Follow her instincts? She wasn't instinctive, she was cerebral. But Colt sounded as though she'd better dig deep and find those instincts, fast.

She'd never seen a strip show or even watched a pornographic movie. How did women strip for their lovers? She walked away, her brain whirling.

And then he was going to…

She looked over her shoulder at him. Eyes gleaming bright, he was the picture of male carnal anticipation, completely pure and innocent in his own way, simple and elemental. He pulled off his shirt. Now naked, he adjusted a pillow behind his back and settled against the headboard.

She took a deep breath. She winked.

A smile spread over Colt's face. Encouraged, she undid the buttons on her work shirt. Turning, she flashed him.

"Yowza, baby!"

She spun away, then glanced over her shoulder and blew him a kiss. She sauntered over to the clock-radio on his nightstand, giving him only peeks at her breasts through the half-open shirt. She fiddled with the radio until she found a mellow jazz station.

She let the shirt drop to her elbows, revealing her breasts. She danced a little to the music, letting the girls bounce and sway. Colt wolf-whistled as she jerked off the shirt and tossed it across the room.

She clapped her hands over her breasts, turned and gave him a mock frown. "No loud noises, please. You distract the performer."

"Oh, sweetheart. The performer is sure distracting me. Come over here, darlin'."

"No way. You get to wait."

"Woo-hoo. She's feelin' her oats, all right."

She winked again, then cupped her breasts and fondled the nipples. Colt's blue gaze was riveted to her chest. She pinched her nipples until they reddened, then brought them up to her mouth so she could lick the tips.

She liked the taste and feel of her nipples on her tongue and gave them a good long bath, until they hardened on her lips. She nipped the peaks. His eyes widened, and a shining drop glistened at the head of his cock. He wrapped one hand around his rod, caressing himself as he watched her.

Picking up his discarded T-shirt, she rubbed it against her naked breasts, then trailed its end over Colt's muscular torso.

He gasped, leaping off the bed to grab her. He tossed her onto the bed face up and buried his face between her breasts. She let him have a lick or two, then squirmed beneath him and pushed him over. She straddled him to rub her nipples against his chest, as always loving the gentle scrape of his hair against her skin. She gave him a wet, open-mouthed kiss.

He groaned. Beneath her, she could feel his erection pulsate against her denim-clad pelvis. She ground against his hard-on, enjoying the rub of that tantalizing bulge against her cunt.

"Oh, baby." Colt fumbled for her zipper. "Let me kiss you."

Maybe he'd forgotten his plan. She threw back her head in triumph.

He pulled her jeans down to her bent knees and buried his face in her muff, seeking her clit. He found it, and sucked it hard to draw it forth. With one hand on her buttock to steady her, he pushed the other hand between her legs, fumbling for her slit.

She pulsed and rocked, letting his finger slip inside her. Abruptly, he let her go, pulling back to blow on her heated pussy. "Yeah, baby. You're so hot you're steaming."

"Aren't you … aren't you gonna finish?" She really needed to come.

"Oh, I'm gonna finish you off real good." He flipped her over so she was sprawled face down over the stacked pillows, her ass high as though presented to his hand. After tugging off her jeans, he spread her knees so he could kneel between them.

The first stinging smack caught her off guard, and she yelped. He laughed. She turned her head and glared at him.

"C'mon, honey. That didn't hurt and we both know it."

"I was surprised," she said, trying to sound dignified and together and adult, as if she did this every day, as if she could handle it. As if.

Another spank rocked her world. A fierce, carnal heat rushed through her. She fisted the bedclothes and bit her lower lip, but nothing could stifle her moan of desire. Her nipples hardened, and she rubbed them against the pillows, hoping to quench the flame.

The third spank fell on her clenched buttocks, searing her. She cried out again, and her hips jerked. His hand pressed against her lower back, pinning her in place.

"How is it, baby?" Colt's voice sounded in her ear, low and rough.

She gasped, unable to answer.

"Can you take more?"

"Yeah," she managed.

"Do you … want more?"

She paused. Her butt burned, but arousal radiated from it in waves, enveloping her pussy with a flame she'd never before experienced. Her clit twitched and throbbed, aching for release. "Yeah. I … I really want to come."

"Good." His hands clenched over her smarting buttocks, pulling her closer to him. Without any more warning, he entered her, driving deep. He opened her wide, filling her all the way to her womb. He surged in and out, with each plunge punctuated by a spank on her butt. They reverberated through her, the sting increasing the pleasure, driving her fast and high.

She started to come, screaming with the fullness of her climax. But he didn't stop, instead continuing to fuck her through one orgasm and into another.

With a hoarse shout, he released, spurting liquid heat into her core. As tremors continued to ripple through her, he let his body sag onto hers in complete relaxation.

Chapter Twenty-One

"Hey, there's something I want you to have." Colt led Dana into a room she hadn't seen before. It was dominated by two large desks, arranged so they faced each other, meeting in the middle of the room. "This is Dad's study. I should say, my parents' office. They share everything, especially their work."

"That's cool."

He opened a closet door and fumbled around its dark interior, extracting a small gray metal box. Opening it, he removed a silk pouch, stood and faced her. His eyes held an odd intensity. "Dana, I, we … in the last day or two, we've figured out how, how this could all work."

"What are you talking about?"

"I'm talking about you and me. Us."

Astonishment swept her. Could it be that Colt's thoughts and feelings were running along the same lines as hers? "There's an, an *us*?" she asked.

"Oh, honey. We already talked about this. You're the lady in my life, so of course there's an us." He took her into his arms and held her tight.

She felt light-headed. "There's an us. This is wonderful."

Colt pulled back so he could look her in the face. "Listen. I need to be here. And you, you discovered a comet. We know you can do your work here, and I need to be here…" He gulped. "Dana, I want to share my life, this life, with you."

Oh, my God. An aching need lanced Dana's heart.

He opened the green pouch and took out a platinum ring set with a row of small, cut stones. "Miners' diamonds," he said. "This ring belonged to my grandmother. Max felt it wasn't Nick's style, so Mom and Dad said I could give it to the woman I marry, if you want it."

Tears burned her eyes. "Thank you," she whispered, reaching for the ring. Then her brain clicked on, and she stopped. "I'm not sure I'm, umm, we're, ready for this, though. It's been such a short time. Other then the elevator incident and a few dinners, we've known each other maybe a … a week. You don't know anything about me."

"I know everything about you I need to know." He put one finger under her chin, raising it so she would have to look into his eyes. She found their crystal blue clarity disconcerting, as though he could look deep into her soul. "I know that I love you. You're everything any sane man could ever want in a wife. You're intelligent, brave, kind, and damn sexy."

How could he be so certain? She pulled away. "Oh, Colt! How do you know we'll be happy? Marriage isn't about two people on vacation screwing on a train and making love in a hot tub. Marriage is being able to live together and be happy every day." She softened her strident tone. "Sweetie, I don't mean to imply I don't care. But marriage? Isn't this a bit hasty?"

He sighed and tucked the ring and its bag into his pocket. "Yeah, it's hasty. So?"

"Marry in haste, repent in leisure."

"True enough. Hell, I've said that myself. But honey, I love you, and I believe that you love me." He hugged her. "If not now, when?" He kissed the top of her head.

"I don't know," she said, feeling helpless and unusually indecisive. "I just don't know if we can make it day-to-day, living together like normal people."

"Wake up, darlin'. We're living together, and have been since you invited me into your train compartment. Isn't that what you want?"

"Well, yes. How else can we tell if our marriage will work?"

He strode up and down the braided rag rug. "Can't you hear yourself? You're talking about our marriage without agreeing to marry. That's crazy. And have you thought about what we've been doing for the last week? Honey, you could be pregnant!"

"Oh, for goodness's sake! What am I, a moron? I can count days, you know."

"Huh? What do you mean?"

"I won't get pregnant," she said, hoping she sounded as pissed off as she felt. Really, the nerve of the man. She rubbed her low back, which had started to cramp. "And the next time we leave the farm we'll need to buy tampons."

"Oh, I see." He looked abashed.

"I won't marry you because I have to. I'll marry you because…" Dana was interrupted by a knock at the door.

It opened. "We're starving," Nicole announced.

"So am I, now that you mention it." For once, Dana was glad that her sister had intruded.

"May I take you out to lunch, madam?" By Nicole's side, Max gave her an exaggerated bow from the waist.

"I don't have any clothes other than what I'm wearing." Dana fingered her blue shirt.

"Jeans are all right for the place we're going," Max said. He gave Colt a shifty little grin.

The four of them hopped into the Wilders' SUV, and Colt, with a faintly annoyed attitude, drove them to the nearby town of Burgsville. Burgsville, a one-road town, boasted a post office, a Mom-and-Pop market, a police station, and very little else. Colt pulled into a dirt driveway in front of a wood-fronted shack at the edge of town.

Dana eyed the building. Its rusty red paint was peeling off warped boards. The dusty, unpaved parking lot was crowded with battered pick-ups featuring gun racks and leashed, whining hounds. Grubby little kids in shorts and overalls teased the dogs with lit sparklers. Light, voices, and twangy bluegrass music spilled out of the dive's double doors whenever they opened to admit a patron, or when the bouncer expelled a bum. Dana blinked; she'd never been to a bar where the bouncer ever had to do anything except look mean.

Although the hot, smoky honky-tonk was crowded, they found four empty stools at the corner of the L-shaped bar near the kitchen, with the Newcombe women in the center, flanked by the Wilder men.

"Hey, Beaver-Diver," Colt said to the T-shirted dude behind the bar.

The barkeep stopped and wheeled abruptly, facing Colt. "Well, young pup, you new to this town?"

"Not really. Can't four thirsty people get beers in this craphole?"

Dana's mouth dropped open. "Colt!" She tugged at his sleeve.

"Well, Colt and Max Wilder, as I live and breathe!" The bartender dove over the bar and swept up the Wilder brothers in a giant bear hug. The males laughed and pounded each other on the back as Dana watched, amazed.

"Dana, honey, this is my friend Bill." Colt wiped his eyes, streaming with laughter.

"I thought his name was Beaver."

They roared. "N-not really," Colt choked out. "'Beaver-Diver refers to his hobby during high school."

Dana reddened. "That is truly gross!"

They laughed harder. "Ain't she a princess?" asked Colt of Bill.

"Oh, yeah, what a honey," rumbled Bill, looking Dana over. His intent gaze lingered on Dana's braless bust line beneath her work shirt, the tails of which were tied around her waist. Nick bridled, no doubt missing the attention.

"Hey, barkeep! Can we get some service down here?" Impatient voices called from the other end of the long, battered wood bar.

"I'm on break! Getcher own damn beers!" Bill yelled down the length of the bar. A redheaded waitress, dressed in a white crop-top and a black miniskirt, glared at Bill as she ducked underneath the counter into the well and started to fill the drink orders. "Mary, gimme four Rollin' Rocks!" demanded Bill. The redhead complied, scowling.

"When you gonna quit hangin' with those useless friends of yourn?" she snapped.

Bill grabbed the bottles out of her hands, twisted off the caps, and served them. Colt drank deeply, and wiped the foam off his stubbly chin with the back of his hand. Bill and Mary continued their argument while Nicole listened with her mouth open in shock, but Max looked more relaxed and happy than Dana had ever seen him.

"This is my bar, woman, and if you don't like how I run it, you know just where you can get off." Bill wiped damp fingers on his grubby apron.

"The hell you say," Mary stormed. "There's jest as mucha my money in here as yourn."

Bill rolled his eyes and resumed his place behind the counter. "What'll it be, folks?" he asked resignedly.

"Four burgers, fries, with everything," Max said. "And keep the beer comin'. All right with you?" He cast a glance at Dana and Nicole.

Nick's eyes were round as she surveyed the scene. "Anything you say, baby."

"That's how I like a woman." Bill's voice was loud enough for everyone to hear. "Cooperative. Compliant. Agreeable. Pleasing."

"What are you, a thesaurus?" asked Mary. Dana was surprised. From the woman's speech patterns, Dana didn't realize Mary knew any three-syllable words. The two women laughed at the same time. Their eyes met, and they laughed harder.

"You ain't from around these parts, are you, honey?" Mary wiped the counter.

"How could you tell?" Dana asked.

"Ain't too many people around here don't come into this bar. You seem like a nice girl. Why you with that low-life?" Mary tucked her bar rag into her apron.

"Colt's a low-life?" Nicole smirked.

"Nah, not really. He's harmless, to the likes o' me. I'm too old."

Dana grinned. "So, he goes for the young ones?"

"Oh yeah, both of them. They were the bad boys of Burgsville High. 'Course, they was always blaming the other for their mischief." Mary laughed.

Bill slapped four plates, laden with greasy fried food, in front of them as Colt said, "Mary, put a lid on it. Dana doesn't want to hear alla that ol' stuff."

"Maybe I do," Nicole said. "I had no idea you two were such local celebrities." She winked at Max.

Mary snorted. "Hard to miss, those two, with all the girls moonin' over them like they was Johnny Depp or somethin'."

Both Colt and Max were definitely red underneath their stubble. "Hmmm," Dana said. "I think I understand."

"Unnerstan' whut?" Colt chewed and swallowed a bite of his burger. He chugged his beer.

"Please pass the ketchup," Dana said, evading.

Colt handed Dana a red plastic bottle. She turned it upside down and squeezed it over both her burger and her fries, enjoying the lush aroma of fried bar food.

"Unnerstan' whut?" he asked.

"Nothing important." She winked at Mary, and both women started laughing again.

"Tell me!"

"Nothing to say, honey." Dana chewed and swallowed. "Look, if you get all upset, you won't digest your food properly."

He nudged her. "Ah am *not* upset!"

"So what are you going on and on about?"

"Ah am not goin' on and on about anything. Ah jus' want to know what you're thinkin'."

"I'm thinking that this is a great burger." She took a big bite.

"Thank you," said Bill precisely. "I flatter myself that our culinary achievements are the equal of any establishment in this county."

Colt and Mary laughed. Dana and Max chewed. Bill cleaned the bar. Nicole said, "So, let's talk weddings.

How come you two didn't tell us?" She fixed them with a penetrating hazel gaze.

"Tell you what?" Dana asked, playing for time.

"I just got a phone call from Mom that you're engaged."

By Dana's side, Colt squirmed. "It's not really official."

"No ring?" Nicole asked.

"There's a ring if she wants it," Colt said, sounding the tiniest bit miffed.

Shit, thought Dana. Now she was really, truly trapped.

"Mom wants you to go to Louisville for engagement photos. She's already set up a sitting at a photographer. She wants to know what colors and flowers you want, and I've already started to design your dress." Nicole took several sheets of paper out of her satchel.

To Dana, every one of the dress designs looked like they were out of someone else's Cinderella fantasy: leg-of-mutton sleeves, tiny nipped-in waists, and lavish, full skirts. "What am I, Bridal Barbie?" she asked.

Nicole looked hurt, and Max said, "Dana, Nickie took quite a lot of her time designing dresses for you." Both shot her accusatory glares.

The pit of Dana's stomach froze colder than Europa's icy seas. A miserable knot appeared in her chest, clenching around her heart. "I'm sorry, but I ... I don't want this." She stood and walked out of the bar.

"Thanks for nothin'," Colt snarled at his brother. He threw a twenty onto the bar and chased Dana.

Outside, she turned on him. "This is your fault. If you hadn't told everyone we were getting married…"

"I know, I know. Don't get mad, okay?"

"I can't do this. If Nicole keeps at me about this ridiculous wedding, I'm going back to Boston. Soon."

"What?" Colt, shocked, looked into her desperate eyes and realized that she wasn't exaggerating. "Oh, baby, don't say that. We just got here."

"Hey, I thought you wanted me to be more assertive about Mom and Nickie."

"I do, but not like this. You're hurting us." Damn. He'd better find a way to keep her here, or their entire relationship could go up in smoke. How could he marry Dana if she hated weddings and intended to walk out on him?

"I love you, but I can't stand this crazy wedding thing. You know how Nickie can get. She's just as obsessive as my mother. I refuse to participate in another multi-media marital production."

He grabbed her. "You said it."

"Said what?"

"That you love me. Whoopee!" He picked her up and swung her around, then gave her a big, wet kiss. He sucked on her tongue, then palmed her sweet butt and brought her closer until his pelvis rubbed against hers. Passion spun through him, fierce, all-consuming, and never-ending.

He had to have her. Now and forever.

A voice behind them called, "Get a room!"

She broke away from him, grinning. "Of course I love you. You're my hero. Of course, you're not an L.G.M., but hey, nobody's perfect…"

He took the green silk bag out of his pocket. "Guess what? Did you know that Kentucky has no waiting period?"

"*Really?*" Her expression continued to brighten.

"Yes, really. Nick and Gabrielle can't plan a big wedding if we're already married."

"Huh." An angelic smile spread over her face.

"Umm, should I ask you again?" He dangled the bag in front of her eyes, swinging it as though it was a pendulum. Her eyes tracked it as though it was a new star. He tried to smother his smug grin, but he was sure he had her.

She winked. "Yes, you can ask."

"Well? Shall we do it?"

She took a deep breath and said, "Yes. Would you put it on me, please?"

"Oh, baby." Relief flooded him. He embraced her, then fumbled at the ring. It didn't fit.

"My God, Colt, your grandmother had tiny hands!"

"Try your pinky finger until we can get it sized." He roped an arm around her shoulders and squeezed her tight, kissing her temple, her cheek, her lips, everything he could reach. "I shouldn't ask, but why the sudden change of heart?"

She pushed the ring onto her smallest finger. "The way you're handling the wedding issue, for one. Nickie got me really upset and you're backing me up, totally. I love you, but I've known that for a while, since the train wreck. What I realize now is that you know me and accept me like no one else ever has, and I love you even more for it." She slid her arms around him and cuddled. "I'm yours, and we'll marry."

~ * ~

The silly little place was called Chapel of the Pines. The suit Colt found in the back of his closet, which dated from his college graduation, didn't fit. His shoulders had broadened, so he wore jeans and a leather jacket.

Dana wore sandals and a white linen minidress she'd grabbed off the rack at a store. She didn't care. She'd marry Colt if he wore rags and if she were dressed in burlap. Nothing mattered but their love. But the Elvis impersonator that Colt had hired to perform the ceremony was a creative touch, she thought.

"How did you know that I really love the Jailhouse Rock period?" she asked Colt.

He grinned. "Because you love bad boys in leather jackets. Like me."

She kissed him as Elvis handed her a bouquet of red roses. "No, I love wild horsemen on big black stallions. Like you."

The End

About the Author:

An award-winning, best-selling traditional romance novelist, Suz uses a pseudonym to protect her privacy. But if you're a romance fan, you've probably read her books or have heard of her, since she's known for layered, compelling novels charged with humor as well as emotion.

Of her journey to the steamier side of writing, Suz says, "I love writing traditional romances, but after several years in the same mode, I felt that I really needed to cut loose as a creative artist and write hot, sexy books that reflect the wilder side of being human."

Suz's books are fast paced, with seductive situations, complicated characters and a whole lot of kink!

Meet LSB Authors At The House Of Sin
Lsbooks.NET

We invite you to visit Liquid Silver Books

LSbooks.com
for other exciting erotic romances.

MOLTEN Silver

Edgier, naughtier – from Summer 2006

Featured Series:

The Zodiac Series: 12 books, 24 stories and authors
Two hot stories for each sign, 12 signs

The Coven of the Wolf by Rae Morgan
Benevolent lusty witches keep evil forces at bay

Fallen: by Tiffany Aaron
Fallen angels in hot flight to redeem their wings

The Max Series by JB Skully
Meet Max, her not-absent dead husband, sexy detective Witt, his mother…

And many, many more!

Another LSB Romance by
Suz deMello…

Seducing the Hermit
4 lips, Two-Lips Reviews

Rock 'n roll deejay Paige Percy rejects the phony life she's led in Los Angeles and travels to remote Takinsha Island, Alaska, determined to make a new life. There, men outnumber women twenty to one, so she's confident she'll snare a casual bedmate or two...she'll need a couple of hot dudes to warm her bed through the long, cold Alaska winter.

But as locals say, the odds are good, but the goods are…odd.

Instead of the jolly, outgoing boyfriends she expects to meet, she falls for Fisher Chugatt, a loner whose agenda doesn't include a relationship of any sort. But Cupid has other plans for this couple. While Paige learns to adapt to the out-of-kilter world of Takinsha, Fisher struggles to banish the shadows in his soul that prevent him from committing to Paige.

The Best of LSB Romance...

The Zodiac Series
22 LSB Authors
   4 print books, each a collection of the Zodiac stories combined into Elements: Air, Earth, Fire, Water.
   http://zodiacromance.com

Ain't Your Mama's Bedtime Stories
Best Anthology of 2003 - The Romance Studio
   R. A. Punzel Lets Down Her hair - Dee S. Knight
   Beauty or the Bitch - Jasmine Haynes
   Snow White and the Seven Dorks - Dakota Cassidy
   Little Red, The Wolf, and The Hunter - Leigh Wyndfield
   Once Upon a Princess - Rae Morgan
   Petra and the Werewolf - Sydney Morgann
   Peter's Touch - Vanessa Hart

Resolutions
4 ½ Stars Top Pick - Romantic Times BookClub
   A Losing Proposition - Vanessa Hart
   Free Fall - Jasmine Haynes
   For Sale by Owner - Leigh Wyndfield
   That Scottish Spring - Dee S. Knight

More Contemporary Romances from LSB...

One Touch
Susie Charles

For Jake Reilly, one touch was all it took, and now he wants more, much more. Now Cassie's unrequited love for him is getting requited—real quick! When he discovers her secret, can he ever forgive her and will their growing feelings be strong enough to survive it?

Plane Jane
Paige Burns and Tiffany Aaron
A He Said, She Said book

Jane Van Poppel isn't looking for Prince Charming, until her rich boss Josh Anderson sweeps her off her feet. Between her insecurities and his family, will Josh and Jane get their happily ever after?

That's What Friends Are For
Bridget Midway

Now in Print!

A former high school cheerleader and a former high school nerd have grown up together and are now best friends. Ned is attracted to Fiona, but thinks she'll always see him as just a big nerd. Fiona is attracted to Ned, but figures a brainiac like him would want an equally intelligent woman by his side.

Can best friends sleep together and still be friends in the morning?

Sacking the Quarterback
Tiffany Aaron

Ten years of playing pro football has gotten Donovan Klasek two bad knees, a bad shoulder and an addiction to pain killers. Now he's free of the addiction and loves working at his bar, but part of him wishes he had another chance at the big game.

Johnni Aitken can rattle off football stats with the best. When she gets a job waiting tables at Donovan's bar, she can't believe her luck. Football is a religion to her and Donovan has been the star in several of her fantasies. What happens when a man beat up by life meets a woman longing to heal his heart?

Simon's Wicked Web
Ava McKnight

Now in Print!

Kate Preston has selected billionaire bad boy Simon Jones as the subject of her final book in a bestselling series of biographies on overindulgent, decadent multimillionaires.

Simon challenges her to take a walk on the wild side with him, though, and Kate finds herself being pulled deeper and deeper into his wicked web. Before the biography is finished, Kate will discover a decadent side of herself she never knew existed... But at what cost to her heart?

Printed in the United States
126516LV00001B/39/P